HOUSE OF FLIES

Also by Graham Masterton

Horror Standalones
Black Angel
Death Mask
Death Trance
Edgewise
Heirloom
Prey
Ritual
Spirit
Tengu
The Chosen Child
The Sphinx
Unspeakable
Walkers
Manitou Blood
Revenge of the Manitou
Famine
Ikon
Sacrifice
The House of a Hundred Whispers
Plague
The Soul Stealer
Blind Panic
The House at Phantom Park

The Scarlet Widow Series
Scarlet Widow
The Coven

The Katie Maguire Series
White Bones
Broken Angels
Red Light
Taken for Dead
Blood Sisters
Buried
Living Death
Dead Girls Dancing
Dead Men Whistling
Begging to Die
The Last Drop of Blood
Pay Back the Devil

The Patel & Pardoe Series
Ghost Virus
The Children God Forgot
The Shadow People
What Hides in the Cellar

The Night Warriors
Night Warriors
Death Dream
Night Plague
Night Wars
The Ninth Nightmare

Short Story Collections
Days of Utter Dread

GRAHAM MASTERTON

HOUSE OF FLIES

An Aries Book

First published in the UK in 2025 by Head of Zeus,
part of Bloomsbury Publishing Plc

Copyright © Graham Masterton, 2025

The moral right of Graham Masterton to be identified
as the author of this work has been asserted in accordance with
the Copyright, Designs and Patents Act of 1988.

All rights reserved. No part of this publication may be: i) reproduced or transmitted in any form, electronic or mechanical, including photocopying, recording or by means of any information storage or retrieval system without prior permission in writing from the publishers; or ii) used or reproduced in any way for the training, development or operation of artificial intelligence (AI) technologies, including generative AI technologies. The rights holders expressly reserve this publication from the text and data mining exception as per Article 4(3) of the Digital Single Market Directive (EU) 2019/790.

This is a work of fiction. All characters, organizations, and events portrayed
in this novel are either products of the author's imagination or are used fictitiously.

9 7 5 3 1 2 4 6 8

A catalogue record for this book is available from the British Library.

ISBN (HB): 9781837931118
ISBN (E): 9781837931095

Cover design: Matt Bray | Head of Zeus
Typeset by Siliconchips Services Ltd UK

Printed and bound in Great Britain by
CPI Group (UK) Ltd, Croydon, CR0 4YY

Bloomsbury Publishing Plc
50 Bedford Square, London, WC1B 3DP, UK
Bloomsbury Publishing Ireland Limited,
29 Earlsfort Terrace, Dublin 2, D02 AY28, Ireland

HEAD OF ZEUS LTD
5–8 Hardwick Street
London, EC1R 4RG

To find out more about our authors and books
visit www.headofzeus.com

For product safety related questions contact productsafety@bloomsbury.com

HOUSE OF FLIES

I

The Reverend Paul Wymarsh lowered his book and reached across to his bedside table for his mug of hot chocolate. He lifted up his book again and took a first sip of chocolate, but as he did so he felt something bob lightly against his upper lip.

When he looked into his mug, he saw that there were three dead flies floating in it. He let out a *'yah!'* of utter disgust, threw back his duvet and climbed out of bed. He had not seen any flies circling around his bedroom. It was late October, after all, and a chilly October too, and by now the fly breeding season was usually over.

He carried his mug into the bathroom, switched on the light, poured the hot chocolate and the flies into the lavatory and flushed it. He saw himself in the mirror over the washbasin, narrow-shouldered and wiry-haired and bespectacled in his green-striped pyjamas, and he thought he looked quite shaken.

He wondered for a moment if he ought to ask God if there was any significance to three flies drowning in his bedtime drink, but then he thought it was far too petty a question with which to bother the Almighty, especially tonight, with so many wars in the world.

In any case, God would probably say *How the hell would I know?* The Reverend Wymarsh knew from experience that God had a sense of humour.

He left his empty mug on the small table on the landing. But as he crossed back to his bedroom, he heard a shuffling sound from downstairs. He stopped and listened, and after a few seconds he heard another sound, as if somebody were softly sweeping the floor.

He switched on the landing light. The sweeping sound gradually faded, but then he thought he heard another shuffle.

'I say! Is there somebody down there?' he called out. He had meant to sound stern and authoritative, but his voice came out strained and clogged up, as if he had a bad cold.

There was no answer, only silence, although the Reverend Wymarsh could hear his heart beating. He had locked both the front door and the kitchen door before he came up to bed, so he was sure that he would have heard anyone breaking in.

Even though he could hear no more noises from downstairs, he knew he would have to go down to make sure there was nobody there. Perhaps he had simply heard the gas boiler switching itself off, or the radiators cooling. The vicarage was early Victorian. The floorboards and rafters had a tendency to creak, and the windows to rattle, but he had never heard shuffling and sweeping sounds before.

Outside, it was raining, but not heavily, only a light patter, and there was no rumbling of thunder.

He went back into the bedroom and put on his corduroy slippers. Then he made his way cautiously downstairs, past the framed pictures of Jesus and his disciples at Gethsemane and of Southwark Cathedral, where the Reverend Wymarsh had been ordained. When he reached the hallway, he switched on the light and listened again. Still silence.

First he looked into the living room, with its antique leather sofa and armchairs and its Gothic stone fireplace. He leaned sideways so that he could see behind the sofa, but there was nobody crouched down behind it, and there were no toecaps protruding from underneath the brown velvet curtains.

He was undecided for a moment, but then he picked up the brass-topped poker from beside the fireplace. Perhaps it was less than Christian for him to look for a possible intruder with a weapon in his hand, but crusaders had carried swords against the infidels, after all.

He checked his book-lined study, and the downstairs lavatory, and the large mahogany wardrobe where he kept his overcoats and hats and shoes. He prodded the coats with the end of the poker, but there was nobody hiding behind them.

Lastly, he went into the kitchen. When the fluorescent light blinked on, he could see that there was nobody there. He tried the door that gave out into the garden, and that was definitely locked. He opened the door to the utility room, where his shirts were hanging to dry, but there was nobody in there either.

It must have been the heating, making those noises. Either that, or mice. Or maybe I'm starting to suffer from tinnitus.

He was about to return the poker to the living room and go back upstairs when he saw something sparkling on the kitchen window, behind the Venetian blinds. At first, he thought it was raindrops, but when he looked closer, he realised that it was five or six flies, crawling up the glass.

He stared at them in disgust, and also in bewilderment. Where in the world had all these flies come from? The kitchen was spotless, because his cleaning lady, Ola, had visited only yesterday. He had left out no food uncovered, or dirty plates that might have attracted flies.

He laid down the poker and opened the cupboard under the sink to take out a can of Raid, which he had bought during the summer to get rid of wasps. He raised the Venetian blind and then sprayed the flies with much more insecticide than was probably needed to kill them.

Almost immediately, the flies dropped off the glass and fell on to their backs on the windowsill, where they waved their legs and spun around and around for a few seconds before lying still. The Reverend Wymarsh tore off a sheet of kitchen paper, wrapped them all up in it, and dropped them into his pedal bin.

He stood in the kitchen feeling relieved but strangely guilty. Even a fly was a life, given by God, and he had just taken half a dozen of them.

He gave one last look around, and then he picked up the poker, switched off the lights, and made his way back upstairs to bed.

Before he closed his eyes, he said, very quietly, 'Lord Jesus, I believe you are the Son of God who died to pay the penalty for my sins. I open the door of my heart and ask you to be my Saviour and Lord. I ask your forgiveness for all my misdeeds.'

It took him nearly twenty minutes to fall asleep, and when he did, he began to dream almost at once that his late wife, Glenda, was playing the piano in the living room. At least, she was sitting in front of the piano and fingering the keys, but there was no sound.

He came up behind her and watched her for a while, and then he said, 'There's no music, Glenda. What's wrong?'

Without looking at him, she said, 'Cancer, Paul. Once you have cancer, nobody can hear what you're playing.'

He laid both his hands lightly on her shoulders and continued to watch her as she carried on running her fingers over the keyboard in total silence. He missed her so much that it made his stomach hurt.

While he was dreaming that he was watching her, his bedroom door opened. A tall figure was standing outside on the landing, a figure that glittered in green from head to foot, as if it were covered all over in tiny shattered fragments of green glass. It stayed there for a few moments, listening to the Reverend Wymarsh murmuring in his sleep, and then it entered his bedroom and stood beside his bed. It was making a constant hissing sound, so soft that it was almost inaudible, like the white noise from a radio.

The figure waited for over a minute, and then it seized the top of his duvet and dragged it halfway downwards. The Reverend Wymarsh instantly woke up, although for the first two or three seconds he was not sure if he was actually awake or if he was still dreaming. He rolled over on to his back and said, '*What—?*'

The figure grasped him by the throat and clenched it so tight that he was unable to say any more, only choke. He struggled and beat with both hands at the mattress, but the figure was not only throttling him but pushing him downwards with such force that he was unable to lift his head off his pillow. His legs were tangled up in his duvet, too, so that it was impossible for him to kick.

It was dark already in the bedroom, but he began to feel a deeper darkness coming over him. He couldn't think about praying to God to save him. All he could think about was the crushing pain in his throat and his desperate inability to breathe. His lungs felt as if they were just about to burst.

His mouth was wide open, gagging for air, so while the figure was still strangling him with one hand, it pinched the tip of his tongue between its fingernails and pulled it out as far as it would go. The Reverend Wymarsh would have retched if his larynx had not been squeezed so hard. He felt a prickling sensation on his tongue, as if flies had settled on it, and then he felt as if flies were starting to crawl inside his mouth, not just a few, but scores of them. He managed to make a thin wheezing sound, but then he blacked out.

The figure kept its grip on his throat until it was sure that he had stopped breathing. Then it pulled his duvet back up, and covered him with it.

It said nothing, but stood there for a while in utter silence, as quiet as Glenda's piano.

2

Jerry had just finished taking a statement from an elderly man who had deliberately run over his neighbour's Samoyed because it never stopped barking.

'Don't get me wrong, I'm an animal lover,' the man told him. 'And I never wanted the poor dog to suffer or nothing. But me and the missus had to put up with that barking more than fifty times a day for three months solid, and we was going totally doolally.'

'Well, don't quote me,' Jerry told him, switching off the voice recorder, 'but I probably would have chucked some poisoned dog biscuits over the fence, long before then.'

The door of the interview room opened and DC Mallett came in, still holding a half-eaten Cornish pasty.

'Sorry to interrupt, skip. Didn't realise you were still *in flagrante*.'

'No, we're all done now. It's all right, Mr Belling, you can go now. I'll be sending your statement off to the Crown Prosecution Service, along with all the witness statements, and I'll be in touch with you when they tell me if they've decided to go ahead with a prosecution. Or not, as the case may be.'

The elderly man lifted his sagging grey raincoat from the back of his chair. As he was struggling into it, he looked as if he were about to say something, but then he changed his mind.

DC Mallett stepped aside so that he could shuffle out of the room.

'Was that the Samoyed Squasher?'

'Yes, Edge. He said he's going to plead guilty if it goes to court, but I doubt if it will. They've got more stabbings to deal with these days than I've had hot dinners. Did you want me for something, or did you just come down to offer me a bite of your pasty?'

'No, Jerry, yes. I mean skip. Sorry – I'm not quite used to your being promoted yet. Which do you prefer? Skip or sarge?'

'Whatever, Edge. You can call me "your majesty" if you like.'

'The Martian's been on the blower,' said DC Mallett. 'He reckons he's got a case that might need you and DI Patel to take a shufti at it.'

'That sounds ominous. Did he give you any details?'

'Not a lot. But he says it concerns that vicar who was found dead yesterday in Clapham. Manually strangled, apparently.'

'DCI Butcher's dealing with that one, isn't he?'

'He is, yes. But there's some question about *when* he was strangled and how long he'd been lying there before they found him.'

'That doesn't sound particularly supernatural to me. But I'll give the Martian a bell anyway. How's that Secret Garden case coming along?'

Jerry was referring to a five-year-old boy whose body had been discovered in the small hours of the morning on top of the slide at Battersea Secret Garden playground. He had suffered multiple injuries, including a fractured skull and broken ribs, and he had obviously been abused over a long period of time.

Edge took another bite of his pasty and shook his head. 'Bugger all so far,' he said, blowing crumbs. 'No witnesses, no CCTV. No children reported missing.'

'What some people do to their kids, it's unbelievable. That's the third one this month.'

Jerry went back upstairs to the office he now shared with Detective Sergeant Ruth Watkins. It was almost three months now since he and Detective Sergeant Jamila Patel had worked on their last case together. It had been a surrealistic investigation into a Fagin-like gang of children being run from a cellar in Vauxhall, and several robberies and murders associated with it.

They had both been given strict instructions never to disclose any details of this case to the media, or even to discuss it with their fellow officers. After they had filed their report, though, Jamila Patel had been promoted to Detective Inspector and Jerry had been promoted to Detective Sergeant, and each of them was now paid nearly £5,000 a year more than they had been before.

Almost every officer in the Met who had any hint of what Jamila and Jerry had achieved called them 'The Ghostbusters', but that was officially frowned on. As Detective Chief Superintendent Herbert Chance had brusquely stated, 'We work with facts. We work with evidence. We do *not* work with figments of people's fevered imaginations.'

Jerry rang Derek Grant, the 'Martian'. He sounded as dreary as he usually did.

'Ah, DS Pardoe. Thanks for calling back so quick. Yes. I'm at Falcon Road, with Dr Crowe. DCI Butcher's here too, but I think it would be a good idea if you could come over and see this for yourself.'

'Mallett told me it was that vicar who was found dead in Clapham.'

'Yes. The Reverend Paul Wymarsh, from St Gratus. There's no question that somebody strangled him – Dr Crowe's one hundred per cent certain about that. The question is when. He held evensong on Saturday, but he failed to show up for communion on Sunday morning. His churchwarden tried phoning him, but when the Reverend Wymarsh didn't answer, he went round to the rectory. He had a spare key, so he was able to get in, and that's when he found him dead in bed.'

'So what's the mystery about when he was murdered? It must have been sometime between evensong on Saturday and morning service on Sunday. That's, what, ten hours max.'

'Like I said, I think you need to come over and see this for yourself.'

'Okay. I just want to grab a bite to eat. I haven't had time for any breakfast yet.'

'Uh-oh. I wouldn't, if I was you.'

It was only a five-minute drive to HM Coroner's Office on Falcon Road. Jerry parked in Afghan Road opposite, but as he dodged across to the other side of the street he narrowly missed being run over by a number 49 bus. *Oh well*, he thought, *at least they wouldn't have had far to carry me to the mortuary.*

He gave a flirty double-click of his tongue to red-haired Kirsty in reception, and she blew him a kiss in return. Then he took the claustrophobic lift upstairs. The Martian was waiting for him in the laboratory, as well as Dr John Crowe, the forensic pathologist, and his assistant Zahir, and DCI Butcher.

Everybody in the Met called Derek Grant 'the Martian' because he was skinny and bald, with huge protruding ears, and he spoke in an other-worldly monotone. Dr Crowe, on the other hand, was tall and flamboyant with tangled grey hair, and he always sounded as if he were playing the lead in a Shakespearean tragedy, even when he was simply asking Zahir to pass him a retractor.

Jerry thought that DCI Butcher could hardly have had a more appropriate name, because he was burly, with florid cheeks and fingers as fat as sausages, and he looked as if he should be wearing an apron and chopping up pork ribs behind a counter.

'So what's the SP?' asked Jerry.

'I'm totally baffled, me,' said DCI Butcher. 'I've never seen nothing like this in all my thirteen years. And I mean, never, with a capital N.'

'Here, see for yourself,' said Dr Crowe in his booming voice. 'I can't say that I've ever come across anything like this either – even in cases of advanced decomposition.'

The Reverend Wymarsh was lying naked on a stainless-steel pathology table, his ribcage protruding like the victim of a famine. Dr Crowe beckoned to Jerry to come closer.

'You see these massive contusions around his neck? He was manually strangled and that was undoubtedly the cause of death.'

'So what's so unusual about that? Strangling doesn't account for too many murders, does it? Only about seven per cent. But that's still about fifty every year.'

'Ah, but what I've never encountered before is *this*,' said Dr Crowe. With his blue nitrile-gloved fingers, he levered down the Reverend Wymarsh's jaw, so that his mouth gaped wide open. Inside, Jerry could see that it was crammed full with black feathery objects, and when he looked closer, he realised that they were flies.

All he could say was, 'Jesus.'

'According to DCI Butcher here, the churchwarden who

found him said that his whole bedroom was buzzing with flies. He opened the window and most of them flew away. But it was only when I started my examination here that I discovered all these flies in his mouth, almost as if he'd been trying to swallow them. At a rough estimate, there must be more than a hundred of them. *Musca domestica*, most likely, the common housefly. I'll be able to count them exactly, of course, once I've photographed them and scanned them, but Derek here thought you ought to see them first-hand, *in situ*.'

He pulled down his surgical mask and blew his nose with a tissue. Then he said, 'It doesn't do you any harm to eat flies, if that's what the reverend was trying to do. They're no different from any other food.'

Jerry peered closer into the Reverend Wymarsh's mouth. He had seen flies crawling over dead bodies before, but never so many, and never filling up a victim's mouth. 'You don't seriously think he was having them for breakfast, do you? That's enough to make a maggot gag.'

'Well, I very much doubt it,' said Dr Crowe. 'But "maggot", that's a most appropriate word, because that's what I simply can't understand,' said Dr Crowe. 'The time period in between the reverend's last appearance at evensong and when he was discovered the following morning was not nearly long enough for him to start to decompose. Even if he had, and a female fly had deposited eggs on him, it takes at least a day for fly eggs to hatch into maggots, or larvae. Then it takes the larvae approximately two weeks before they become pupae, and a further six days for them to emerge from the pupae as fully developed flies.'

'Right, thanks. I think I've seen enough now,' Jerry told him. He was beyond grateful that the Martian had warned him not to eat anything before he came here. 'So what you're telling me is that these flies were all grown up before the Reverend Wymarsh was strangled?'

'Yes. No question about it.'

'If that's the case, where did they come from, and how the hell did so many of them get into his bedroom? And even more to the point, how did so many of them manage to fill up his gob?'

'We have absolutely no idea,' said the Martian. 'That's why I called you. I've already been in touch with Professor Gregory Yearling. He's an entomologist up at Oxford, and he's going to come down later today and examine these flies for us. He'll be able to let us know if there's anything unusual about them, although Dr Crowe says they seem to be perfectly ordinary, so far as he can tell.'

Jerry took a last long look at the Reverend Wymarsh. The Martian had not said so directly, but Jerry knew why he had called him. He obviously suspected that there could be some less-than-natural cause for the swarms of flies that had filled up the reverend's bedroom when he was strangled. Maybe their appearance had been nothing more than a freak of nature, but what, exactly? Maybe the Reverend Wymarsh had been breeding flies, although God alone knew why he should be.

'Let me have a word with DI Patel,' said Jerry. 'She probably knows more about flies than I do. I'll give you a bell later.'

DCI Butcher said, 'There's a caff up the road. Let's go and have a coffee and I'll fill you in on the rest of this shitshow.'

Jerry was about to follow DCI Butcher out of the laboratory when he saw a single fly emerge from the Reverend Wymarsh's mouth and crawl over his lower lip.

Jerry looked over at the Martian and the Martian could

only shake his head. Even now, some of the flies were still alive.

'It's not only the bloody flies that's got me scratching my head,' said DCI Butcher, as they sat down in the blue plastic chairs in Al's Place Café. He had ordered a bacon sandwich, but Jerry still felt as if he could taste flies in his mouth, and contented himself with a cup of black coffee.

'So what else?' he asked DCI Butcher.

'Most of all, how did the perp gain access to the rectory, and how did they get out again afterwards? Both doors were locked. The front door was the old-fashioned type, and needed to be locked from the outside when it was closed. The kitchen door still had the key in it.'

'Windows?'

'All closed.'

'Any fingerprints or footprints?'

'Don't know yet. But the Martian's team will be checking the door handles and the banisters and the floors with UV. They'll also be testing the reverend's bedcovers for DNA because the perp must have pulled them up to cover him.'

'But you have no idea at all how the perp got in, or how they left?'

'Absolutely none, Jerry. Not unless they came down the chimney like Santa.'

DCI Butcher's bacon sandwich arrived, and while he was taking his first wolfish bites, Jerry thoughtfully sipped his coffee.

'What about motive? Do we know of any threats that anyone's made to the Reverend Wymarsh? Any personal problems?'

DCI Butcher chewed and swallowed, and then he said, 'DI Baker and the rest of the team are over at St Gratus right now. I've got them taking statements from the two assistant priests and the parish administrator and anybody else involved in the church – you know, just to find out if the Reverend Wymarsh might have trodden on anybody's toes. He was widowed, but we'll be looking into the possibility that he might have started up a new relationship, and if so, who with.'

'Do we know of any religious sects in Clapham who might have it in for Christians?'

'Only a bunch of Druids, and you could hardly call them terrorists.'

'Druids believe in human sacrifice, don't they? It was Druids who made those wicker men, wasn't it, and stuffed people inside them, and burned them alive?'

'I don't think the Druids in Clapham would be up to that. They're about ninety years old, most of them, and they couldn't make a wicker shopping basket, let alone a wicker man. I can't see any of them breaking into a rectory in the middle of the night and strangling the vicar. They're probably all asleep by half-past eight, smelling of cocoa.'

Jerry finished his coffee. He realised that the Martian and DCI Butcher had called him in because the murder of the Reverend Wymarsh did appear to have some supernatural elements about it, but maybe that was only because they couldn't work out how it had been done, and it needed more than routine policework to solve it. To be fair, though, he had no idea himself how the perpetrator might have managed to break into the rectory, or where those swarms of flies might have come from, and what they signified, if anything.

'Like I told the Martian, I'll go back to the station now and have a rabbit with DI Patel,' he told DCI Butcher. 'I can't guarantee that she'll have any more of a clue than me, but she knows a lot more than I do about ghoulies and ghosties and things that go bump in the night.'

DCI Butcher wiped his mouth, screwed up his paper napkin and tossed it on to his plate. 'I hate investigations like this. I fucking hate them. Give me an out-and-out shooting any day of the week.'

3

It had started raining again by the time Brenda and her little boy, Michael, arrived at Wandsworth Cemetery. It was only a fine drizzle, though, and today was the only day that Brenda had been able to get off work. Michael should have been at school, but Brenda had rung them and told them that he had an earache.

Actually, it had been a year yesterday that her husband, Philip, had been killed. His van had been struck from behind by a 20-ton truck on the M25 because the truck driver was texting on his phone. When Brenda had arrived at the hospital, the mortuary assistants had not allowed her to see him.

As they walked along the path between the hundreds of grey gravestones, Brenda was carrying a bunch of thirteen white roses, one for every year that she and Philip had been married. Michael's memorial offering was a bag of Haribo jellies because his father had always managed to sneak one whenever he was eating them, and winked at him, and laughed.

When they reached Philip's grave, however, Brenda was concerned to see that it was cordoned off with blue-and-white police tape. Three uniformed constables in yellow high-viz jackets were standing beside it, as well as a cemetery officer.

Philip's marble headstone was still standing, but when she came closer Brenda saw that his grave itself had been dug up, and that it was surrounded by heaps of dark soil and gravel.

'My God, what's happened?' she asked the policemen. When she looked down into the grave, she saw that the coffin was still lying there, but its lid was tilted to one side and Philip's body had gone. All that remained was the green good-luck gnome that Philip had always taken with him to work, and which she had asked the undertakers to tuck into his coffin beside him.

'Sorry, madam,' said one of the constables. 'Is this someone you knew?'

Brenda was so shocked that she found it difficult to speak.

'That was my husband. That was – where is he? What's happened to him?'

'I'm afraid there's been an unauthorised exhumation,' said the cemetery officer. He had thick-rimmed glasses and a ginger moustache, and he looked so much like Brenda's old geography teacher that she almost thought it could have been him. 'It occurred sometime during the night.'

'Who did it? What for? Where have they taken him?'

'I'm afraid we have no idea who could have wanted to disinter your husband's remains, or how they did it, or why. And neither do we know where they could be now.'

'We're waiting for the crime scene specialists to show up,' the constable told her. 'The detectives dealing with this case will be here in a minute too.'

Michael started to cry, tightly clutching his bag of sweets. 'Where's Daddy? Where's he gone?'

Brenda's eyes filled with tears too, but she put her arm around him and said, 'Don't worry, sweetheart. The police will find him for us.'

'But why did they take him? Why? He's dead, Mummy! He's dead!'

Brenda turned to the constables. 'I'd better take him home. Look – here's my mobile number. Please call me as soon as you find out anything.'

'Of course, madam. In any event, the detectives will be wanting to talk to you. Could you give me your address as well?'

Brenda took hold of Michael's hand and together they walked back towards the cemetery gates. Brenda was unable to stop herself trembling and she stumbled twice. Michael was still sobbing and kept turning his head to look back at Philip's desecrated grave. A forensic services van had just arrived, closely followed by two unmarked cars.

It took less than ten minutes for Brenda to drive to their semi-detached house on Broomwood Road, but all the way she felt as if were dreaming. Because it was only drizzling, the windscreen wipers flopped from side to side with a series of rubbery squeaks. Michael had stopped sobbing, but as soon as she opened the front door he kicked off his shoes and ran up to his bedroom without saying a word.

Brenda hung up her raincoat and went into the living room, still feeling unreal. A large framed photograph of Philip stood on the bookcase, and he was smiling as if he knew where his body had been taken, and was trying to make up his mind if he should tell her. He had always been a joker.

Brenda dropped down on to her knees and let out a howl like a bitch in pain.

Because it was still drizzling, DI Simon Fairbrother returned to sit in his car while the three-strong forensic team carried out their preliminary examination of the grave and its surrounding area.

DS Audrey Morrison and DC Iniko Okeke remained standing outside, but DI Fairbrother had only just recovered from three weeks of Covid and he was not keen to risk a relapse.

All the same, he switched on his windscreen wipers now and again, so that he could clearly see the forensic technicians as they climbed in and out of the grave in their white Tyvek suits, like three giant snowmen. He could also see them taking samples from the heaps of soil and gravel and circling around the adjacent gravestones, scanning the grass with UV lamps for footprints.

He had already talked to the cemetery officer, but the cemetery officer had only been able to admit that he was clueless. He was waiting now for the forensic team to give him their initial assessment, and then he would take DS Morrison around to interview Mrs Brenda Harris, the widow of the missing deceased. Maybe she would have some idea why his remains had been disinterred.

All he had discovered so far was that Philip Harris had been buried here about a year ago, but that only made the removal of his remains even more mystifying. Who on earth would want to steal a body that was already starting to decompose?

DI Fairbrother knew that the rate of decomposition could vary greatly, depending on whether a body had been embalmed or not, and whether the coffin was wood or metal. Sometimes, holes were drilled in coffins to speed up the rate of decay, but some bodies took up to ten years or even longer before they were reduced to a skeleton. However he had been buried, though, DI Fairbrother reckoned that Philip Harris would have been in a fairly slimy state by now.

Another half-hour passed, and then one of the forensic technicians came up to his car and tapped on the window. When he put the window down, the technician peeled off his face mask.

'Hi, Steven,' said DI Fairbrother. 'Got anything to tell me?'

'Not a lot. I think the right word for this particular shout is "bamboozling". We're going to be here for a few more hours yet, I can tell you. We may even have to come back tomorrow, after we've done some more tests in the lab.'

'What are you bamboozled about, if you don't mind my asking?'

'Principally, the condition of the coffin lid and the way the soil was deposited.'

'Steven – somebody dug him up, for whatever reason. What's so bamboozling about that?'

'The point is that nobody dug him up. Not so far as we can tell.'

'What do you mean? If nobody dug him up, how was he taken out of his coffin?'

'He wasn't taken out. It doesn't look that way, anyhow, although we'll be running a lot more tests, like I say. What I'm telling you is that everything points to the coffin lid being broken open from inside and the soil being scrabbled away upwards, by hand.'

'What? He broke out of his coffin himself? That's impossible. He'd been dead for a year.'

'I know, but if by some miracle he was capable of digging, he wouldn't have had too far to dig. The coffin was buried only a little more than three feet deep. That's the minimum allowed by the Local Authorities' Cemeteries Order, provided the soil is of suitable character. You know, not too sandy, nor nothing like that.'

DI Fairbrother stared at the technician as if he were mad.

'Steven – didn't you hear what I just said? He'd been dead for a year. He was probably half rotted. You've seen those zombie films. He probably looked like one of those, only worse. And you and I know there's no such thing as zombies. The only walking dead that I know of is that old biddy who cleans the toilets back at the nick.'

The technician gave him a Gallic shrug. 'I'm only telling you what the evidence tells us. We found numerous abrasions on the inside of the coffin lid. They look very much like fingernail scratches, as if the occupant had been struggling to get out. And that's not all. If somebody else had dug him up, the gravel that was spread on top of his grave would be underneath the excavated soil, instead of the other way about, which it was.'

'Well, all right,' said DI Fairbrother. 'But I think I'll wait until you've completed your lab tests back at Lambeth Road. I'm pretty sure you'll find there's some rational explanation for the evidence you've come up with here. I mean – other than a dead body deciding he'd had enough of lying in a box under the ground and wanting to go for a quick pint. If I believed that, I'd have my team out right now, searching all the local boozers.'

He shook his head. '*Occupant*, Steven, for Christ's sake! He wasn't an occupant. He was a fucking stiff.'

Brenda was still deeply in shock when DI Fairbrother and DS Morrison went round to her home to talk to her. She sat with her hands clasped together, staring at the photograph of Philip, and she answered their questions in a whisper, as if she didn't want him to hear what she was telling them in case he was embarrassed.

'Everybody liked him,' she said. 'I can't think of anybody who would have wanted to do him harm. He was always making people laugh.'

'What business was he in?' DI Fairbrother asked her. 'He wouldn't have upset anybody in his particular field of work, would he? He might have got up someone's nose without even knowing it. That can happen.'

'He runs an ironmonger's shop. Well – he *used* to run it. Harris's Hardware, on Garratt Lane. But I really can't imagine that he ever made anybody angry enough to dig him up out of his grave, especially a whole year after he was buried.'

Brenda's lips puckered with grief, and tears started to slide down her cheeks. DS Morrison sat down on the sofa next to her and put her arm round her shoulders.

'I missed him so much when he died,' wept Brenda. 'But at least I could go to his grave and lay flowers on it and know that he was there, resting in peace. Now I have no idea where he is, or why anyone would be so cruel as to take him away. He's dead! Why couldn't they leave him alone?'

DS Morrison said, 'We're going to do everything we can to find out what's happened to him, Mrs Harris, believe me. Don't give up hope. We'll find him, I promise you, and we'll give him a second funeral, so that he can go back to sleeping undisturbed.'

As they drove back to the station, DI Fairbrother said, 'That was a bit rash, wasn't it, telling her that we'd definitely find him?'

'Well, maybe. But who's going to want to keep a decomposing body? The smell alone would be enough to put you off.'

'I don't know. There's no accounting for taste. My missus loves Limburger cheese and that stinks worse than a corpse any day.'

4

Jerry was parking his car behind Lavender Hill police station when another car drew up almost silently beside him and Jamila Patel climbed out. The man who was driving it climbed out too – an Asian-looking man with a neat beard and a light grey suit.

'Hey, too long no see!' Jerry told Jamila with a smile, and then nodded towards the driver. 'You all right for the fare?'

'Oh, this isn't an Uber,' said Jamila. 'This is my partner, Ashish Desai.'

'Your partner? You didn't tell me you had a partner.'

'Ashish and I only got together after you and I last worked together. He's a surgeon. Come and say hallo to Jerry, Ashish.'

Ashish came around his car and shook Jerry's hand. Jerry looked down at his shoes. He always checked out people's shoes first, because they invariably gave away so much. Ashish was wearing shiny black John Lobb shoes, recognisable by their distinctive double buckle, and Jerry knew for a fact that they cost over £1,000 a pair. It was then that he gave Ashish's car another look. Although it was a dull grey colour, it was a BMW M series, a top-of-the range electric saloon that cost at least £165,000.

Jerry was tempted to say, *Make a few bob then, do you,*

Ashish, cutting people up and stitching them back together again?

Instead, he said, 'Nice to meet you, mate. Make sure you take good care of Detective Inspector Patel, won't you? She's very special.'

'Of course,' said Ashish, resting his hand on Jamila's shoulder, as if he could sense Jerry's jealousy. 'Although I am sure she is capable of looking after not only herself, but me too. In medical college they did not teach us karate, or how to fire a gun.'

'Still, I expect you're pretty handy with a blade,' said Jerry.

Ashish gave Jamila a kiss on the cheek and told her that he would see her later. When he had driven off, Jamila said, 'He is a fine man, Ashish. He comes from a good family too.'

'Not like my Maureen, then. Her old man's been in and out of Wandsworth prison so often they're thinking of installing a revolving door for him.'

'You haven't told me about Maureen, either.'

'Well, it's on and off. I think she preferred her pet Pomeranian more than me, but he's dead and I'm still alive and at least I don't bark and piss on the kitchen floor.'

They went upstairs to Jerry's office. DS Watkins was sitting by the window, frowning at her desktop computer. She was a big woman, with a tight blonde bun. Jerry liked her a lot because she had a coarse sense of humour. He introduced her to Jamila, and Jamila gave her a quick, polite smile.

'Fancy a coffee, ma'am?' Jerry asked her.

'No, no thank you. I have just had one with Ashish. Tell me, what is all this about flies?'

'I'm not sure at all, to be honest with you. It may be a case for some kind of insect expert rather than us. Maybe David Blaine as well. You know, that escapologist. Somehow, the perp managed to enter the rectory even though all the doors were locked, and they were *still* locked when he or she left – although it was almost certain to have been a "he", judging by the size of the bruises on the reverend's neck.'

Having said that, he looked over at DS Watkins, and thought to himself that she could easily strangle any man with one hand while admiring her nail polish on the other.

Jerry described the state of the Reverend Wymarsh's body and the flies that were crammed into his mouth. Jamila listened to him, frowning, and then she said, 'Do you know what that reminds me of? It reminds me of vetalas.'

'What are "vetalas" when they're at home?'

'They are Hindu demons who carry out their evil deeds by raising the dead. They get corpses to steal and murder for them, and when the corpses appear they are almost always surrounded by flies. Well, because they are rotting, and they attract flies.'

'Yes, but why would a Hindu demon want to strangle a vicar in Clapham? And how would it get here from India, for a start?'

'I couldn't tell you, Jerry. I'm only saying that I'm reminded of vetalas, not that it actually could have been one.'

'Maybe we should check if there's any similar kind of spook in Christian culture. But before we start doing that, we really need to know if the Reverend Wymarsh had annoyed anyone enough for them to want to break into his rectory and murder him – or if maybe he was killed by terrorists. You know, some of those religious nutters who think that Jesus was the Devil in disguise.'

'There are plenty of those, I'm afraid,' said Jamila. 'Especially in Redbridge.'

'DCI Butcher's questioning just about everyone who

knew the Reverend Wymarsh,' said Jerry. 'Apart from that, the Martian's bringing down some fly expert from Oxford University. I don't think there's much point in us chasing after some legendary demon until we've heard something conclusive from both of them.'

'If it was a vetala, then we're going to need a Hindu priest, because vetalas are supposed to be trapped in a limbo between life and death, and the way to dismiss them is to give them a funeral service. I met a Hindu priest once when we were in Tooting – Sham Sunder. He could recite mantras and scatter ashes and turmeric and salt, and that would do the trick.'

Jerry sat for over half a minute looking at Jamila without saying anything. He almost hoped there would be no rational explanation for the Reverend Wymarsh's murder, so that they could work together again. He had grown to love her in a way that he had never loved any other woman. Maybe it was the secret knowledge they had come to share between them, that countless other worlds existed, apart from our own – some worlds that were ordinary, some that were bright and blissful, but others that were terrifying beyond all human understanding.

At the same time, he was willing to admit that he was mostly attracted by her self-possession, and her dark-brown eyes, and the sweet smell of Qamar perfume that she always wore.

'Did you have anything to eat with your coffee?' he asked her.

'Only some biscuits, why?'

'I thought it would be a good idea if we went over to Falcon Road so that you could have a butcher's at the reverend for yourself. But he's in the sort of condition that will probably make you regurgitate.'

'I have a strong stomach, Jerry. You know that. Have you ever seen me bring up my breakfast?'

Although her eyes were fixed on her PC screen, DS Watkins had obviously been listening to them. 'Talking of dead bodies, have you heard about that body that was half-inched last night from Wandsworth Cemetery?'

'You're joking.'

'No, DI Fairbrother's put out a call for any witnesses. Whoever it was, they dug up the grave, opened the coffin and made off with the deceased.'

'Bloody hell. Who would want to do that?'

'Don't ask me, Jerry. Maybe they wanted a nice ripe corpse to fertilise their vegetable patch.'

Jamila stood up. 'I must say that you have an unusual sense of humour, DS Watkins.'

DS Watkins didn't look away from her PC screen. 'You know what they say about this job, ma'am. You have two alternatives. Either you laugh like a drain or you go off your nut.'

Jerry drove them up to the coroner's office on Falcon Road. This time, he refrained from giving Kirsty his usual double tongue-click, but she smiled at him all the same and gave him a little finger-wave.

When they went upstairs, they found that Dr Crowe's assistant, Zahir, was waiting for them in the corridor outside the forensic laboratory. In one hand he was holding two surgical masks, and in the other an open jar of Vicks VapoRub.

'Started to pen-and-ink already, has he?' asked Jerry. Both he and Jamila knew why he was offering them the masks and the VapoRub.

'It is extraordinary,' said Zahir. 'He is bloating well before we expected him to. We have never seen a cadaver decompose so rapidly. From "fresh" to "bloat" in under two hours.'

Jamila and Jerry each poked their fingertips into the jar of VapoRub and dabbed some under their nostrils. The strong fumes of camphor and eucalyptus made Jamila give a tight, suppressed sneeze, and Jerry said, '*Gesundheit!*' before sneezing himself.

'*Al-hamdu Lillaah!*' said Jamila.

Dr Crowe was waiting for them in the laboratory. He, too, was wearing a surgical mask, but Jerry could tell by the way he stared at them how disturbed he was. A green sheet was draped over the pathology table to cover up the Reverend Wymarsh's body, but in spite of that, and in spite of the VapoRub under their noses, Jerry and Jamila could still smell putrefying flesh, or at least they imagined they could.

From experience, Jerry knew he would still be smelling it when he went to bed that night, and he would probably have nightmares about rotting corpses.

Dr Crowe said, 'I've already contacted Detective Chief Inspector Butcher about this development, and he's on his way back here. I have to admit that I have never seen such rapid decomposition in the whole of my career. Of course, I've never come across a cadaver that was infested with so many flies – not in the way that this one is.'

'Maybe when he gets here the fly expert will be able to tell us why he's gone off so fast,' said Jerry. 'There has to be some explanation for it.' He nodded towards the green sheet. 'Any chance of taking a look? I think DI Patel needs to see what we're dealing with here.'

'Of course,' said Dr Crowe. Then, 'Zahir – would you do the honours?'

Zahir drew back the sheet and folded it up. When Jerry saw how dramatically the Reverend Wymarsh had changed since his previous visit, he could hardly believe he was looking at the same dead body.

'Fucking hell,' he said, under his breath.

Jamila whispered, '*Mārā prabhu.*'

Instead of the emaciated figure that Jerry had seen before, here lay a hugely inflated parody of a man. His belly was grotesquely swollen and his arms and legs were blown up like the sausage-shaped balloons that party entertainers twist into animals.

The gases that had built up inside him had forced the liquids inside his bowels out of his mouth, his nostrils and his anus. His lips were covered in foul-smelling chocolatey froth, and there was more brown froth bubbling between his buttocks.

The skin over his stomach was stretched so thin that it had become pearly-white and translucent, and Jamila and Jerry could see scores of black flies swarming underneath it and laying eggs inside him.

'The flies made their way down from his mouth into his oesophagus,' said Dr Crowe. 'Under normal circumstances, I would have exterminated them. But of course these are not normal circumstances, not by a long chalk, and we need Dr Yearling to be able to examine them while they are still alive and going about their business.'

Even as they were talking, the Reverend Wymarsh's belly ruptured, just below his navel. There was a soft, putrid exhalation of hydrogen sulphide, carbon dioxide and methane, and his belly collapsed. At least a dozen flies came crawling out of the sagging rupture in his skin and began to spread out all over him, over his bony chest and into his grey pubic hair. Some of them started to fly around the laboratory, and Jerry had to flap his hand at one that was flying towards his face.

'I wish I could spray them,' said Dr Crowe, swatting two or three of them away, just like Jerry. 'Unfortunately, I can't contaminate the body until I've completed my whole examination. And I don't want to kill any of them before Dr Yearling has had a chance to take a look at them.'

'Can you think of any medical reason why the reverend's body should have decomposed so quickly?' asked Jamila.

Dr Crowe shook his head. 'Perhaps it was something he ate, although I don't think that's very likely. I've sent a sample from his bowels to be analysed, as well as his liver and his kidneys and his blood. I'm guessing it could be some mutated form of *Clostridium perfringens* bacteria, which causes gas gangrene, but I won't be able to tell for sure until all my tests are completed.'

Jerry turned to Jamila. 'Have you seen all you want to see? I'm beginning to feel a touch queasy, to be honest.'

'Yes, I think we can go,' Jamila told him. Then, to Dr Crowe, 'Thank you for showing us the reverend's remains. We look forward to your conclusions.'

'I doubt if you're looking forward to them half as much as I am,' said Dr Crowe.

When they reached the lobby, they found that DCI Butcher was standing there, waiting for the lift to come down.

'Oh, hi there, guv,' said Jerry. 'Come to see the rotting reverend, have you? You're in for a treat, I can tell you that for nothing.'

'I'm glad I've caught you both,' said DCI Butcher. 'I was going to call you anyway after I'd been here. Mallett's been checking the CCTV from around St Gratus at the time when the Reverend Wymarsh was done in.'

'Spotted anything helpful, has he?'

'Yes, he has. And it's confirmed my first feeling that this is definitely a case for you two to look into. A bit on the weird side, if you know what I mean.'

'How weird, exactly?'

'Mallett will show you for yourselves when you go back to the station. But the CCTV picked up a highly suspicious character approaching the church up Rectory Grove at about eleven thirty in the evening. What's weird is that when Mallett tracked this character's progress back to where he'd come from, he couldn't believe how fast he'd been walking. He managed to track him back down Rectory Grove as far as Clapham Common, but he lost him there, because he must have crossed the common on one of the footpaths, and they're not covered by cameras. He's still checking the CCTV around the perimeter of the common to see if he can find where he entered it.'

'So he's a fast walker,' said Jerry. 'I don't see what's so weird about that.'

'You will when you see the CCTV. He's walking fast but he's not moving his legs.'

'Not moving his legs? You're having a Turkish, aren't you?'

'Maybe he was wearing a pair of those electric roller-skates,' said Jamila.

'That's what we wondered, to begin with,' said DCI Butcher. 'His movement's very similar – you know, almost like he's rolling along the pavement. But you can clearly see from some of the video footage that he's not wearing anything on his feet except what look like socks.'

'But he's not moving his legs at all?'

'Not once. Not on any of the footage we've seen so far, anyway.'

Jerry gave Jamila a look that suggested that maybe DCI Butcher was right, and this was a case the two of them should investigate. He had called it 'a bit on the weird side', but from the rapid decomposition of the Reverend Wymarsh's body and now the information that a suspect had somehow been running towards the rectory without moving his legs, it was clearly way beyond weird.

Jerry's old grandfather would have called it 'well rummy'.

5

George was tying the swivel on his fishing line when he saw a pale object floating in the middle of the pond. He was short-sighted and at first he thought it might be a log. Last week had been stormy and many of the birch trees around Wandsworth Common had lost their branches.

When he stood up and put on his glasses, however, he realised that it was a human body, face down in the water. Two ducks were swimming past it, but they ignored it.

He looked around. The only other people in sight were three schoolboys who were kicking a ball to each other and an elderly woman in a bright-pink coat who was walking her dog. He took his phone out of his anorak pocket and pressed 999.

'Emergency. Which service, please?'

'I don't know, love. I'm fishing at Wandsworth Common pond and I think someone's gone and got drowned.'

'What makes you think that, sir?'

'Well, they're bobbing around in the middle of the pond and they haven't come up for air.'

'All right, sir. Please stay where you are and emergency services will be with you in a few minutes. Please don't enter the water yourself.'

'I wasn't going to, miss. It's bloody freezing cold and they're well past saving, whoever they are.'

George stayed by the side of the pond, clapping his hands and shuffling his feet to keep warm. After fifteen minutes, three police cars and a police van appeared in the road beside the common, their blue lights flashing, followed by a black coroner's ambulance.

Nine officers came across the grass towards him, two of them wearing black wet suits and helmets.

'Thanks for your call, sir,' said a young inspector. 'So – where's our floater?'

George pointed out to the middle of the pond. The ducks had returned and were circling around the body and appeared to be pecking at it.

'Go on,' the inspector told the two officers in wet suits. 'Fish it out before there's nothing left of it.'

The officers waded into the pond. In the middle of it, the water came up to their shoulders.

They shooed the ducks away and then they slowly dragged the body to the side of the pond, lifting it out through the weeds with its arms dangling down. Two coroner's assistants had wheeled a trolley across the grass, and the officers lifted the body up on to it and turned it over. It was then that they could see from his shrivelled penis that he was a male, although he was badly decomposed.

His eye sockets were empty and his nose had rotted away, leaving two triangular holes. His pallid skin was stretched over his ribcage and his pelvis, and his feet were like fleshless claws. He was baring his teeth in a maniacal grin because he had no lips.

'Blimey,' said one of the officers. 'He looks like he's been dead since last Christmas.'

'Well, I don't think you're far wrong,' said the inspector.

'And he didn't drown here, either accidentally or intentionally, there's no mistake about that.'

'I was here only two days ago,' said George. 'He certainly wasn't floating around here then.'

The inspector bent over the man's body so that he could examine it more closely, his hand cupped over his nose and his mouth. Then he stood back and said, 'I reckon he was deceased long before he was dropped into the pond. Weeks, even months. It could be that someone was afraid his body was going to be discovered, and was trying to dispose of the evidence. I've come across that before.'

'Not a very clever way of doing it, though, was it?' put in one of his officers. 'They would have been much better off chucking him into the Thames. At least the tide would have carried him away.'

'We'll be taking him to Falcon Road,' said one of the coroner's assistants, a smart young black man in dark glasses. 'You'll be wanting a forensic postmortem, won't you, and Dr Crowe's there just now.'

'Of course,' the inspector told him. 'Cause of death isn't obvious, is it? No stab wounds or bullet holes so far as I can see. He could have been suffocated – or poisoned, if there's still any trace of it left in his system.'

He turned to George. 'Thank you again for alerting us, sir. If I could take your contact details, in case we need a short statement about how you first discovered the deceased. You can carry on now with whatever you were doing.'

George looked across the pond, which was faintly rippled by the breeze. Three forensic technicians had arrived in their white snowman suits, and they had already started to comb the edges of the pond for any sign of tyre tracks in the grass or footprints in the mud.

'I was just about to start fishing,' said George. 'But, you know, I think I'll give it a miss for today. As a matter of fact, I don't think I'll ever be able to fish here again. Never.'

Jamila and Jerry found Edge in the canteen when they returned to Lavender Hill. He was having a cup of tea and a corned beef sandwich, with the racing pages of the *Sun* spread out on the table in front of him.

'Don't you ever stop filling your face?' Jerry asked him.

'Got to keep my strength up. I've entered myself for the London marathon, and I'm in training.'

'That's over twenty-six miles, Edge. When do you ever get the time to train?'

'I haven't actually started any running yet. I'm training myself mentally. The brain burns up just as many calories as the body.'

'Well, talking of bodies, do you want to show us all this CCTV footage?'

Edge slurped the last of his tea and picked up the second half of his sandwich. They went together up to the communications room and sat down in front of one of the monitors. It was dim and silent in there, with two female officers watching nine different screens.

'So – have you had any luck finding out where the suspect might have come from?' asked Jamila.

'Not yet. As I'll show you, the first sight of him is coming out of the north side of Clapham Common, but I still haven't been able to see where he entered it. Two of the cameras on the west side of the common were out of action, one by Broomwood Road and the other at the end of Nightingale

Walk. They still are. I was having a quick break and then I was going to search a bit wider.'

He switched on the monitor and they could see the suspect leaving Clapham Common on the north side and heading up Rectory Grove towards St Gratus church.

For some reason, the CCTV cameras had been unable to focus on him in any detail. He was taller than average height, but his outline was blurred, and he reflected the light from the street lamps so that he appeared to shine – even, at times, to glitter. Jamila and Jerry could see that DCI Butcher had been right: although he was making his way up Rectory Grove as fast as if he were running, his legs were not moving at all.

'Gordon Bennett,' said Jerry. 'He's flying along. How's he doing that? Just like you said, ma'am, he's not wearing roller-skates. It's not too clear, is it, but it looks like his feet are dragging along the pavement.'

Jamila peered at the monitor closely, with her eyes narrowed. 'I've never seen anything like this in my life. Is he wearing some kind of special suit, made of tin foil? It's covering his head as well as his body. He looks like an alien out of a science-fiction film.'

'I've tried focusing on him sharper,' said Edge. 'But this is the best I could get. His outline's all kind of flickery, isn't it?'

They sat and watched as the suspect reached the rectory by the side of St Gratus church. Although the CCTV camera was some distance away, they could see him standing in the porch for a few moments, and then they could see that he opened the front door and disappeared inside. The time was 11:37.

'So how did he get in?' asked Jerry. 'More important, how did he get out? According to Butcher, that door was locked when the churchwarden went in to find the reverend dead, and it had to be locked with a key after it was closed.'

'We can see him come out,' said Edge. He fast-forwarded the CCTV footage until the suspect reappeared in the rectory porch, exactly sixteen minutes and twenty seconds later. He turned to face the door as if he were locking it, and then he made his way back down Rectory Grove, as fast as he had before. He turned into Clapham Common, and that was the last recording of him.

At that time of night, only a few people had been walking up and down Rectory Grove, but almost all of them had stopped and stared at the suspect as he went sliding past them. At least one of them had taken out her phone to take a video of him, but by the time she held it up he had vanished into the darkness.

'Has anybody reported seeing him?' asked Jamila.

Edge chewed and swallowed the last of his sandwich and shook his head. 'Gillian's been checking social media to see if anybody's posted a picture or a video of him, but nothing so far.'

'Right, then, we'll let you crack on with your searching,' Jerry told him. 'I think it's worth posting an appeal for witnesses on Facebook and Instagram and X. I know it was late at night, but somebody must have seen him before he started crossing the common. You couldn't really miss a shiny bloke whizzing past you without moving his legs, could you, even if you were pissed as a newt.'

'I'll let you know as soon as I pick him up again,' said Edge. 'It might take some time, though. He could have come from any direction at all.'

Jamila and Jerry went downstairs to Jerry's office. DS Watkins had gone out on a shout, but she had left behind the lingering smell of her Ariana Grande perfume spray.

'So, we're going to take this case on?' asked Jerry.

Jamila nodded. 'Yes. But not only because DCI Butcher wants us to. He is not a stupid man, but he has obviously recognised that with this investigation he is way out of his depth.'

'And we're not?'

'We may be. But we have successfully dealt with cases that are equally strange, haven't we? And I am very curious to find out who or *what* this suspect might be. Is he anything like a vetala? I'm sure that you want to know too.'

'Well, I do, for sure. I was just wondering that even if we locate him, maybe we'll need to rent a couple of e-scooters to catch up with him.'

'Jerry – are you ever serious?'

'Always. But like Ruthie said, you either laugh in this job or you go off your head. Especially when you're supposed to be nailing a shiny bloke who strangled a vicar and stuffed his mouth full of flies.'

Jamila called DCI Butcher to tell him that she and Jerry would agree to be involved in the investigation into the Reverend Wymarsh's murder.

'What did he say?' asked Jerry, when she had put down her phone.

'He said "thank the Lord". He's over at Falcon Road right now, because the entomologist has come down from Oxford, and he said that the entomologist is just as baffled as he is. He'd like us to go over there, if we can.'

'I was thinking about a coffee, but okay.'

They drove to Falcon Road and this time Jerry managed to park right outside. Dr Crowe was waiting for them in an office next to the laboratory, along with his assistant, Zahir, and Professor Yearling.

Jerry thought that Professor Yearling had exactly the right looks for an investigation that might have some kind of supernatural element. He was lean, and beaky-nosed, with grey swept-back hair, and he had a crimson handkerchief arranged like a florid rose in the breast pocket of his three-piece suit. He could have been the twin brother of the horror actor Peter Cushing.

He shook their hands. 'Detective Chief Inspector Butcher has been telling me that you two have teamed up before on some rather strange cases.'

'Yes, and this one is *very* strange,' said Jamila. She turned to DCI Butcher and said, 'We have just seen the CCTV footage. We are as bewildered as you are. Why does the suspect shine like that, and how can he run so fast without moving his legs?'

'I don't have the foggiest,' said DCI Butcher. 'Not only that, we've got another bit of a mystery here. Do you want to tell them what's bothering you, professor?'

Professor Yearling sat down at a desk at the side of the office and opened up his laptop. When he switched it on, an enlarged photograph of a fly appeared.

'This is one of the flies that I retrieved from the throat of the deceased,' he said, in a very precise tone of voice, as if he were giving a lecture.

Dr Crowe interrupted him. 'For now, we've stored the reverend's remains in the negative temperature fridge. However, we've left the flies in his mouth and his trachea and his abdomen until we know more about them and where they came from.'

'I can understand why Dr Crowe assumed that the flies are *Musca domestica*, or houseflies,' Professor Yearling continued.

'These, unusually, have red eyes like houseflies. Actually, though, they are a variety of *Conicera tibialis*, commonly known as "coffin flies". They are given this name because they are found almost exclusively in buried bodies.'

'How do they get into buried bodies?' asked Jamila. 'If the coffin is six feet underground and sealed, it seems impossible.'

'Sometimes flies will enter bodies in mortuaries, before they are buried. They will crawl into the nostrils of the deceased or into their mouths, and then they will lay their eggs. Most morticians will plug up a body's orifices to prevent this from happening, but it is not always possible.

'Apart from that – this fly, the *Conicera tibialis*, is capable of digging down over six feet under the earth to lay eggs on a body, especially if the casket has collapsed or there is any kind of aperture through which they can enter it. They can fit through unbelievably small spaces.'

'But the Reverend Wymarsh wasn't in a coffin when he was killed, was he?' said Jerry. 'He was lying in his bed in his jim-jams, reading a book by the look of it. What were these coffin flies doing in his bedroom, if they're only found in buried bodies, like you say?'

'That's why I'm puzzled,' Professor Yearling told him. 'One might possibly have expected to find a few *Sarcophaga carnaria* in a dead man's bedroom, or "flesh flies" as most people call them. They feed off carrion and dung and so forth. But it would have been unusual, even so, especially since there were so many of them. And of course these weren't flesh flies at all.'

'Do you have any theories about how these coffin flies might have come to fill up the reverend's mouth?' asked Jamila. 'Any ideas at all, even if they're far-fetched?'

'None, I'm afraid. Well – not unless the perpetrator who

strangled him came into his bedroom carrying a whole bottle full of flies and tipped them down his throat.'

'I was going to have a coffee and a doughnut,' said Jerry. 'For some reason, I've changed my mind.'

6

As soon as evening prayers were over, Sister Teresa left the convent and went next door to the guest house that was run by the nuns.

St Rita's House was almost fully booked up, as usual, but she had to prepare a bedroom on the third floor for a guest who would be arriving tomorrow from Canada.

Clapham Road was unusually empty of traffic, and there was a strong south-west wind blowing, which made Sister Teresa's veil flap like a seagull's wing. When she reached the top of the steps in front of the guest house, she turned and looked around. Sheets of newspaper were scuttling across the road and the street lights were flickering, which gave her the feeling that something strange was in the air.

She was only twenty-two, but her sensitivity to the world around her was the reason that she had joined the Franciscan convent. Ever since she was a small child she had been frightened by changes in the weather, or by unexplained noises, or what had appeared to be coincidences, like the same number appearing again and again. She had become a postulant because she thought that God might be able to explain to her what was happening in her life, and reassure her that she was not alone, and not in any danger.

Her mother had begged her not to become a nun, because she was attractive, and well-educated, and creative, and she had a promising future as a commercial artist. Her fears, however, had been overwhelming.

She entered the guest house. She could hear music playing and there was a smell of chicken casserole from this evening's dinner. Although the rooms were simply furnished and the facilities were basic, St Rita's House was popular because it was always clean, and the nuns were welcoming, and it had Wi-Fi, and it was cheap.

First of all, she went to the laundry cupboard and collected clean sheets and pillowcases and folded them over her arm.

As she was waiting for the lift, an elderly couple came out of the dining room, both of them deeply suntanned.

'Evening, sister!' the husband greeted her, in a broad Australian accent. 'Bit late to be changing beds!'

'It's never too late to do the Lord's work,' said Sister Teresa. 'Did you enjoy your meal?'

'Really yummo, thanks. As per usual. Do you know, this is the third time me and Doris have stayed here? You can stuff your Ritz, if you'll excuse my language.'

'Good night and God bless,' said Sister Teresa as the lift door opened and she stepped inside. It was the guest house motto.

The room she had to prepare for their Canadian guest was on the third floor, overlooking the back yard. It had a single bed and an armchair and a washbasin, and a framed picture on the wall of St Rita of Cascia flying high in some thundery clouds.

Sister Teresa set the clean linen down on the chair and stripped the bed of its sheets. There was a stain on the lower sheet that was probably semen. So many people are so lonely, she thought, and I would be lonely too, if it weren't for God. Even then, she had sometimes begun to wonder if God was really listening to her. He must have to attend to such a never-ending babble of prayers, day and night, century after century.

She had once had a boyfriend, Raymond, for a little over three months, and she could still remember how safe and wanted she had felt in his arms. But one day Raymond had gone up to Manchester for a job in IT and never come back. She had sent him message after message, and tried to call him again and again, but he had never replied. It had made her feel that she was nothing, and a nobody.

Once she had changed the sheets and straightened the brown candlewick bedcover, she sat down on the end of the bed and closed her eyes. She felt exhausted. The nuns always rose at 5 a.m. for silent meditation, followed by prayer. After breakfast this morning, Sister Teresa had spent the day at St Christopher's children's home in Wandsworth, helping the staff with their thirty-five orphans.

The children loved her, and several would simply sit next to her and hug her. She loved them, too, but she found it was emotionally draining to give them endless affection, apart from helping to cook their lunch and clean their bedrooms and go shopping for them.

She lay back on the bed with her eyes still closed. If she could rest for only ten minutes, that would help to restore some strength in her. She thought about some of the children she had been talking to today, especially little Margaret, who was only seven years old but had been abused by her stepfather. Margaret's innocence had been taken away from her, and she would never be able to forget what had been done to her. Sister Teresa had tried to tell her that as far as God and his angels were concerned, she was still pure.

She had meant only to rest, but she fell asleep, so deeply that she had no dreams. Ten minutes passed, and then another ninety.

She was still lying there sleeping when the bedroom door opened. A hand reached inside and switched off the light. Then the door was opened wider, and a figure stepped into the room. If Sister Teresa had been awake, she would have seen that the figure momentarily reflected the light from the landing outside, and that it sparkled, as if it were covered head to toe in sequins. But then it closed the door behind it and the room was in total darkness.

She was woken up instantly, though, when the hem of her habit was dragged forcibly upwards, right up as far as her hips.

She gave a choking cry and tried to raise her head, but then two strong hands were clamped around her neck and a thumb was pressed painfully hard on her larynx.

She couldn't scream, but she twisted and kicked and she struggled so violently that the figure climbed on top of her, and pinned her down with its weight.

She could see nothing but blackness. The grip on her throat was so tight now that she was unable even to gasp for breath. Weakly, she tried to lift her knee so that she could hit the figure in the groin, but her leg was tangled up in her habit.

Inside her brain, she pleaded for God to save her. But she could feel that the blackness was swallowing her up, and after seven minutes it swallowed her up completely.

The figure released its grip on her throat and waited for

a further few moments in case she took another desperate breath, but she lay still. When the figure was sure that she was not going to move any more, it bent its head forward and pressed its mouth against hers, pushing its tongue between her lips. It stayed there for almost a quarter of a minute. Then it stood up and pulled up her habit even further, so that it could reach the waistband of her thick cotton tights. It tugged them off and dropped them on the floor, and then it bent its head forward again and clamped its mouth between her thighs. Again, it stayed there for almost a quarter of a minute.

Eventually, it raised its head and climbed off the bed. It opened the door so that it could see Sister Teresa lying with her arms outstretched as if she had been crucified. The light from the landing showed that the bedroom was swarming with flies, pattering against the window and crawling up the curtains. Sister Teresa's face was crimson and swollen and her eyes were bulging from their sockets. Flies were crawling in and out of her veil.

The figure quietly closed the door and went back down the stairs, almost floating. Once it had left the guest house, it turned right and started to make its way southwards, towards Clapham Common, moving so fast and so smoothly that passers-by turned their heads to stare at it.

Jamila was buttoning up her coat, ready to return to Redbridge, when the phone rang.

Jerry picked it up and said, 'Detective Sergeant Pardoe. How can I help?'

'I saw your appeal on Instagram,' said a woman's voice.

'You know – asking if anybody had seen a man in a shiny suit who looked like he was roller-skating.'

'What, and you have?'

'Yes, about twenty minutes ago – just as we were coming out of Stockwell station. My boyfriend said I shouldn't bother to call you because he was probably only one of those street performers, you know, the ones who pretend to be statues and that.'

Jamila gave Jerry a little hand-wave and was heading for the door, but Jerry shook his head and pointed to his phone to indicate that this call could be important, and she should wait.

'What's your name, love?' he asked the woman.

'Jemima – Jemima Philbrow. We were on our way back home after seeing that Van Gogh exhibition.'

'And you saw this man only about twenty minutes ago? Can you describe him?'

'On Instagram you said he was wearing something shiny, but it was more like he was covered in this light grey fluff. It was all over him, this fluff, right from his head to his toes, even his face.'

'Fluff?'

'Well, that's what it looked like. Grey, and fluffy, but a little bit shiny.'

'How tall would you say he was?'

'About average. Five-nine, five-ten.'

'And which direction was he heading in?'

'Down towards the common. And he was going really fast – as fast as if he was roller-skating, like you said in your post. But I couldn't see any roller-skates, and when you roller-skate you move your legs, don't you? He wasn't moving his legs at all. I just couldn't believe it. He was going so fast, and he was weaving in and out of all the people who were waiting for a bus. They were all just as surprised as I was, I can tell you that.'

'Did you see where he went?'

'No. He was gone so quick. And of course it's dark. And to be honest with you, he frightened the life out of me. I think he frightened my boyfriend as well, but he didn't like to admit it.'

'Okay, Jemima. I'm making a note of your number in case I need to talk to you again. But I really appreciate your call, thank you.'

Jerry put down his phone and gave Jamila a look that said *What the hell are we dealing with here?*

'So what was that about?' Jamila asked him.

'Another shiny geezer who speeds along without moving his legs. Well, he was fluffy rather than shiny, according to this young lady. She saw him only twenty minutes ago whizzing past Stockwell station, heading south.'

'If he went past Stockwell station, it's more than likely that we have him on CCTV.'

'Let's go up and take a look, shall we? I was going to go up there anyway, to see if Edge was having any luck.'

Jamila looked at her watch. 'Ashish is coming to pick me up in a minute, but I don't think he'll mind waiting. He's always so calm. I suppose you have to be, when you're a surgeon.'

They took the lift up to the communications room. As they went up, Jamila peered at herself in the mirror and patted her hair and said, 'I wonder if this is the same man. If it is, perhaps he's committed another offence, and that's what he was running away from.'

'Come on. It must be the same man. I can't imagine there's two geezers who look like that. Not unless they're twins.'

They entered the communications room and Edge raised his hand in salute.

'Evening, ma'am. Good timing, skip. I was just about to come down and see you. I've finally managed to pick up our suspect leaving Clapham Common.'

'He's been seen again this evening, Edge,' said Jerry. 'Only about half an hour ago, going past Stockwell station. We've had a call from a member of the public.'

'You're joking. Really? I've managed to find footage of him making his way from Clapham Common south-westwards down Thurleigh Road, but as soon as he reaches Wandsworth Common – woof! – he disappears again.'

Edge played back the CCTV footage so that they could see the sparkling suspect gliding along the street towards Wandsworth Common.

'I've been sent dashcam footage from a 319 bus, which shows him crossing over Bolingbroke Grove and going into the common. But he definitely doesn't come out the other side of it, even though it's pretty well covered by CCTV. I've also got dashcam footage from two 219 buses, from round about the time he would have reappeared, but there's no sign of him. Not a dicky bird.'

'So perhaps he could have spent the night on the common?' asked Jamila. 'Maybe sleeping rough, although it's hard to imagine how he could be doing that. He's not the least noticeable person in the world, and the Parks Police would have spotted him, surely, or one of that Enable lot who take care of all the bushes and the trees. But anyway, he's reappeared this evening, and you definitely should be able to find footage of that.'

'Did you hear that they've recovered the body of a male from the pond at Wandsworth Common?' Edge asked him.

'Well, yes, of course,' said Jerry. 'We had a heads-up from DI Watson at Wimbledon. It was on the news, too. But that can't be our man. According to Watson, the geezer they found in the pond was badly decomposed, like he'd been brown bread for literally months. Watson's theory is that someone chucked his body in the pond because it had been hidden somewhere but they were panicking that it was going to be found.'

'Right,' said Edge. 'Let's take a look at the CCTV footage from Stockwell station. What did you say – about half an hour ago?'

He was still scrolling through the pictures from Clapham Road when Jerry's phone rang. It was DCI Butcher.

'Pardoe? I've got some rather bad news for you, I'm sorry to say. Another homicide, and the MO's almost identical to what was done to the Reverend Wymarsh. I'm afraid it looks like another one for you and DI Patel.'

'Oh, you're joking.'

'I'm afraid not. A nun's been found dead at St Rita's guest house, next to St Rita's convent. The cause of death isn't one hundred per cent certain yet, but it looks like a possible strangulation and she's covered in flies. And not just a few flies, either. Bloody hundreds of the buggers.'

'St Rita's guest house? Where's that?'

'Clapham Road, about half a mile south of the Oval.'

Jerry lowered his phone and looked across at Jamila. 'It's Butcher. And from what he just said, you might well have been right about our shiny geezer doing it again. A nun this time, and apparently she's got flies crawling all over her.'

'*Hē bhagavāna*,' said Jamila. 'I cannot even begin to imagine what we are up against here.'

***

Ashish was waiting for Jamila in the reception area. He looked tired.

'I'm so sorry, Ashish,' Jamila told him, taking hold of his hands. 'There's been a possible homicide reported and Jerry and I have to attend.'

'Will you be long?' asked Ashish. 'I can wait for a while, although I have to be up early tomorrow. I have to carry out a heart bypass.'

'I really don't know. It could be hours. But don't worry. I'll take an Uber back to Redbridge.'

Ashish frowned at Jerry over Jamila's shoulder as if he had planned this deliberately, but he said, 'Very well. But call me when you're safely home, won't you?'

Jerry drove them to St Rita's House. He was tempted to joke to Jamila that from the look Ashish had given him, he would be shit-scared to have him operate on his heart, but he decided to keep his mouth shut. He had learned from bitter experience that if you want to steal a woman from another man, you don't slag the other man off. That only makes the woman defensive about him, and it also makes her feel that you're criticising her taste in men.

It took them only a little over ten minutes to drive to St Rita's House. Four patrol cars with flashing blue lights were already parked outside, as well as a forensic van and a black coroner's ambulance. A van from Sky News was there too. The pavement had been cordoned off, although only a small crowd had gathered because it was so late.

A constable lifted the crime scene tape for them so that they could duck underneath it, and then they went up the steps and into the guest house. DCI Butcher was in the hallway, talking to the Mother Superior of St Rita's convent. When Jerry came closer, he could see from the Mother Superior's swollen eyes that she had been crying.

DCI Butcher introduced Jamila and Jerry, and then he said, 'The victim's up on the third floor. Sister Teresa, twenty-two years old, birth name Susan Lawrence. She joined the convent nineteen months ago.'

'She was so sweet and so shy,' put in the Mother Superior. 'She suffered from chronic social anxiety disorder, but she was especially good with orphans. I can't think why anyone would have wanted to do her any harm. She wouldn't hurt a fly.'

She pressed her hand to her mouth. 'Oh, Lord! Please forgive me! I shouldn't have said that, should I?'

'I'll take you up and you can see her for yourself,' said DCI Butcher. 'Have you both got Covid masks? Good, because you're going to need them. You don't want to – you know.'

Jerry knew he had been about to say 'swallow a fly' but had stopped himself.

They went up in the lift together to the third floor. The landing was brightly lit with halogen lamps and the bedroom door was open. They could see two forensic technicians in their Tyvek suits, bending over the young nun's body on the bed. A third technician was shuffling around the bedroom on her hands and knees, methodically examining the carpet with an ultraviolet torch.

The air was swarming with flies, so that the technicians had to keep batting them away. Flies were still crawling up the curtains and the walls and all over the bedcover.

'We can't spray the buggers yet because it might compromise any samples,' said DCI Butcher. 'But come in and see what's been done to her.'

Jamila and Jerry entered the bedroom. Sister Teresa was staring blindly at the ceiling, with flies clustered in her eyelashes. Flies were crawling in and out of her nostrils too.

Her mouth was wide open, and just like the Reverend Wymarsh, it was filled up with flies. Some of them obviously dead already, but it looked as if others were struggling to get past them and make their way further down her throat.

'This is what knocked me for six, though,' said DCI Butcher. He nodded to one of the technicians, who lifted Sister Teresa's habit. Her legs were bare and her pale thighs were parted. Her vagina was crammed with dozens of flies, even more than her mouth. They were crawling through her pubic hair, all over the lips of her vulva and down to her anus.

Jamila immediately turned away, and even Jerry looked for only a few moments longer. DCI Butcher nodded again, and the technician dropped Sister Teresa's habit to cover her up.

'Where in the name of everything holy did all those flies come from?' said Jamila, as they went back down in the lift. She was trembling with shock, and with anger. 'And who would have defiled that poor young woman like that? And how?'

Back in the hallway, DCI Butcher said, 'She'll be sent over to Falcon Road so that Dr Crowe can carry out a postmortem, and that professor can tell us what kind of flies they are. But as for *who* and *how*, I'm relying on you two to find that out, because I'm damned if I even know where to start. I've never seen anything like this in my whole career.'

'Well, we could be making some progress already,' said Jerry. He told DCI Butcher about the CCTV footage that Edge had found of the shiny figure making its way down to Wandsworth Common, and the report they had been given about a similar figure gliding this evening past Stockwell station.

DCI Butcher shook his head. 'This definitely sounds like a case that's up your street, rather than mine. I mean, God almighty. It sounds like this perp's not even human. More like a fucking ghost.'

7

The next morning, David was over half an hour late arriving at his delicatessen. His wife, Adina, had been suffering from one of her sick headaches and so he had offered to take their three-year-old daughter, Talia, to her kindergarten.

He was not unduly worried about being late. He knew that his assistant, Miriam, would have opened up the deli on time and that she would have started to take the meat and sausages and bowls of cholent out of the fridge and arrange them in the glass display cabinets under the counter.

It was raining when he arrived at the corner of Wandsworth Road and The Chase. Someone had left a battered maroon van in his usual space, and so he had to drive further down the road before he could find somewhere to park. He hurried back to the corner with his jacket pulled up over his head.

When he reached Kaplan's Kosher Deli, however, he stopped, and stared at the front windows with a sense of total unreality, as if he were still in bed at home and having a nightmare. He simply could not believe what he was looking at.

Both of the windows were covered by a mass of flies, thousands of them. There were so many that they looked like living net curtains. Even the small circular window in the door was obscured by flies.

Shaking, David pushed open the door and entered the deli. Flies were carpeting the floor and climbing up the walls and creeping over the half-dozen tables where customers could sit and eat. Flies had even managed to find their way inside the glass display cabinets and were swarming all over the plates of kosher chicken and salt beef and the bowls of pomegranate brisket and kugel.

The air was filled with flies, too, and David had to swat them away from his face.

'Miriam!' he shouted. 'Miriam! Are you there?'

There was no answer. Miriam must have come into work this morning because she had taken all the food out of the fridge, but David wondered if the flies had suddenly invaded the delicatessen and she had left in a panic. If that was what had happened, though, surely she would have phoned him. And where did all these thousands of flies come from? He kept Kaplan's Deli scrupulously clean, and he was regularly visited by health inspectors, and a *mashgiach* to check that all the food he was offering was strictly kosher.

'Miriam?' David called out. There was still no answer, so he went through to the kitchen, covering his mouth with one hand and flapping the other hand from side to side to keep the flies off. The kitchen, too, was filled with flies, crawling over the work surfaces and even climbing in and out of the sink. The fridge door was wide open and he could see flies clinging to the shelves.

His heart was beating so hard that he thought he might suffer a cardiac arrest. He was tempted to turn around, leave the delicatessen and call the police, and an exterminator too. But where was Miriam? The door to the storeroom at the back of the kitchen was closed, and he had to make sure she wasn't hiding inside. Maybe she had shut herself in there, and simply hadn't heard him, and that was why she hadn't answered.

He opened the storeroom door. It was dark inside, so he switched on the light. The shelves on either side were stacked with tins of kosher beans and anchovies and apple sauce, as well as bags of kosher flour and matzo meal.

At the end of the storeroom was a blank wall, and David let out a '*dah!*' of sheer shock. Spreadeagled against the wall was Miriam, completely naked, with flies swarming all over her.

Her long dark hair had been loosened from its usual buns and was straggling down to her shoulders. The palms of both hands had been nailed to the wall, and her ankles had been crossed over and fastened to the wall with a single nail too.

David slowly approached her. At first he thought she was dead, but as he came nearer she opened her eyes.

'*David,*' she whispered, and as she opened her mouth, three flies crawled out. They clung to her lips for a moment, rubbing their legs together and fluttering their wings, as if to dry themselves, and then they flew off. '*David, help me.*'

'Dear God, Miriam, I will. Look – I can't pull you down, I'll only hurt you more. I'll call for an ambulance. Here, I'm doing it now. Hold on, sweetheart. Try and hold on.'

He prodded out 999.

'Emergency, which service?'

'Ambulance. As quick as you can, please. Kaplan's Kosher Deli on the corner of Wandsworth Road and The Chase. A young woman's been seriously injured.'

'The ambulance will be on its way. Can you tell me the nature of her injuries? Is she in any immediate danger?'

David looked up at Miriam, who was gazing at him like a wounded angel staring down from a cloud. Another fly crawled out of the side of her mouth.

David's eyes filled up with tears, so that his vision became blurry. He had never felt so helpless in his life.

'She's nailed to a wall!' he told the emergency operator. He was almost screaming. 'She's been crucified!'

Jerry was sitting in the Lavender Hill canteen with a plate of fried eggs, sausages and baked beans. Maureen had stayed overnight, and when she stayed overnight she usually cooked breakfast for him, but this morning they had argued because Maureen had taken such a long shower that she had used up all the hot water.

When Jerry had complained, she had told him that he could always take a shower at the station, and stormed off. He had no idea if he would ever see her again.

He had taken his first mouthful of baked beans when his phone warbled.

'Pardoe? Where are you?' It was DCI Butcher, and he sounded urgent.

'Having a bite of brekkie, guv. What's up?'

'Get yourself over to the corner of Wandsworth Road and The Chase. Kaplan's Kosher Deli. Like, *now*. There's been another assault with a load of flies. Even more flies than ever this time, but the victim's still alive. Just get here, pronto. I'll be calling DI Patel and giving her the heads-up too.'

Jerry looked down at his plate and thought, *shit*. He used a paper napkin to pick up one of the sausages, and then he pushed back his chair, stood up and hurried out of the canteen. Bimpe the cook watched him go but all she could do was shrug. She had seen too many officers have to rush off and leave their meals half eaten, although she was sad to see Jerry go. She liked him a lot, and that was why she had given him an extra egg.

It took Jerry less than five minutes to drive to Kaplan's

Kosher Deli. Two patrol cars were parked on the pavement outside, and an ambulance and a forensic van were double-parked in The Chase. He parked his own car close behind the forensic van and climbed out, taking a last bite of sausage and crumpling up his napkin.

DCI Butcher was standing outside the front door of the deli, with a blue Covid mask under his chin. He waved his hand towards the windows, which were still teeming with flies.

'Bloody hell,' said Jerry.

'It's worse inside,' said DCI Butcher. 'Got your mask, I hope? Come and take a look. The victim's a young woman who works in the deli. Can you believe she was nailed to the wall in the storeroom. They're just trying to get her free now.'

Jerry followed him into the delicatessen. The arrival of so many people had stirred up the flies into a frenzy, and the air was thick with them, pattering against the walls and the windows. As they made their way through the kitchen and into the storeroom, both Jerry and DCI Butcher had to flap their hands furiously from side to side like windscreen wipers.

Jerry felt several flies catching in his hair, and as he reached up to tug them free, another fly flew into his left ear.

'Jesus,' he said, shaking his head to dislodge it.

The storeroom was crowded with three uniformed police officers, two forensic technicians and a female paramedic, as well as David.

Miriam was still nailed to the wall, although a red checkered tablecloth had been tied around her to cover her nakedness. The nails had already been removed from her ankles and her right hand, but her left hand was still pinned against the plaster. One of the forensic technicians was holding her upright, while the other technician was standing on a box and using a hand-held hacksaw to take the head off the nail that protruded from her palm.

Miriam's eyes were closed, but the paramedic was keeping her finger on her pulse. She had already stuck a thick sterile dressing over the hole in her right hand.

'Miriam, *ahuvati*,' said David, over the harsh sound of sawing and the rustling of Tyvek suits. 'Hold on, Miriam. It won't be long now and we'll have you free. Don't worry, you're going to be fine. *Hashem yevarech otha*.'

Miriam's eyelids flickered, and she whispered, 'Where am I?'

It was then that the head dropped off the nail, and between them the paramedic and the forensic technician were able to lift her down from the wall. Another paramedic had wheeled a trolley into the kitchen, and Jerry and DCI Butcher stood back while Miriam was carried out of the storeroom and laid down on it, with a blanket to cover her.

'Where will you take her?' asked DCI Butcher, his voice muffled behind his mask. 'St George's?'

The paramedic had been flapping the flies away, but he managed to give DCI Butcher the thumbs-up. Then he wheeled Miriam away, with David following close behind.

Jerry was sitting with David in the waiting room at St George's Hospital when Jamila arrived. They were watching the BBC London news, which had already reported that a woman had been assaulted in Kaplan's Kosher Deli, and that the whole delicatessen had been teeming with flies.

'It's like one of those insect hotels in there,' the TV reporter had said, standing in front of the delicatessen windows. 'Except – as you can see – *this* insect hotel is mind-bogglingly overcrowded.'

The softly spoken Indian doctor who was taking care of Miriam had come down to inform Jerry that it would be several hours before she was in a fit state to be questioned. The wounds in her hands and ankles had been dressed and she was being given dopamine treatment for shock, but she was still unconscious.

Jamila walked in, took off her plastic rain hat and shook it. 'Isn't it *ever* going to stop raining?' she complained. 'If I was a Christian, I would be thinking about building an ark by now.'

'This is Detective Inspector Patel,' Jerry told David. 'She and I will be working together to track down whoever it was who attacked your Miriam. And also to find out where all those effing flies came from.'

'I still can't believe it,' said David. 'It was worse than a nightmare. I mean, who would want to nail an innocent young woman to a wall?' He turned to Jerry. 'I didn't think to ask you before, but did that doctor tell you if she'd been sexually assaulted?'

'No, he didn't,' said Jerry. 'Apart from the nails in her hands and her ankles, the only other injuries he mentioned were some really bad bruises on her thighs and her forearms. They could well have been the result of her struggling, and being lifted up against the wall.'

'She'll be given a full forensic examination in due course,' Jamila put in. 'Meanwhile, the most important thing is for her to recover. And, of course, the next most important thing is to identify her assailant and make sure he can never hurt any other young woman like that, ever again.'

David shook his head. 'Whether you find him or not, that's

my business down the Swanee, for definite. It's been on the news twice since we've been here. Who's going to want to buy food from a deli that was full of flies, *lemá'an hashém?* Kaplan's Insect Hotel.'

Jamila said, 'Please excuse us, Mr Aaronson. I have to have a private word with DS Pardoe here. We need to get this investigation moving as quickly as possible.'

She beckoned Jerry to join her outside the waiting room, and they crossed over to a quiet corner of the reception area. Jamila was almost always placid, even in the most stressful of situations, because she believed that there was an answer to every mystery, no matter how baffling it appeared at first. This morning, though, Jerry thought she looked unusually agitated.

'So what's on your mind?' he asked her. 'I wonder if you've been thinking what I've been thinking.'

'Very possibly. I was thinking on the way here that these two murders and this assault on this poor young woman all have one thing in common, which is religion. A vicar, a nun, and now a crucifixion in a Jewish delicatessen.'

'Well, yes, that occurred to me too,' said Jerry. 'But what's the motive? We're talking about three different religions here, aren't we, so what's the connection? An Anglican vicar, a Roman Catholic nun, and a Jewish girl. Like, who's going to be next? Maybe a Buddhist, or a Mormon. Or one of those nutters who thinks the world's going to come to an end next Tuesday.'

'I'm sure the religious element is important. But I also believe that the presence of all these flies has great significance. I have no idea what that significance could be, or how so many flies can appear like that, in such a short space of time. But I have the feeling that if we can find the answer to those two questions, then we'll understand who's been committing these attacks, and why.'

'So far as we know, it's that shiny geezer, isn't it? I've already got Edge checking the CCTV from Wandsworth Road to see if he's been picked up entering that deli this morning. And maybe we should go back and have another chat with that insect professor, if he hasn't shot off back to Oxford already.'

'There's someone else I feel we should talk to,' said Jamila. 'His name is Father William Devine, and he is the parish priest at Our Lady Help of Christians in Ilford. He knows more about the supernatural side of religion than anybody I have ever met.'

'How'd you come across him, then?'

'A woman in Ilford was beaten nearly to death two years ago because her husband said that she was possessed by a fallen angel and he was trying to exorcise it. Certainly, the woman's behaviour was very strange, even after she had recovered from her beating, and so Father Devine came to see her. He's an official exorcist.'

'Blimey. The woman's head didn't swivel round, did it?'

'No. I'm not sure what Father Devine actually did, but the woman was much more stable after he'd visited her. We prosecuted the husband for GBH, of course, but Father Devine gave evidence on his behalf, saying he would have had every reason to believe that his wife was possessed.'

'All right, then. Let's go and ask him if he's got any idea what's going on.'

They were about to go back into the waiting room when Jerry's phone rang. It was Edge.

'Hi, skip. I've been through all this morning's footage from the camera opposite Kaplan's Deli, and guess what?'

'Go on, Edge, enlighten me.'

'Just before seven o'clock, the lens of the camera on the corner of Wandsworth Road and The Chase got covered up, so everything after that's a total blank.'

'What do you mean, "covered up"? Covered up by what?'

'Flies, skip. Flies.'

8

Canon Roger Williams was sitting at his desk with his eyes closed, almost asleep, when there was a polite knock at the open door of his sacristy.

He opened his eyes and saw that it was Zedd, a Czech handyman who came around regularly to fix any problems with the roof tiles or the plumbing or to tidy the oratory graveyard.

'Sorry if I disturb you, sir,' said Zedd. He was very tall and thin, with a bushy beard and a man bun.

'Oh, that's quite all right,' Canon Williams reassured him. 'I was up for most of the night with one of my parishioners, a poor old gentleman of ninety-seven years old. He was taking his last breaths before the Lord lifted his soul up to heaven, but that didn't happen until five past five this morning.'

'The rain is stop and the sun shines,' said Zedd. 'I was think maybe to cut down the grass in the graveyard. It is very high now.'

'Of course. I thought of calling you yesterday to give it a trim, but it was raining so hard that there didn't seem much point.'

'Okay. I do it now. And maybe I also fix those broken bricks in the graveyard wall.'

Once Zedd had gone back outside, Canon Williams stood

up and wearily went into the oratory to stand in front of the altar. The Oratory of St Mark the Evangelist was elaborately decorated, with a gilded screen behind the altar with representations of the twelve disciples, and stained-glass windows, and statuettes of Mary and Joseph in little alcoves.

Canon Williams crossed himself and asked God yet again to give him strength. He had been married before he was ordained, but eighteen months after his ordination his wife had left him. He had heard only last month that she had married again, and it had given him a pang and a sense of loneliness that even God's companionship had not yet completely assuaged. He still wore his wedding ring, though, because it gave him some comfort.

He had been appointed parish priest here in Wandsworth less than a year ago, after the previous priest had died, but he had already made many friends among the parishioners, and he found that comforting too.

He returned to his sacristy and sat down to write some notes for next month's parish magazine. He had written only 'Time flies, and already we have found ourselves in Advent, preparing ourselves once again to celebrate the birth of our Saviour' when Zedd appeared in the doorway, and this time he was too flustered to knock.

'Zedd? What's wrong?'

'It is dug up, sir! The grave of the Canon Walach!'

'Dug up? What do you mean?'

'All dug up, sir, and the coffin broke open, and the canon gone!'

Canon Williams dropped his pen, pushed back his chair, and followed Zedd outside to the small graveyard that lay beside the oratory. It was overgrown with grass and weeds, and most of the tombstones were weathered and topped with moss. Nobody had been buried there since 1938, except for the parish priests who had served there. Canon Walach had been Canon Williams' predecessor, and he had died at the age of only fifty-nine of congestive heart failure.

His grave was on the far side of the cemetery, overshadowed by a firethorn bush that was clustered with bright orange berries. His grey marble gravestone was still there, but as Zedd had said, the grave itself had been dug up, and there were heaps of dry soil on either side of it.

Canon Williams looked down and saw that the coffin was empty, its lid broken and tilted to one side. A stained white cushion still bore the impression of Canon Walach's head.

'I can't believe this,' he said. 'Graverobbers, in this day and age?'

'I look here in the graveyard yesterday afternoon,' said Zedd. 'Everything was okay then, so somebody must dig him up in the night.'

Canon Williams crossed himself and then hurried back to his sacristy to call the police.

Steven the forensic technician climbed out of the grave and smacked soil off his gloves.

'Don't tell me,' said DI Fairbrother. 'He was just like the other one. He got fed up with lying there in the dark and he dug himself out.'

'Spot on,' said Steven.

'What? You're joking, aren't you? Because I was.'

'I wish I had been. But, no. The coffin lid was definitely forced open from the inside, and the way the excavated soil is stratified shows us without any doubt that it was dug out from the coffin upwards. It's exactly the same as we found at

Wandsworth Cemetery. Look at all those clumps of grass on top of the soil. If the grave had been dug out from ground level downwards, that grass would have been underneath it, because it would have been dug up first.'

'I don't know what the hell to make of this,' said DI Fairbrother. 'Talk about the Day of the Dead.'

'I can't work it out either, to tell you the truth,' said Steven. 'We're still testing the coffin and the samples of soil from Wandsworth, but we haven't yet come up with any explanation of how the deceased managed to dig himself out of his grave. He'd been dead for a year, hadn't he, so there was no question of him being buried alive.'

He narrowed his eyes to read the inscription on the gravestone. 'Do we know how long ago this bloke was buried – this Reverend Father Kaczimicz Walach?'

'About a year, so the priest told me. I'll be going inside in a minute to have another chat with him. Apparently, they stopped burying their parishioners here back in the thirties, because the graveyard was getting overcrowded, but they still bury their parish priests in this small corner they have left.'

Steven looked down into the grave again. One of his fellow technicians was still kneeling in the coffin, shining a UV lamp on its broken lid.

'I'll tell you my best guess,' he told DI Fairbrother.

'Oh, yes. And what's that?'

'I reckon we're dreaming this. We're going to wake up soon and find out that it never happened.'

DI Fairbrother puffed out his cheeks. 'Jesus Christ, Steven. That would solve all of our problems.'

He went back into the oratory and found Canon Williams lighting candles on the altar.

'For Father Walach,' said Canon Williams. 'I didn't know him well, but he was always good-humoured, and very traditional, like me. A staunch believer in the *ad orientem* mass.'

'We're still not sure how his remains were disinterred,' said DI Fairbrother. 'But just for the record, do you happen to know if he'd upset anybody, before he died? If he'd made any enemies, for whatever reason? Or if he'd had threats – say from another religious community? You have to admit that this is a pretty rough area.'

'He had no enemies that I know of, detective inspector. Not unless you count Satan, or one of his demons.'

Jamila and Jerry had been planning on having lunch at Mien Tay, the Vietnamese restaurant only a minute's walk down Lavender Hill. Jamila particularly liked their salt, pepper and garlic tofu. Jerry always chose their chargrilled quail with honey and garlic because Maureen, he said, would never be able to cook him anything like that. She could rustle up a passable English breakfast, with scrambled eggs and grilled tomatoes, but that was about the limit of her culinary talents.

As they were buttoning up their coats, though, Jamila's phone rang.

'Well, yes, we can,' she said, 'if you really can't make it later.'

'We can what?' Jerry asked her, as she put her phone back in her pocket.

'That was Dr Crowe. He said he needs us to come over to Falcon Road so that he can show us what happened to that poor nun. He says he also has something else that we might find relevant.'

'And he wants us to go over there now? Mien Tay closes at three and I could eat the trunk off a dead elephant. With or without garlic.'

'He says he has to go to Reading this afternoon to carry out a postmortem on two children who died in a house fire.'

'Well, all right,' said Jerry. 'I can't say I envy him, I must say. I've already seen enough of the dear departed for one lifetime.'

They drove to Falcon Road and Jerry parked on a double yellow line right outside the coroner's office. Upstairs, they found Zahir waiting for them with surgical masks and Vicks VapoRub, as before.

'Watch out... there are still some live flies buzzing around,' he warned them. 'Also, we do not know if the deceased might be carrying some infection.'

Inside the forensic laboratory, Dr Crowe was sitting at his desk, tapping with two fingers at the keyboard of his laptop. Sister Teresa was lying on the examination table, covered up to her chin with a sheet. Her face was white, but she looked as beautiful as a marble sculpture of a Vestal virgin.

Parked on the opposite side of the laboratory was another trolley with a body on it, but it was completely covered by a green sheet.

'Ah, you two, glad you could make it,' said Dr Crowe, prodding his keyboard one more time and closing his laptop. He stood up and went over to the examination table, looking down at Sister Teresa with an expression that was almost fatherly.

'What an unfortunate young woman,' he said in his theatrical voice, as if it were the first line in one of Shakespeare's plays. 'She dedicated her life to God, but went to meet him far sooner than she deserved.'

He paused, and then he said, 'You will notice that I have removed the flies from her mouth and her oesophagus, and from her vagina too. A few of them had climbed up as far as her cervix.'

'It's totally horrifying,' said Jamila, shaking her head. 'How many flies altogether? Have you counted them?'

'One hundred and six. And I was sure they were the same variety of flies that we found in the mouth of the Reverend Wymarsh – *Conicera tibialis*. Professor Yearling went back to Oxford yesterday evening before she was brought in, but I emailed him a picture of one of the flies and he confirmed it.'

'How the hell did they get inside her?' asked Jerry.

'That's another thing I can tell you,' said Dr Crowe. 'I found some light bruising around her mouth and around her vulva, which indicates that her assailant pressed his mouth against both of them with considerable pressure. There is even an indentation caused by incisors, so he was almost biting her. I can only assume that while he was doing so, he was somehow filling both her mouth and her vagina with these swarms of flies. Don't ask me how – unless he himself was filled up with them.'

'You're sure it was a "he"?' said Jamila.

Dr Crowe folded the sheet down from Sister Teresa's chin. They could see then that her neck was purple with massive bruises.

'Oh, yes. Her assailant left DNA on her mouth and her vulva and I was quite quickly able to determine from the Y chromosome in its amelogenin gene that it was almost one hundred per cent male. Apart from which, there are not many women who would have been able to contuse her neck as badly as this.'

'Fingerprints?' asked Jamila.

'Yes. A thumbprint on her larynx and three more around the side of her neck. They've been lifted and I've already sent them off to Lambeth Road to see if there's any comparison on file.'

Dr Crowe respectfully folded the sheet back over Sister Teresa's neck.

'I'll be writing up a complete postmortem report for you and I should be able to send it to you first thing tomorrow. But meanwhile, there's something else I have to show you. I didn't want to jump to any conclusions without further evidence, but it does strike me that it might have relevance to your investigation into these flies.'

He led them across the laboratory and Zahir lifted the sheet off the body on the trolley. Jamila gagged, and Jerry said, 'Holy shit.'

It was a man's body in an advanced state of decomposition, his flesh blotchy green and black. Some of his ribs had ripped through his papery skin. His face had the appearance of a ghastly laughing carnival mask.

'This is the gentleman who was retrieved from the fishing pond on Wandsworth Common,' said Dr Crowe. 'We've identified him as Philip Harris – the same Philip Harris who was disinterred from his grave at Wandsworth Cemetery two days ago. Although, as you know, there is some speculation that he somehow magically managed to dig himself out.'

As they stood looking at Philip Harris's body, three or four flies circled around and settled on his face. Zahir flicked them away with his notepad.

'DI Fairbrother's handling this one,' said Jerry. 'So where exactly do we come into it? Apart from the possibility that he dug himself out of his own grave. That's a touch on the spooky side, I have to admit.'

'Flies have adhesive pads on their feet called pulvilli,' said Dr Crowe. 'These are covered with setae, which are tiny hairs with curved spatula-like tips. It used to be thought that these hairs alone were enough to give flies their grip, so they could cling on to walls and ceilings. But later it was discovered that they actually produce a glue-like substance composed of sugar and oils, and it is this adhesive substance that allows them to walk around vertically and upside down.'

'So why don't they get permanently stuck?' asked Jamila.

'Because the adhesiveness of the glue varies according to the surface they've landed on, and when they want to fly away they have a pair of claws on each foot to peel their footpads free.'

'Fly Glue,' said Jerry. 'Sounds like something you could bottle and sell to home decorators. Stick it on your hands and knees and then you could climb up there and paint your ceiling without needing a stepladder.'

'What is the relevance of this?' asked Jamila.

'The relevance is that I discovered traces of this substance all over Mr Harris's body, from his head down to his feet. The water in the fishing pond was extremely cold, only two or three degrees above freezing, and it had not had time to wash all traces of the substance away before his body was retrieved. I also found microscopic traces of scratches all over him, head to foot, and these matched the kind of scratches made by the claws of *Conicera tibialis* when they prise themselves free from anything yielding they might have landed on, such as human skin.'

'So what you're telling us is that at some point Mr Harris's body was totally covered in flies?'

'Yes. And despite the condition of his remains, this happened recently.'

Jamila was silent for a few moments, looking down at the rotting body of Philip Harris. He was staring back at her with his hollow eye sockets and his hideous Joker-like grin, as if he were taunting her. *Go on, ask it, I dare you.*

'This is pure conjecture,' she said. 'But if he was totally covered in flies, and I suppose we're talking about thousands of them – could they collectively have had the strength to lift him up, and enable him to move around?'

'It would certainly take a great number,' Dr Crowe told her. 'A single fly can lift 10 milligrams, or about 110 millionths of a pound. So it would require at least five million to lift him, although there would not have been room for all five million to cling directly on to his skin. Mind you, the only figures I have is for houseflies. It's possible that coffin flies may have the capability to lift a fraction more.'

'And if they all flapped their wings at once?'

'Then, who knows? Maybe he would have been able to move. But as you say, this is pure conjecture.'

Jerry swatted another fly away. Then he turned to Jamila and said, 'If he was covered all over with flies, and they were all flapping their wings, he wouldn't have needed to move his legs, would he? He would've been flying.

He paused, and then he said, 'This is our shiny geezer. I bet you.'

9

Gerald came back into the funeral home, shaking raindrops from his large black umbrella.

'Thank God we've got that fixed,' he told Nadia. 'You can just imagine what it would have been like if we'd tried to drive to the crem tomorrow morning with a flat front tyre. That Mr Herbert would have done his nut.'

Nadia gave him a tight smile. It was she who had spotted this evening that one of the front tyres on their Etive electric hearse had been punctured. She was meticulous in everything she did, from dressing bodies for burial or cremation to dressing herself. At work she always wore a black tailored suit, and her black hair was always tightly tied back with a black silk ribbon. She was almost as pale as the clients who were lying in the refrigerators at the back of the funeral home.

Gerald dressed formally, too, with a black suit and a grey striped waistcoat, but he always looked like the best man who had drunk too much at his brother's wedding, with his hair sticking up, his cheeks flushed, and his bow tie askew.

'You've finished casketing Mrs Herbert?' he asked Nadia.

'Yes, but I had to cut that lovely silk gown down the back to make it fit. She was probably more than a stone and a half lighter when she last wore it.'

Gerald nodded towards a pair of emerald-green high-heeled

shoes that were standing on Nadia's desk. 'Her daughter brought those in, did she?'

'She said they were her mother's favourite. They're Valentino Garavani and they must have cost at least six hundred. I'll take them across to the children's charity shop next week. There's no way in the world that I'd be able to jam them on to her feet.'

'Not that she'll be walking anywhere,' said Gerald, although his tone was sad and respectful rather than joking. He always treated the deceased with the greatest care, making sure they were well dressed and that they appeared to be sleeping peacefully – even those who had been smashed up in car crashes or hit by trains.

He hung up his raincoat and was about to go into the back room when the doorbell rang. He went across to open the door and found a big, stocky-looking man standing outside. Because it was still raining, the man's thinning hair was sticking to his scalp, and the collar of his camel overcoat was turned up. His eyes were near-together and his lips were pursed as if he were angry about something.

'I'm sorry, we're closed,' Gerald told him. 'We're open again tomorrow at nine.'

'Oh, you're *closed*, are you?' the man replied. 'The people you've got in here, they need their kip, do they?'

'I'm sorry, but I can't help you this evening, I'm afraid,' Gerald repeated. 'Not unless it's something really urgent.'

'Oh, it's urgent all right. There's nothing more urgent than being dead, is there? When you're dead you need to do what needs to be done pronto, before you're too far gone, if you know what I mean.'

As the man was talking, a fly flew in through the door, and then another, and then three or four more. Gerald tried to swat them away with his hand, but they circled around the reception area, and one or two of them disappeared into the back room.

'I don't know what you mean, I'm afraid,' said Gerald. 'Now I'm really going to have to shut this door before any more flies come in. I can't imagine where they're coming from, not in this weather. Why don't you call again at nine o'clock tomorrow?'

'Because it's urgent, like I said,' the man told him. 'The grim reaper doesn't wait for nobody, does he? And neither do his flies.'

He lifted one hand as if he were making a signal to somebody standing behind him. Gerald stepped back, taking hold of the door and attempting to close it, but the man jammed his foot against it, staring at Gerald with an expression that was both threatening and triumphant.

'Get out of here,' said Gerald. 'Sod off before I call the police.'

'Ooh!' the man retorted. 'That's not very nice language for a funeral director, is it?'

He lifted his hand again, and snapped his fingers, and this time more flies flew in through the door, and then more, and then suddenly a swarm of thousands of flies came pouring into the funeral home. There were so many that they looked like a thick black blanket rippling in the air, and their zizzing noise was almost deafening. Nadia screamed and jumped up from her desk, wildly waving her arms to keep them away.

The flies covered the lampshades and the pictures on the walls and clung to the purple velvet curtains. Gerald staggered back, flapping his hands, but hundreds of flies clustered all over him. They covered his face, crawling all over his lips and into his nostrils and blinding his eyes. He could feel them in his hair and tickling inside his ears and even creeping inside the collar of his shirt.

He slapped his hands against his face, again and again, trying to crush them, but even when some of them dropped off he could feel more landing on him. He didn't shout out or call for Nadia to help him. He was afraid that if he opened his lips, the flies would crowd into his mouth. He could already feel them crawling around inside his sinuses, and he was holding his breath, terrified that he might suck some of them down into his lungs.

Blindly, he stumbled backwards, colliding with the chair in front of Nadia's desk. The chair tipped over and he fell over it, hitting his head on the side of the desk. Nadia had sat back down again, but now she too was covered completely in shimmering flies. She had opened her mouth to scream for help, and now the flies were pouring down her throat and choking her. She was gagging and trying feebly to spit them out, but there were too many of them.

The man in the camel overcoat stepped over Gerald's legs and made his way to the open door that led to the cooler room. The flies followed him in a cloud, although none of them settled on him.

Refrigerators lined each side of the room. The man went over to the left side and pulled out the first sliding drawer. The body of a red-haired woman lay inside in a white paper gown, her head raised on a block to prevent purge seeping from her nose and mouth. The man took hold of the hem of the gown with both hands and ripped it apart. Underneath she was wearing only a pair of plastic knickers, again to prevent fluids seeping out.

Once he had torn the paper gown off her, the man stepped to one side, and the swarm of flies immediately settled on her, furiously buzzing, as if they were fighting each other for a place to cling to her skin. Within less than a minute, her entire body was a mass of flies, some of them still crawling over each other, and all of them beating their wings, so that it looked as if her skin was shimmering silver.

Meanwhile, the man slid out another drawer, in which a bearded grey-haired man was lying, and then a third and fourth drawer, containing the bodies of a teenage boy and a balding middle-aged man, both of whom looked as if they had been the victims of a catastrophic car crash.

As soon as he had pulled them out, thousands more flies began to settle on them, until they too appeared to glitter from head to foot.

At last the man raised his one hand again and said something that was unintelligible, but sounded like a command.

The woman was the first to sit up. She raised her upper body and then heaved herself sideways off the refrigerator drawer so that she appeared to be standing upright on the floor. The teenage boy was next, rolling himself off the drawer and almost falling over. Then the two men, standing side by side but both swaying slightly in their fly-speckled shrouds as if they were drunk.

The man beckoned, and the four silvery figures followed him out of the refrigeration room and into the office. Nadia was still sitting at her desk, but her head was tilted back, and even though her eyes were open she was staring blindly at the ceiling. The last few flies were emerging from her mouth, fastidiously wiping their legs together to rub off her phlegm and her saliva, and then flying away.

Gerald was lying on the floor, facing the skirting board. He was breathing, but keeping his lips tightly closed and trying again and again to snort flies out of his nose. As before, the man climbed over him and the four silvery figures followed, although they floated over him rather than lifting their legs.

The man opened the door of the funeral home. He paused for a moment as if he were making sure the street was deserted, and then he stepped out into the darkness and the rain. His sparkling entourage of four dead people came after him and as they made their way along the shining wet pavement together, they weaved and circled around him as if they were being carried by an unfelt wind.

Jerry was about to put a frozen butter chicken curry in the microwave when his doorbell rang. When he opened it, Maureen was standing on the landing, with raindrops dripping from her pink hooded Puffa jacket.

'Oh, it's you,' said Jerry.

'Well, who did you expect, unless you've got some other floozy I don't know about?'

She pushed past him into the narrow hallway of his flat and unzipped her jacket. She unzipped her boots, too, and levered them off.

'Don't I get a kiss, then?' she demanded, looking up at him. Without her boots, she was only five foot three inches tall.

Jerry took her in his arms and kissed her. Greedily, she kissed him back, pushing her tongue into his mouth and giving him a taste of her cherry-flavoured lip gloss. After their ferocious argument yesterday, Jerry was surprised that she was so passionate, but he wasn't going to complain, especially when she started fondling the front of his trousers.

They had met six months ago when Jerry went into his local Oxfam charity shop to donate his old CDs, and Maureen had been working behind the counter. She was not the cleverest woman he had ever dated, but she was pretty, with a tangled mass of curly blonde hair, and she was funny, and she was very energetic in bed.

They went through into Jerry's living room. The television news was on, and as usual the room needed to be tidied up. A dismembered copy of the *Sun* newspaper was spread all over the couch, and a rickety wooden clothes horse was standing in front of the bookcase, crowded with socks and underpants and pyjamas.

'Have you eaten?' asked Jerry, picking up the newspaper pages from the couch and folding them up.

'I'm not hungry. Not for food, anyway. I wanted to see you, that's all.'

She sat down on the couch and crossed her legs. She was wearing a short black woollen dress and glossy black tights, and a circular silver pendant around her neck.

'How about a drink? I've still got some of that Pinot left.'

'I wanted to see you, that's all.'

'Are you sure? I'm going to help myself to a beer.'

She smiled at him but said nothing, and there was a strangely remote look in her eyes. When she didn't answer him, he went into the kitchen, opened the fridge, and came back with a can of Tyskie Polish beer. He popped it open and sat down next to her. She continued to smile, but her eyes still appeared to be focused on something in the distance.

He lifted up the silver pendant around her neck. It was engraved all around with stick-like symbols, and it was surprisingly heavy.

'So where'd you get this?' he asked her. 'Bloody weighs a ton, doesn't it?'

'It takes care of me.'

'What does that mean?'

'It tells me what to do.'

Jerry took a swig of his beer. 'I still don't understand, love. Did someone give it to you?'

Maureen took it back from him. 'Don't let's talk about me. Let's talk about you.'

'I only asked where you got it from. I've never seen anything quite like it. It looks like some kind of magical what-do-you-call-it – talisman.'

Maureen leaned forward and started to stroke Jerry's thigh, as if she were stroking a pet cat. With each stroke, her fingertips came higher and higher, towards his crotch.

'What case are you working on at the moment?' she asked him.

'What's that got to do with the price of Mars bars?'

'I'd like to know, that's all. You always say you're working on something really unusual, but you never actually tell me what it is.'

'There's not much I can tell you about it, love. It's all a bit of a pig's dinner at the moment. Even Jamila and me don't really have a scooby what's going on.'

'Is it very dangerous?'

'Dangerous? Why are you asking me that?'

Jerry put down his can of beer on the coffee table. Maureen was continuing to stroke his thigh, so he took hold of her wrist and stopped her. Apart from what she was asking him, there was something in her tone of voice and the way she was looking at him that distinctly unsettled him.

Why was she so keen to know what case he was currently involved in? She had never shown much interest in his detective work before. And why had she asked him if it might be dangerous, as if she knew somehow that it could be?

'You look really knackered, that's all,' said Maureen. 'You

ought to have a rest. When was the last time you had any time off?'

'What are you trying to say to me?' Jerry asked her.

'I'm saying that maybe you should stop working on this case and take a holiday.'

'You don't know a thing about it, love.'

Maureen leaned forward even further and kissed him. 'I don't want any harm to come to you, that's all. And I'm worried that it will.'

'Why? What makes you think that?'

Maureen smiled and kissed him again. 'Shall we go to bed? After yesterday, we've got some making-up to do, haven't we?'

'You're confusing me, I've got to tell you.'

'Will it confuse you if I give you a sucky-blow-blow?'

Jerry shook his head in amusement. 'I was just about to heat up a chicken curry, but if you put it like that—'

He was woken by his phone ringing. He lifted his head from the pillow, reached over to his bedside table and switched on his lamp. His digital clock showed him that it was 5:05 a.m.

He picked up his phone and at the same time he reached beside him to feel for Maureen lying next to him, but to his surprise she wasn't there. He sat up, tossed back the duvet and said, 'Hallo?'

It was Jamila on the phone. 'Jerry,' she said, 'I'm sorry if I've woken you. But I've just had a call from DCI Butcher.'

Jerry stood up and saw that the bedroom door had been left about an inch open, as if Maureen hadn't wanted to wake him up by closing it completely. He went out into the hallway and saw that her pink Puffa jacket was no longer hanging up and her boots had gone.

'There's been a serious assault at a funeral director's – Lettice & Pray on Merton Road. One fatality – a female partner – and one serious injury – a male partner. He's still in a coma at St George's.'

Jerry switched on the light in the kitchen to see if Maureen had left him a note. 'So where do you and me come into it?'

'Four bodies were taken from the refrigerators at the back of the funeral home. Four!'

'Jesus! How many perps did it take to pull that off? And what the hell did they want four bodies for? Not unless they were cannibals and they were feeling a bit peckish!'

'Jerry, there's nothing funny about this. DCI Butcher called me because the female partner who was found dead was choked by flies. Some of them were still down her throat when she was found. And the male partner still had flies crawling out of his nose.'

Jerry went into the living room, but there was no note from Maureen there either.

'So far we haven't been able to find any witnesses,' Jamila went on. 'Of course, we'll be checking all the CCTVs and doorbell cameras along Merton Road, but I expect you're thinking what I'm thinking, and what DCI Butcher's thinking, which is why he called me in the first place.'

'*Flies*,' said Jerry. He felt a deep sense of inevitability that made him shiver. 'Maybe that's how four stiffs got nicked from out of a funeral director's, all at once. Maybe they weren't carried out. Maybe they simply walked out – or *flew*, rather. Maybe we're looking for more of our shiny geezers.'

'When can you get to Merton Road?' asked Jamila. 'I'll meet you there as soon as you can.'

Jerry saw himself reflected in the mirror in the hallway. He was naked and covered in tiny red scratches, and he thought of how fiercely Maureen had made love to him last night, biting his neck and his earlobes and digging her fingernails into him. For one split second, he had even been worried that she was going to bite off the end of his penis – so much so that he had grabbed hold of her hair and pulled her head back.

'Okay,' he told Jamila. 'But I think this is going to be one of those days.'

10

'Right – do you all have your test papers?' Martin called out. 'Sandra – I think you've dropped one of yours on the floor. Yes, it's down by your bag, dear.'

Martin always looked forward to half-term exam time. It gave him a few hours' peace to catch up with the latest Detective Mouton novel and to stare out of the window and think about his life. He would be thirty-seven in February, and he wondered if he was going to be spending all his remaining years trying to teach basic maths to teenagers who were more interested in TikTok.

To be fair, the students at St Juliana's Church of England School were comparatively well behaved and gave him very little trouble. He knew of five teachers who had quit their jobs at state secondary schools because of violence and swearing from their students. If the teachers punished them by giving them detention or extra homework, their parents would turn up at the school and threaten them with even more foul language.

Martin returned to his desk. A fly had settled on his open register, and he flicked it away. 'You have an hour and a half to complete all your answers,' he reminded the twenty-two young students sitting in front of him. 'If you get stuck on one question, remember what I told you. Go on to the next question and return to it later.'

A boy at the back of the class put up his hand. 'Sir – what do we do if we get stuck on all of them?'

'Then leave the room quietly, close the door behind you, and go and apply for a job at McDonald's.'

The class all laughed. Then they started to work on their test papers and the classroom fell silent. Martin prodded his phone to send a message to his wife, Jeanette, telling her that he would pick her up at six to go shopping. After that, he opened his detective novel to chapter 5 and began to read.

There is no question, monsieur – Georges Marat was deliberately infected with hepatitis C. It was that filthy woman – Mademoiselle Crasseux.'

He had just turned the page when he saw that Satya Yadav appeared to be waving to him. He stood up and walked down the aisle to her desk.

'Satya – did you need something?'

'No, sir. These flies keep landing on my test paper, that's all.'

While she spoke, three flies settled on her desk, and two of them started to crawl across her test paper. Martin picked up the test paper and shook them off, but they kept on circling around Satya's head.

'I'll go and see if Gordon the janitor's got some fly spray,' Martin told her. 'Meanwhile, you can have an extra ten minutes to finish your test.'

'Can I have an extra ten minutes too, sir?' asked John Peebles, who was sitting at the next desk. 'Satya's really been putting me off, flapping her arms around like that.'

'All right. In fact, the whole class can have an extra ten minutes.'

Jesus, he thought, looking up to the picture of Christ

hanging over the classroom door. The Lord was smiling benignly, his halo shining and his arms outspread, surrounded by lambs. The same picture hung in every classroom at St Juliana's, and a massive crucifix hung at the end of the dining hall.

When Martin opened the classroom door, he found to his surprise that a man was standing there, facing him. The man was wearing a long camel overcoat and a brown trilby hat, and he was staring unblinkingly at Martin as if he had a bone to pick with him and had been waiting for him to appear.

What startled Martin the most, though, was that the air in the corridor behind this man was thick with flies, hundreds of them, maybe even thousands of them, and they were buzzing so loudly Martin was surprised he hadn't heard them in the classroom. Some were crawling up the walls and across the ceiling, and more of them were covering the windows, blocking out the daylight.

'Excuse me, who are you?' Martin demanded. 'And where the hell did all these flies come from?'

'Teachers need teaching a lesson, too, now and then,' the man replied. He had a distinctly East End accent, pronouncing it 'toychers'. 'That's what these flies have come here for.'

'I think you'd better get out of here – you and all these bloody flies.'

'That's not very friendly, is it? I thought you Christian lot were supposed to welcome everybody, no matter who. I bet your mate Jesus would give you a bollocking if he was to hear you talking to me like that.'

'Just get out of here,' Martin repeated. 'I'm calling for the janitor right now.'

He turned around and made his way back between the rows of desks to fetch his phone. All the students looked at each other in bewilderment, and then looked behind them at the man standing in the open doorway.

Martin called the janitor's number, but the phone rang and rang and there was no reply. While he was trying to find out where the janitor might be, the man in the camel coat stepped into the classroom. He raised his right hand, like a priest giving a blessing, and said something in a garbled language. He finished by hoarsely shouting out, '*Boro!*' and as soon as he did, the flies came pouring in from the corridor, filling the air. The students screamed and shouted and jumped up from their desks, scattering their test papers, but even though they frantically tried to beat the flies away, their faces and their hands were soon covered. Flies were tangled in their hair and crawling up their sleeves, and every time they tried to cry out, flies flew into their mouths and clustered over their tongues and their teeth. Several students vomited, splattering the floor with half-digested scrambled eggs speckled with flies.

Martin put down his phone, marched up to the man in the camel coat and said tersely, 'Get out of here. Get out of here now.'

'I'll go when I'm good and ready,' the man replied. Martin could hardly hear him over the buzzing of the flies and the crying and gagging of his students. 'I've come in here for the same reason that *you* come in here – to teach you Christians a lesson.'

'I'm not telling you again,' said Martin. He stepped up to the man and tried to push him in the chest, but the man seized both of his wrists and stared at him with an expression that was half derision and half utter hatred. Martin could almost have believed that the man held a burning personal grudge against him.

'I told you. I'll go when I'm happy that my little soldiers have done what they came here to do,' the man told him.

Martin tried to twist his hands free, but the man was much stronger than he was, and only tightened his grip.

'I'm warning you. I'll call the police.'

'The filth? You think that bothers me?'

'Let go of me.'

'All right, sunshine, I will. But only if you promise not to go for me again. Otherwise you'll get a shiv up your arse before you can blink.'

Martin shouted, 'Out of here! Everyone out! Go to the playing field!'

Still wailing and waving their arms to try and keep the flies away, his students all scrambled to the back of the classroom, and for a moment three or four of them became jammed together in the doorway in their panic to get out. The man released his grip on Martin's wrists, rubbing his own hands together as if he were washing them, and giving him a laconic smile.

'I'll be slinging my hook now, you'll be happy to hear. I've done what I come here to do.'

'And what was that? Don't tell me that all you wanted to do was terrify my students? What in the name of God was the point of that?'

By now, all Martin's students had managed to leave the classroom, and he could see them outside, gathering together by the corner of the tennis courts. Most of the flies had flown out, too, leaving only a few of them still circling around the desks and crawling across the discarded test papers.

The man raised his trilby hat to adjust it slightly, and then replaced it. 'You'll find out,' he told Martin. 'Give it a day or two. You'll find out.'

With that, he turned and walked quickly off along the corridor. Martin felt a tickling sensation on his left hand, and when he lifted it up, he saw that a fly was crawling across it. He smacked it with his right hand, crushing it, and it dropped down dead to the floor.

'I mean – who nicks dead bodies?' DCI Butcher demanded, as if he were the irritated victim of some practical joke. 'Every other perp I've ever come across just wants to get shot of the bloody things.'

Jamila and Jerry had arrived to meet him at Lettice & Pray. The funeral home was on Merton Road, which was only a little over two miles away from Lavender Hill police station. It was on a corner site at a road junction, with a collection of urns in one window and a Remembrance Day display in the other, with a Union flag and poppies.

Several media vans were already parked on the opposite side of the road, including Sky News, and a police tape had been strung along the pavement.

They had found DCI Butcher in the refrigerator room at the back, along with DC Spooner. Three forensic technicians were shining hand-held lasers on the four drawers, which were still hanging open.

'I don't think there's any question about it,' said DCI Butcher. 'This was carried out by the same perps who did for the Reverend Wymarsh and Sister Teresa and nailed that poor Jewish girl to the wall. It's just hard to work out what the motive is, do you know what I mean? I know it seems like it's religious, but if it is, it's totally random. And fuck knows where they get all these flies from. Watch where you're walking... there's plenty of them still on the floor.'

Jamila looked around and shivered. 'How many bodies are here altogether?'

'Eleven, before four of them were half-inched. So there's seven left, and one of them's supposed to be buried this afternoon. Some hopes of that.'

'The four that were taken, do we know their identities?'

'Yes. We've got all their details. One middle-aged bloke who died of a heart attack, one sixtyish bloke and his teenage grandson who were killed together in a car accident, and a woman who had stage four cervical cancer.'

'Bloody hell,' said Jerry. 'And people think there's a God.'

'Did any or all of them have religious connections?' asked Jamila.

'Apparently, one of the men was a part-time churchwarden at St Botolph's, but I don't know if the other three were into anything holy. We're still in the process of contacting their relatives. Not an easy job, as you can imagine. Fancy having to say to some grieving husband that his wife's body's been nicked.'

One of the forensic technicians came up to them, a small Indian woman who looked like a child dressed up as a snow fairy.

'We're nearly done here, chief inspector,' she told him, her voice muffled behind her face mask. 'We've found matching fingerprints on all four of these refrigerator drawers that were left open. The same fingerprints don't appear on any of the other drawers, so there's a good chance that they belong to whoever it was who removed those four deceased individuals. We've taken DNA samples, too, from the same drawers, and we'll be checking them against our records back at Lambeth Road.'

'What about the flies?' asked Jerry.

'We'll be sending samples of them to Professor Yearling, but we'll be testing them, too, to see if they contain any stimulants, or any other kind of chemical. Maybe we'll find something in their digestive systems to give us an indication of where they came from.'

Jamila and Jerry and DCI Butcher left the cooler room and went back into the office. The wall behind Nadia's desk was covered with an enlarged photograph of a sunset over a beach. Jerry found a mural like that a bit mawkish. Lettice & Pray's customers wouldn't need to be reminded that all days come to an end.

'We've got the media outside with their tongues hanging out,' said DCI Butcher. 'So what are we going to tell them?'

'Do they know that bodies have gone missing?'

'Not yet. Only that the staff were attacked, one of them fatally. And a member of the public told them that the whole place was filled up with flies.'

Jamila looked out through the front door. Outside she could see TV reporters and their camera crews and a small crowd of bystanders gathering on the pavement opposite.

'All you should tell them for now is that we are carrying out a thorough forensic investigation of the crime scene, and that we hope it will tell us who was responsible for this attack and why they did it.'

'And what if they ask about the flies?'

'Just say that we're consulting expert entomologists to find out where they might have come from.'

'So you don't think we should tell them about the bodies?' said DCI Butcher. 'Maybe they could ask their viewers to keep an eye open for them.'

'I don't think it's a good idea until we know more,' said Jamila. 'We don't want to stir up a whole lot of ghoulish speculation on social media. This case is extremely strange, and it might even have some supernatural elements, but it needs routine investigation, step by step. We don't need any distractions.'

Jerry coughed. For some reason, he was feeling light-headed and unwell. He put it down to his wild romping last night with Maureen and the fact that he had not yet had any breakfast.

'If you're right, guv, and it's the same perps, those four bodies could well have left here under their own steam. Or by fly-power, anyway. And if we tell *that* to the media, they're going to think we're totally off our nuts.'

'DC Mallett is already checking the CCTV from all around here,' said Jamila. 'That should give us some idea of what really happened, and how those bodies were taken away. But in the meantime, Jerry's quite right. The less we say about this, the better.'

Jerry coughed again, and his stomach gave an audible groan. He felt nauseous, but he had nothing to bring up, only phlegm and saliva. There was a box of tissues on Nadia's desk, so he pulled one out, turned his back on DCI Butcher and Jamila, and spat into it.

'Jerry?' asked Jamila. 'Are you all right?'

Jerry nodded. 'I think I'm suffering from an overdose of weirdness, that's all.'

11

Once it had stopped raining, Hester took her black Labrador, Nigel, for a walk around Battersea Park. It always took them at least an hour to make their way around the park because Nigel stopped and sniffed at every tree and every lamp-post and every rubbish bin.

She had adopted him from Battersea Dogs & Cats Home to keep her company after her husband had died three years ago. She had called him Nigel because that had been her husband's name.

She walked past the playground and along the path that was densely lined with beech trees. Nigel sniffed at one tree after another, occasionally lifting his leg to leave a trace of his own identity for the next dog to sniff.

Where the woods were the thickest, though, he suddenly lifted his head as if he could smell something on the breeze. He stood completely rigid, and when Hester tugged at his lead he refused to budge.

'Nigel, come on, I don't have all day!' Hester protested. She tugged at his lead again, but succeeded only in making him take two or three staggering steps sideways. His head remained lifted, his ears folded back, and she could tell that he was breathing in deeply.

'Nigel, for goodness' sake!' said Hester. She wound his lead in shorter, but when she tried to pull him further up the path, he started to pull her in the opposite direction, into the woods, and he was really straining hard.

'All right, then, you awkward cuss! Let's find out what you can smell! Honestly, you're as stubborn as your namesake used to be!'

She bent down and unclipped his lead. Nigel bounded off between the trees, and she followed him, raising her arm to stop herself being scratched by branches. Even though it was late autumn and most of the trees had shed their leaves, it was still gloomy in here, away from the path. At last Nigel stopped, and sniffed at a heap of damp leaves.

'So what can you smell here that's so attractive?' Hester asked him.

Nigel ignored her, and started to dig up the leaves as furiously as if he were trying to find a buried bone.

It took him only a few seconds to reveal the corner of a polythene bag, and as he kept on scrabbling more leaves away, Hester could see that it was about the size and shape of a squarish carry-on suitcase. She found it difficult to see what was in it, because the polythene was blurred inside with condensation; but once Nigel had clawed away the last few leaves around it, he sat down and looked up at her, panting, his eyes bright, as if to say, *Go on, open it!*

Hester thought: *What on earth is this, and what is it doing here in Battersea Park, and who buried it, and why?* She was reluctant to touch it, in case it was some kind of bomb. But when Nigel could see that she was not going to try and find out what it was, he stood up again and gripped the folded-over top of the polythene bag between his teeth, and started to wrench at it, jerking his head from side to side.

'Nigel! No!' Hester shouted at him. 'Bad dog! I said *no!*'

Nigel was always obedient, because Hester had trained him well, and now he stopped biting the polythene bag and stood back, although he was quivering in the same way he did when he was approached by a female on heat.

He had managed to rip open only a few inches of the bag, but Hester could see what was inside. She had trained as a nurse in her twenties, and she could recognise a shoulder socket, even when it no longer had an arm in it.

There was something else she could recognise: the foul smell of a decomposing body.

She reached into the pocket of her coat and took out her phone. As she prodded out 999, Nigel started to circle around the bag, but when she got through to the emergency operator and started to explain what he had found, he stopped circling. He turned his head away, lifting his nose into the breeze and sniffing.

'Thank you,' Hester told the operator. 'We'll stay here and wait for the officers to come.' Then she looked round at Nigel and said, 'What on *earth's* the matter, you incorrigible dog? What can you smell now?'

Nigel made an odd whining sound in his throat and started quivering again. He stayed like that for a few seconds, his nose pointing towards the woods, before he suddenly launched himself off.

'Nigel! Come back! *Heel*, Nigel, *heel*!' Hester screamed at him, but he ignored her and vanished between the beech trees and the bushes.

'Nigel!' she screamed again, but she didn't want to go chasing after him and leave this polythene package untended. She was almost sure that it was a human torso. From the smell of it, and the yellowish colour of the moisture inside the package, she guessed it had been lying here for at least a week, possibly even longer. Because of that, she wasn't too worried that whoever had buried it was still lurking around somewhere.

She waited, clapping her woolly gloves together and shuffling her feet to keep warm. She called Nigel again, but there was still no sign of him. He had never behaved like this before, and she could only hope that he would reappear when he started to miss his treats. She usually gave him a few little star-shaped biscuits to chew when they were out walking.

After less than fifteen minutes, she heard voices, and two plain-clothes detectives came walking through the trees, a man and a woman. They were accompanied by four officers in uniform, all wearing high-viz vests.

'Mrs Hobbs?' asked one of the detectives. 'I'm Detective Inspector Fairbrother and this is Detective Sergeant Watkins. I gather you've found something rather untoward.'

'Yes. It's there. I was taking my dog for a walk and he sniffed it out and dug it up.'

'Your dog?'

'He's not here at the moment. He's run off somewhere.'

DI Fairbrother went up to the package and crouched down beside it. Then he stood up and pulled a pair of blue nitrile gloves out of his pocket. He tugged them on and then he crouched down again and carefully lifted the torn flap of polythene where Nigel had bitten it.

'Is that what I think it is, guv?' asked DS Watkins.

'I'm afraid it is,' said DI Fairbrother. 'Can you call forensics?'

He stood up again and looked around the woods. 'The question is, whoever this is, where's the rest of them?'

As if he had been given his cue in a play, Nigel appeared through the bushes. He was carrying something in his mouth, something large and round and pale, the size of a football, and it was swinging from side to side as he approached them.

'Nigel!' snapped Hester. 'Where have you been? And what on *earth* have you got there?'

As Nigel came closer, however, she could see what it was, even though it was badly decomposed. It was a man's head, and it was swinging because he was holding its long white hair between his teeth.

The man's eye sockets were hollow and underneath a drooping white walrus moustache he looked as if he were snarling.

'God Almighty,' said DI Fairbrother. 'Don't tell me he's dug up Albert Einstein.'

When Jamila and Jerry returned to Lavender Hill police station, Jerry excused himself and went straight to the toilet.

He retched and spat again and again, and when at last he managed to stop, he stood holding on to the washbasin and looking at himself in the mirror.

Jesus Christ, you look terrible. His face was pale and glistening with sweat, and he felt as if he had swallowed a live hedgehog and it was stuck in his throat, so that he was breathless. He guessed he must have picked up some infection, but he couldn't think what, or from where. Not unless Maureen had Covid, and hadn't bothered to tell him. But this didn't feel like Covid, and he had recently been vaccinated. This felt more like some disease that you might contract from being stung by a mosquito or bitten by a rat, or maybe from eating a vindaloo that was well past its sell-by date.

After a few minutes he left the toilet and went up to the communications room, where Jamila was talking to

DC Mallett. As he came in, Jamila took one look at him and said, '*Upara svarga!* Jerry, you look really ill! Why don't you go home? Maybe even see a doctor?'

'No, no, I'll be all right in a bit,' Jerry told her, even though his voice was hoarse and he was short of breath. 'I might knock off a bit early today, but it's probably only something I ate. Either that, or Maureen's given me the bubonic plague.'

He sat down. 'What's the SP, Edge? Picked up any pictures of our body snatcher, have you?'

Edge turned around and brought up an image on his TV monitor. There was no street view though. The screen was completely obscured by a cluster of dark-grey blurry objects, all moving around, and when Edge brought them sharply into focus, Jerry could see that they were flies.

'This is the footage from the camera directly opposite Lettice & Pray at the time when we reckon the bodies were taken. The flies covered the lens for seventeen minutes and eleven seconds. Then – look – they all fly away, but after they've gone all you can see on Merton Road is normal traffic and four or five pedestrians.

'Next, though, this is the footage from the camera covering the roundabout with Brathway Road, a couple of hundred yards to the south. And what do we see? Again, nothing, because the lens is covered with flies. They stay for four minutes and six seconds, and then they're off.'

'You could almost believe that they were *told* to blot out those cameras,' said Jamila, shaking her head.

'Well, as mad as it seems, they might have been,' Jerry put in. 'But in a way, they're showing us where these body snatchers buggered off to, aren't they? All we have to do is follow the cameras covered with flies and see where they take us.'

'I'm afraid that doesn't really help,' said Edge. 'The last

camera that was covered by flies is outside St Michael's Church in Southfields. I've checked all the cameras for more than half a mile around there, although there aren't that many, but as far as I can tell the flies didn't cover up any more of them.'

'And you've made sure that this wasn't just a diversion?' asked Jamila. 'The bodies weren't taken away in another direction altogether?'

'No, ma'am. No dead bodies appear on any other CCTV footage on Merton Road around half past six – either being carried or walking by themselves. But there's another thing. The time-lapse in between the flies covering up one camera and then covering up the next one matches the pace of someone on foot – about three miles an hour, maybe a little faster. So you may be right. Maybe the perps actually *trained* them to cover the cameras, so that they could walk away from the crime scene undetected.'

He sat back and spread his hands, as if he were appealing to the Lord to give him an explanation. 'Totally fucking bonkers, I know. I never heard of flies being trained before, have you? But why else were they doing it?'

Jerry closed his eyes. 'I think I need to go and lie down,' he said, in a voice as rough as sandpaper.

12

On Sunday morning, the pews of St Gratus were crowded, and there was even a camera crew from ITV London News to record the special memorial service for the Reverend Paul Wymarsh.

It was a stone-cold day, and it had started off with a dense November fog. As the parishioners waited for the service to begin, however, and the organist played a soothing voluntary, the sun gradually came out and shone down through the stained-glass windows, each depicting one of the fourteen stations of the cross.

After about fifteen minutes' delay, the Bishop of Southwark appeared, the Right Reverend Christopher Knight, white-haired and bespectacled. He was not wearing his mitre or his ceremonial robes, but only a plain black suit with a purple vest and a silver crucifix.

'I apologise for my tardiness,' he told the congregation. 'The police wished to ask me some more questions about the unfortunate demise of the Reverend Wymarsh. And it is the Reverend Wymarsh who we have gathered here today in the sight of the Lord to honour, and to respect, and to grieve.

'There is still no explanation for his brutal murder, but the police believe it may be associated in some way with his devotion to the church. As you all know, Paul Wymarsh was a man of the utmost generosity, and he gave his heart and soul to his parishioners, and to anyone who called on him for help, whether their need was material or spiritual.

'Sadly, he also gave his life, long before his time.'

The bishop opened the hymn book on the podium in front of him. 'Let us begin with a hymn that is appropriate to the unexpected brightness that illuminates St Gratus this morning, in Paul Wymarsh's memory – "I Watch the Sunrise Lighting the Sky".'

The organist played the first rousing notes and the congregation began, raggedly, to sing. The bishop sang along, too, in a voice that varied wildly between a growl and a falsetto. The first verse of the hymn said that the sunrise cast 'paranoia shadows' but that the singer could always rely on the Lord for protection.

As they came to the chorus, a fly landed on the bishop's hymn book, and he flapped it away. Even a fly was a living creature, after all, created by God. But then another fly landed on his podium, and another, and flies started to circle around his head. He stopped singing and flapped his hands again and again, but more and more flies appeared, all buzzing and sparkling in the sunlight from the stained-glass windows.

The tall churchwarden stepped up to the podium, and he too started flapping at the flies. 'I'm so sorry, Your Excellency. I can't think where they've come from. I'll go and open the doors and with any luck they'll all fly out.'

The organist carried on playing the hymn, but the singing died away as the congregation saw that the bishop was being assailed by so many flies. The churchwarden walked quickly to the back of the church and flung open both the double oak doors. As soon as he did so, though, a huge swarm of flies poured inside, thousands of them, like a dark waving blanket.

Their buzzing was so loud that it almost drowned out the organ.

Everybody in the congregation shouted and screamed in horror. They waved their arms to keep the flies out of their eyes and they scrambled hysterically to extricate themselves from between the narrow pews, scattering hymn books and tripping over hassocks. Some of them were dropping down to their knees, overwhelmed by so many flies that they were blinded and choking, and their fellow parishioners were climbing over them in their panic to escape.

The shrieking and buzzing in St Gratus was deafening, and the organist had collapsed on to his keyboard, so that the church reverberated with one deep, endless, thunderous note, adding to the feeling of doom. The churchwarden tried to separate the people who were jammed in the doorway, pushing and shoving each other to get out, even though flies were crawling over his face, too, and he had to keep spitting to stop them climbing into his mouth. He was thinking: *This is what hell must be like.*

He turned around to see if Bishop Knight had managed to escape into the vestry. To his alarm, he saw that the bishop was still standing behind his podium, with his head thrown back and his arms outstretched. He was covered up to his neck with glittering flies, and even more flies appeared to be trying to cling on to him.

Amid the screaming and the clatter of pews being knocked over, as well as the endless rumbling of the organ, the bishop began to rise up into the air. His arms were still outstretched, like Jesus being crucified, but the expression on his face was not one of martyrdom. It was absolute terror.

He rose slowly from behind his podium, higher and higher, until he had almost reached the vaulted ceiling. He floated there, high above the congregation, and those who were able to brush the flies out of their eyes stared up at him in disbelief.

Almost a whole minute went past. The bishop remained suspended in the air, his body a mass of flies. Beneath him, the last few parishioners pushed their way out of the doors and into the open air. Only the churchwarden remained, his hand cupped over his nose and mouth to keep the flies from creeping in.

'Oh Lord!' the bishop wailed. 'Oh dear Lord, save me from this insanity!'

A few more seconds passed, and then suddenly the flies all burst away from him, like shotgun pellets. He dropped more than fifteen metres into the aisle, and the churchwarden heard his skull crack as it hit the terracotta tiles.

'Bishop Knight!'

The churchwarden hurried up the aisle and knelt down beside him. The bishop was lying on his back, staring up at him. Blood was trickling from the side of his mouth and his eyes were misty.

'This is the Devil's doing,' he whispered. 'You mark my words, Colin. This is the work of Satan himself.'

Jerry's alarm went off that morning at a quarter past eight. Usually, he woke up at six, but he had felt so rough last night that he had allowed himself an extra two hours in bed. In any case, he and Jamila had received no significant updates from Derek Grant or from DC Mallett and so they had arranged to put back their next meeting until at least twelve thirty in the afternoon.

Jerry's T-shirt and shorts were drenched in chilly sweat and he was shaking as if he had a serious case of flu. He folded back his wrinkled duvet and sat up, but his legs felt too weak for him to climb to his feet straight away, and he sat there for nearly five minutes before he was able to summon up the strength to go to the bathroom.

He took his phone with him, and while he sat on the toilet he called Jamila.

'It's Jerry, guv. Listen, I'm sorry, but I'm feeling well Moby Dick. One minute I'm freezing and the next minute I'm sweating conkers.'

'I think you should see your doctor,' said Jamila. 'Maybe you've picked up Covid from someone.'

'It's Sunday. The surgery's going to be closed.'

'Then stay in bed, drink plenty of water and keep warm. Take some ibuprofen. If it gets any worse, go to A & E.'

'I'm sorry. I never usually get sick. I haven't even had a cold since the week after the Queen snuffed it.'

'You don't have to be sorry, Jerry. Catching an illness is not your fault. Just take care of yourself and give me regular heads-up on how you're doing.'

In the background, Jerry could hear an irritable Ashish saying, 'Who is that, Jamila? It is not your work, is it? Come on – your eggs are getting cold!'

Still shuddering, Jerry dragged off his T-shirt and shorts and took a shower. Once he had dried himself, he put on a fresh T-shirt with the Arsenal crest on it and a clean pair of boxers. Then he crept back into bed like a wounded animal and lay there with his teeth chattering, feeling as if he might die before the end of the day.

By the early afternoon he was suffering a blinding headache and every muscle in his body was aching. His skin began to itch, too, and when he lifted up his T-shirt he could see that his stomach was covered in circles of angry red spots, some with tiny black specks in the centre.

He managed to sit up again, and he saw that he also had red spots on his legs, all the way down to his feet. *This is fucking serious*, he thought. He climbed out of bed, pulled open his chest of drawers and took out the navy-blue tracksuit that he had last worn when he tried to run the London Marathon five years ago. Once he had struggled to put it on, and pushed his feet into his battered old trainers, he left his flat and drove to St George's Hospital in Tooting. It was only four miles away, but his eyes were watering so that he had to keep blinking to see where he was going, and he had to grip the steering wheel tightly to stop himself from trembling.

At the corner of Nightingale Lane he drove through a red light, and thought, *If I saw myself doing that, I'd pull me over, and give myself a fucking hard time.*

Once he had found a parking space outside St George's Hospital, he limped into the emergency department. He went up to the front desk and told the receptionist that he had come out in a rash. He held up his hands to show her the spots, and as she stared up at them over her upswept spectacles, she said, 'Oh. Another one. I'm afraid you'll have a bit of a wait.'

'Sorry. What do you mean, "another one"?'

'We've had over a dozen this morning, all with the same kind of skin complaint. The doctor will see you as soon as she possibly can.'

Jerry went through to the waiting room. He found it crowded with teenage boys and girls, although it was almost completely silent, because most of them were prodding at their phones, and the few who didn't have phones were sitting with their eyes closed, or their heads resting in their hands. At the far end of the waiting room Jerry saw a thirtyish man with sandy hair and a short herringbone overcoat, and he too was staring at his phone. The seat next to him was empty, so Jerry shuffled his way between the teenagers and sat down.

He noticed at once that the man had angry red spots on the backs of his hands, the same as his. Jerry lifted up his own hands, turning them this way and that, and said, 'Hey – I see you've caught the dreaded lurgy too.'

'Heavens above,' the man said, lowering his phone. 'Where did you pick yours up from?'

'Don't ask me. Yesterday evening I started to feel like shit and this morning I was covered in them. How about you?'

'Pretty much the same. And all these young people here have broken out in spots too. I'm their class teacher at St Juliana's C of E school. Their parents phoned me early this morning and I recommended that they fetch them here. Most of their parents are still here at the hospital but the doctor advised them not to sit in close proximity, in case they're contagious, so they're waiting in the canteen.'

'Do you have any idea where you and all your kids caught this from – these spots and everything?'

'Well, I do, actually. I've already mentioned it to the doctor. She took some blood from me and two of my students here and she said they'll be doing some tests.'

'So what do you think caused it?'

The man looked around, as if he were making sure that nobody else was listening to him.

'You won't repeat this, will you? It's just that my head teacher gave me strict instructions not to tell anyone about it, in case it got around that St Juliana's was the breeding ground for some kind of epidemic and we had to close down while the whole school was fumigated. I mean, they've gone now, even if they gave us this infection.'

'Who's gone?'

'The flies. There were thousands of them. Millions! They filled up my classroom and crawled all over us. But after a while they all flew away.'

Jerry stared at him. 'The *flies*? Haven't you seen the news lately? You should have called the police straight away.'

'I have seen the news, yes, and I did think of calling the police. But you don't know my head teacher. Strict isn't the word! Apart from that, I didn't really associate those reports I saw on TV with all the flies that came into our classroom. There were simply so many! It was like something out of the Old Testament.'

He looked up to the ceiling as if he were begging for divine guidance. '"For if you will not let my people go, I will send swarms of flies on you, your officials, and your people, and into your houses; and also the land where you live shall be filled with swarms of flies."'

'Jesus,' said Jerry. 'Don't tell me that God's doing this!'

13

One of the boys in the waiting room raised his hand and said, 'Sir, I think I'm going to be sick.'

'Okay, Peter. The toilets are right outside, on the left. Ishan – do you think you could you go with him? I know you feel almost as bad, but just in case.'

Once the two boys had left the room together, Martin shook his head. 'I'm praying that this isn't serious. I don't have any idea what kind of infection those flies could have given us.'

'Well, maybe this is luck or maybe it's coincidence, but I'm a detective based at Lambeth nick, and at the moment I'm investigating several incidents in which flies seem to have played a significant part. Pardoe's the name. Jerry Pardoe.'

'Martin Baker,' said Martin. 'Same as the ejector seat. I won't shake your hand, if you don't mind, in case we have different varieties of spots, and we cross-infect each other.'

'We might, but your spots look just like mine, don't they? And if you're feeling as crappy as I do, then I'm pretty sure we're suffering from the same sickness. But listen – tell me what happened? How did the flies get into your classroom?'

'I was supervising an algebra test. First of all, one or two flies flew in and started to buzz around the students and land on their exam papers. There's a transom window over the door, which is open for ventilation, and I presume that's how they got in. But when I went to see if the janitor had some fly spray, I found this strange man standing in the corridor right outside and the whole corridor was an absolute mass of flies. I couldn't even begin to put a number on them. The walls and the ceiling were black, and they were even blocking out the light from the windows. And the noise – my God, it was like a hundred chainsaws!'

'Can you describe this man?'

'He was about five foot eight or nine, I'd say. Maybe forty-five years old. He was wearing a trilby hat and a light brown overcoat. He had what I suppose you'd call a cockney accent.'

'Would you be able to assist a police artist to make a likeness of him?'

'I think so, yes. He had quite distinctive features. He looked like some kind of rodent, if you asked me to describe him.'

'What did he say to you, in this cockney accent?'

'I can't remember everything. I was quite numb with shock, to tell you the truth. But he did say several times that he had come to teach us Christians a lesson.'

'Right – as soon as you've finished here, I'd like you to come to Lavender Hill. I know you're feeling like shit warmed over. I am too, but this is urgent. I wish to God you'd called us as soon as this happened, but if we can identify who this geezer was who showed up at your school with all these flies, maybe we can find out where the hell they're coming from.

'If he said he'd come to teach you Christians a lesson, it sounds as if it could be a case of religious terrorism. I suppose you can just be thankful that he attacked you with a load of flies, and not with a bomb full of ball-bearings.'

Jerry was called in to see the doctor before anyone else in the waiting room, and when he entered her office he saw why he had been allowed to jump the queue. The doctor was Arisha Nadeem, a specialist in rare infectious diseases. He and Jamila had consulted her several times in the past when they had been baffled by cases that involved inexplicable illnesses, such as a woman who had shed whole layers of skin like a snake and a man who had repeatedly vomited gallons of dark-green liquid.

She was probably well over fifty years old now, Dr Nadeem, but her black hair was elegantly cut in a bob and her caramel-coloured skin was smooth and she had a grace and a calmness about her that made her seem to be much younger.

'Detective Jerry Pardoe,' she smiled, as Jerry sat down. 'I am so sorry to learn that you too have been afflicted with this rash.'

'Actually, I'm Detective Sergeant Pardoe now, and Jamila – she's Detective Inspector Patel. The powers that be promoted the both of us, even though I'm sure they didn't have the faintest notion what the bloody hell we were up to most of the time. Maybe that's why.'

'Please – show me your hands. Yes, I can see that you have the same nummular lesions as the rest of the patients waiting outside. You have also been feeling as if you have a severe case of flu – headache, temperature, shivering, vomiting, nasal congestion?'

'That describes it exactly. Do you know what it is?'

Dr Nadeem nodded. 'I believe so, Jerry. We have managed to complete some preliminary tests on the blood samples that I took a little earlier. We have further tests to carry out, but I am reasonably sure that I have identified the cause of your rash.'

'What? Is it some kind of allergy?'

'No, it's not an allergy. It's a disease. And it's most unusual, because it's a variety of a complaint that still exists in southwest Asia and sub-Saharan Africa and the Caribbean. The interesting thing is that *this* variety was supposed to have died out over a hundred and fifty years ago. It was last mentioned in the journals of a doctor who was helping to treat army officers when the French took over Indochina in the middle of the nineteenth century.'

A hardback book was lying open on her desk, and she slid it across so that Jerry could see the black-and-white photograph of a thin moustachioed man sitting naked on a wooden crate, his entire body covered with dark circular spots.

'That was taken in 1858,' she said. 'Myself, I spent two years in Sri Lanka at the Nawaloka Hospital in Colombo, and that's where I first came across any mention of this variety. I was having to deal with the modern form of it, and I wanted to see how it was treated in the past.'

'Unbelievable,' said Jerry. 'If I had a brother – which I don't – this poor geezer would look exactly like him. Well – maybe he wouldn't have grown himself a dot and dash and be sitting on a box in the nuddy.'

Dr Nadeem closed the book. 'It wasn't until 1875 that a German scientist called Robert Koch identified the disease as a bacterium – *Bacillus anthracis*. It forms spores, which are usually transferred from infected animals to humans. In the eighteenth century it was called "wool-gatherers' disease" because farm workers and butchers would catch it from sheepskins and cowhides. Humans can be infected through cuts or lesions on the skin, or through eating diseased meat. The spores can also be inhaled, or swallowed in tainted saliva.'

'*Bacillus anthracis?* Is that what I think it is? Anthrax? Is that what I've got?'

'That's right, Jerry. I'm afraid so. But – as I told you – it's a variety of anthrax that hasn't been diagnosed in over a hundred and fifty years. The only treatments back in those days were enemas, or opium, or mercury, all of which were useless, of course. But the later variety can be cured very quickly and effectively with antibiotics, and I'm confident that this variety will respond to antibiotics too. That's what I'm going to give you, and all those poor schoolchildren out there.'

'I'm trying to think how I could have caught it. Between you and me, my girlfriend scratched me a bit the other night.'

'Well, it's possible that you were infected that way. The older variety was more contagious, almost like STDs.'

'What about those schoolkids? Did their teacher tell you about all the flies that invaded his classroom?'

'Yes, he did. I haven't completed all my blood tests yet, but I think it's highly likely that those flies were responsible for carrying this infection. He told me that they covered the children's faces and lips and some of them even crawled into their mouths. That would have been enough for them to inhale or swallow any spores.'

Dr Nadeem stood up and went across to a side table, on which she had set out rows of plastic trays with hypodermic syringes and small bottles of antibiotics.

'Since you've probably contracted cutaneous anthrax through the scratches on your skin, Jerry, I'll be giving you a shot of procaine penicillin, which you can follow up with doxycycline, and that should help you to recover quite quickly.'

'What about the kids?'

'It's more likely that the children are suffering from inhalation anthrax, so I'll be injecting them with ciprofloxacin. That's what we use to combat mutant strains of anthrax – ones that we're not sure of – like the ones that might be used in acts of terrorism, or biological warfare.'

Jerry watched her as she filled a syringe with penicillin.

'Do you think this might have been terrorism?'

'I couldn't say for sure, but anthrax has been used for terrorism several times in the past, although mostly in America. The last incident that I know of was immediately after 9/11. A number of letters were sent out in the US mail, all polluted with anthrax spores. Five people who received those letters died and seventeen became seriously ill.'

'So… you think it's possible that someone might be deliberately using these flies to kill off people they've got a grudge against? We've already guessed that they've got it in for anyone religious – the victims so far have been vicars and nuns and Jews. And these kids outside, they come from a Church of England school, don't they? Their teacher told me that some geezer turned up along with the flies and made threatening noises about Christians.'

'Jerry – it's beyond my remit to confirm that they were deliberately infected. I'm afraid that is something for you to find out.'

'I don't know. Like, infecting a letter, that's one thing. Letters don't go buzzing around the room, do they? These are *flies*, for Christ's sake. How do you catch flies and cover them in anthrax?'

'Jerry, I have no idea. Now, roll up your sleeve. You're going to feel a little prick.'

'That's what all the girls say.'

Jerry had returned to his car and was about to leave the hospital car park when his phone warbled. It was Jamila, and she sounded breathless.

'Where are you? Have you seen the news?'

'I'm at St George's Hospital. I've just come out of A & E.'

'A & E? Jerry – what's wrong?'

'I wasn't only feeling rough, guv, I started to break out in these horrible red spots. It turns out I've caught a type of anthrax, believe it or not. And there's a whole bunch of schoolkids here, and they've all gone down with it too. It seems like their classroom got invaded by a bloody great swarm of flies, and Dr Nadeem reckons that's probably how they got infected. I was going to call you about it as soon as I got home.'

'This is unbelievable. Do you know what has happened? About an hour ago, St Gratus church was filled up with flies. It happened during this morning's communion.'

'You're kidding me.'

'I only wish I was. The Bishop of Southwark was holding a memorial service for the Reverend Wymarsh, and I know this sounds like a fantasy, but apparently scores of flies all settled on him and they lifted him up into the air.'

'They *what*? You're having a laugh, aren't you?'

'No, Jerry. There were dozens of witnesses. The flies lifted him almost up to the ceiling and then they dropped him. His skull was fractured when he fell and by the time the paramedics arrived, he was dead.'

'Jesus. We've seen flies that can make dead people walk. But flies that can raise people up into the air? What the hell are we dealing with, guv? This is sheer fucking madness, excuse my French.'

'How are you feeling? Are you well enough to meet me?'

'I'm going home to change but I'll be over at the nick in a little while. The teacher at St Juliana's said some geezer showed up at the same time as all the flies and made threats against

Christians. I'm hoping the teacher can help us to identify him with an EvoFIT. By the way – who's the SIO at St Gratus?'

'Butcher. But he called me almost straight away, as soon as he'd been told about the flies. He said it definitely sounded like another weird investigation for me and you.'

'Okay. Give me an hour. Just at the moment I look like I've been sleeping in a cardboard box on Oxford Street. I feel like it, too.'

Still feeling cold and shivery, Jerry drove back to his flat. He had found out now that he was suffering from anthrax, but what he couldn't work out was how he had contracted it. Maybe Maureen had already been carrying the disease and passed it on to him, either sexually or by digging her fingernails into his skin. Dr Nadeem had said that the older strain could be contagious, like chlamydia or gonorrhoea. Then again, maybe a fly had landed on him after she had left him asleep and infected one of his scratches with anthrax spores.

And what about the flies that had invaded St Gratus church and lifted the bishop up into the air? *I mean, holy crap!*

He was still trying to get his head around what Jamila had told him when he let himself into his flat, prised off his trainers and switched on the television news. The first item was about more fighting in the Middle East, but then he saw a Sky reporter standing outside St Gratus. Behind the reporter, the entrance into Rectory Grove was cordoned off with police tapes, and four squad cars and a forensic van were parked outside.

'The detective inspector in charge of this investigation has been unusually tight-lipped,' said the reporter. 'On the other hand, I've been talking here to more than a dozen members of the congregation who were inside the church when the Bishop of Southwark met with his fatal accident. Some of them even have video footage, which they took with their phones, to prove that what happened was not a case of mass hysteria.

'According to every witness I have interviewed, the service to honour the Reverend Wymarsh had just begun when St Gratus was suddenly filled with literally hundreds of flies. Somehow those flies managed to cling on to the bishop and lift him to a considerable height above the floor, and then drop him. Paramedics arrived in less than fifteen minutes but sadly they pronounced the bishop dead.

'There has been no official explanation yet as to how a swarm of flies could have possibly raised the bishop up high enough for him to suffer a fatal injury when he fell. But this gentleman here was one of the congregation who saw it happen. What was your reaction, sir?'

The reporter turned to a grey-bearded middle-aged man, who was blinking furiously as if he were still suffering from shock. 'I'll tell you – it was like something out of a horror film. I couldn't believe it even though I could see it with my own eyes, and I still can't believe it, even now. You know that scene in *The Exorcist* when the girl floats up off the bed? Well, that was nothing compared with this. That poor bishop was so high up he was almost hitting his head on the rafters.'

An elderly woman in a maroon duffel coat said, 'I thought the Rapture was beginning, and the bishop was being taken up to heaven, and that the rest of us would follow. But perhaps God realised that bishop wasn't as pure as he pretended to be, and dropped him, and decided that he didn't want his congregation either. I'm mortified – absolutely mortified! I could be up there with the angels by now, and my late husband too.'

Jerry kept watching the news as he stepped out of his tracksuit bottoms and tugged his top off over his head. More and more members of the congregation were being interviewed, all shocked, and all telling the same story. It was impossible, but they had seen it for themselves.

Jerry thought: *Where in the name of God are these flies coming from, and how can they make dead people walk and living people fly? Not only how, but why?*

With a little luck, they might manage to identify and track down the man in the trilby hat and the light brown coat that Martin Baker had told him about. But Jerry wasn't going to count on his luck, because he rarely had any. The sole of his trainer had fallen off before he had managed to complete even half the London Marathon and apart from that he had never won more than £3.50 on the lotto.

He tried to call Martin Baker. His phone rang and rang without him answering but almost immediately after Jerry had stopped ringing, he called back.

'Sorry, detective. The doctor's just finished injecting the last of my class now, and the rest of them have all gone home with their parents. I have to admit that I'm still not feeling one hundred per cent myself, but I'll come to Lavender Hill if you want me to. It won't take too long, will it?'

'Brilliant. I'll send an Uber for you.'

After he had arranged a taxi to go to St George's to pick up Martin Baker, Jerry called Maureen. Her phone rang and rang, too, but there was no answer, so he left a message for her. He guessed that she could have gone to see her sister, and forgotten to take her phone. If he still couldn't get in touch with her by the time he had finished at the station, and he felt well enough, he might drop round to see her. She lived not far away in a flat overlooking Clapham Common. He suspected that their relationship might have reached the end of the road, but he still had feelings for her, and at least they could give each other a last kiss goodbye.

Upstairs at Lavender Hill police station, Martin Baker sat in front of the computer screen for over half an hour while Vera Browning, the facial identification officer, showed him scores of expressionless faces on the EvoFIT database. Jamila and Jerry sat on either side of Martin to give him support.

Martin was shivering and kept rubbing his hands together to keep warm, but he had promised Jerry that he would do his best to pick out a likeness of the man who had brought all those flies to his classroom. Dr Nadeem had told him that he and his students could have suffered permanent brain damage, or even died.

Vera Browning was infinitely painstaking. She was plump and calm, like a kindly kindergarten teacher. She made no complaint when Martin asked her to narrow the cheeks of the face that he had finally selected, and then widen them a little, and then narrow them again, as well as raising the eyebrows slightly and making the chin a touch more pointed, and then not quite so pointed. Then she sat and waited patiently while he stared for nearly half a minute at the black-and-white image that she had created on the screen from his description.

At last, he sat back and said, 'That's him. That's exactly him. Bloody hell. I can almost hear his voice.'

He put on a cockney accent, and said, '"*I've come in here for the same reason that you come in here – to teach you Christians a lesson.*"'

'Is that what he told you?' asked Jamila.

'Those were his exact words. I'll never forget them.'

At that moment, DCS Herbert Chance came into the room. He was still wearing his dress uniform and all his medals because he had been attending an afternoon reception for EU police officers at Clarence House.

'EvoFITting, are we? Found who you're looking for?' He leaned over Jamila's shoulder and squinted at the computer screen.

He was silent for a moment, and then he reached into his pocket and took out his horn-rimmed spectacles. Once he had put them on, he said, in his soft, hoarse voice, 'Now, *there's* a face I haven't seen for a while. I thought he was still banged up in the Scrubs.'

Jamila turned around. 'You know him?'

'Know him? Oh, yes. That's Vincent Narrow. He headed up the most violent gang of housebreakers you could ever imagine. He was sent down for sixteen years at least.'

'I've heard of him,' said Jerry. 'Him and his gang, they used to break into wealthy people's houses and keep the owners prisoner, sometimes for days, while they totally stripped the place of everything that was worth anything.'

DCS Chance took off his spectacles. 'That's right. They took jewellery, furniture, paintings. Even carpets, if they had any value. But one houseowner died after he'd been tied up in a chair for nearly a week. No food, no drink, sitting in his own mess. Narrow should have been hanged for that.'

Jerry frowned at the rat-like face that was staring at him out of the computer screen.

'Let out on parole, was he, or did he escape?' he asked DCS Chance.

'Must have been paroled. If he'd escaped, we would have heard about it, for sure.'

'The question is, though – he's a professional housebreaker,' said Jerry. 'What's he doing with a bloody great swarm of flies, infecting kids in a C of E school and giving out threats against Christians?'

DCS Chance shrugged. 'Perhaps he wanted a change of career. Sometimes I feel like jacking this lark in for good and all and running a pub.'

Jerry and Martin Baker both left Lavender Hill to go back to their respective homes and recover. Meanwhile, Jamila stayed at the station and contacted the Parole Board. It turned out that Vincent Narrow had been released on licence from Wormwood Scrubs prison nine months ago, eleven years into his sixteen-year sentence. His supervising officer gave her Narrow's address, and so she sent officers around to see if he was home. When they knocked at the door, there was no reply. His neighbours said they hadn't seen him for at least a week.

PC Barrett in the communications room tried to locate Narrow's smartphone, but there was no trace of it.

Jamila also tried to track down some of Narrow's old gang of housebreakers, but they had all served their time and melted away into obscurity, except for one, who was still in the open prison in Ford, in Sussex. She was able to phone him, but he told her that he had heard nothing from Narrow for more than ten years, and didn't want to, either. 'Them days are gone, thank God. We was like a pack of rabid dogs. Someone should have put us down.'

14

Jerry slept deeply for nearly nine hours. He dreamed about flies and Maureen and mysterious hooded riders on horses with impossibly long legs, like the Martian tripods in *The War of the Worlds*.

He had called at Maureen's flat on the way back from Lavender Hill, but when he knocked at her door there had been no answer. He had sent her a text message telling her that he had tried to visit her and then he had gone home and collapsed on his bed without even taking off his shoes.

He felt much less shaky when he woke up, and his spots were starting to fade. Once he had showered and dressed, he went into his kitchenette and brewed himself a mug of espresso. He was trying to decide whether to make himself a sausage sandwich for breakfast when his phone rang, and it was Jamila.

'Jerry? How are you feeling?'

'Almost back to normal, thanks. Still a bit spotty but the headache's gone and I don't feel like I've gone fifteen rounds with Muhammad Ali, like I did yesterday.'

'Muhammad Ali died years ago.'

'That's probably why I felt so bad. So – what's the SP?'

'I've had a call from Dr Crowe,' said Jamila. 'He's been

examining that head and torso that were found in Battersea Park.'

'Do we know who that was yet?'

'Not yet. Nobody of that age has been reported missing and the face was so badly decomposed that it couldn't be identified. They'll be sending an image of it to Len Makepeace, that reconstruction artist, to see if he can make a clay model of it.'

'So why did Dr Crowe call you about it? What's it got to do with us?'

'When he was carrying out chemical tests on the torso, he found traces of bacterial contamination from flies. And he said that it wasn't just a single fly. The contamination was all over the torso and appears to have been left by literally dozens of flies.'

'Oh, bloody hell.'

'He's asked if we can go to Falcon Road so that he can show us exactly what tests he's completed.'

'Okay. When? I can come now if you like. I was thinking of making a sausage sandwich, but I think I'll forget about it. Jesus. This case is the best diet I've ever been on.'

With a rustling sound, Dr Crowe's assistant, Zahir, lifted the thick black plastic sheet that was covering the torso. When she saw it, Jamila retched and turned away.

It was a man's chest – an elderly man, because the hairs around his nipples were grey, and even though the skin had decomposed until it had become black and leathery, they could clearly see that it was wrinkled with age. He had been decapitated between his vertebrae C_4 and C_5, so there was a stump of his neck remaining. Both arms, however, had been completely removed, leaving only their sockets.

Jamila had retched because the man's body had been sawn in half between his ribcage and his pelvis, leaving his bowels bulging out of his abdominal cavity. His intestines had turned green and slimy, with black blotches on them, and dozens of pale beige maggots were crawling all over them.

'Blimey,' said Jerry. 'Haven't you got any of that bug spray? I had maggots in my dustbin and I can lend you some if you like. It works a treat.'

'We've left them untouched on purpose,' Dr Crowe told him. 'They appear to be coffin fly larvae, but we've asked Professor Yearling to take a look at them for us. What's unusual is that this man must have been killed at least two weeks ago, maybe more, and yet the larvae must have hatched very recently. I would say no more than two days ago.'

'Have you been able to establish *how* he was killed?' asked Jamila.

Jerry said, 'I don't think having his bonce cut off would have done him much good.'

'Actually, the indications are that he was strangled before he was dismembered,' said Dr Crowe. 'His arms were forcibly twisted off, by the look of them, but the hemicorporectomy was performed with a chainsaw.'

'Do you still have his head here?'

'Yes. We sent a 360-degree image of it to the reconstruction artist and he's working on it now. Zahir – the head, please.'

Zahir went across to the refrigerator in the far corner of the laboratory and lifted out a large polythene box. He placed it on a small metal trolley and wheeled it over to Dr Crowe. Then he prised off the lid so that Dr Crowe could reach inside and lift out the victim's head. The hair on top of the head was white and long and unkempt – the hair of a man of seventy years old or over who rarely visited a barber or who even cut his hair himself.

His face was hideously rotten. His jaw had dropped open so that his blackened tongue was hanging down over his lower set of teeth like a giant slug. His nose had gone, exposing his triangular nasal cavities. His eye sockets were hollow and his cheekbones were gleaming white through tattered skin, which indicated that his facial flesh had probably been pecked at by birds.

'As you can see, it would be fairly pointless posting a picture of him in this condition and expecting anybody to identify him,' said Dr Crowe. He was sounding more Shakespearean than ever. 'As you know for yourselves, though, Len Makepeace is something of a magician when it comes to reconstructing faces. It doesn't seem to matter to him how badly they're decomposed, or crushed, or incinerated. He seems to be able to come up with a recognisable likeness at least seventy per cent of the time.'

'You told me you had found evidence that the victim had been covered with flies,' said Jamila. 'But when? You say these larvae hatched quite recently.'

'Yes. As I mentioned to you before, flies use a sticky secretion of sugars and oils to stick to whatever surface they've landed on, as well as leaving drops of faecal matter behind. I was able to date some of this secretion and some of this faecal matter to three to four weeks ago, but there was also evidence that more flies had settled on his torso very recently – probably after it was abandoned in Battersea Park.'

'Couldn't leave the poor bugger alone, then?' said Jerry.

'No. But what interests me is that coffin flies like to feed on dead flesh, so it doesn't surprise me that they were attracted to his decomposing torso. But the older residue would indicate that they were crawling all over him while he was still alive, or only just deceased. It's not possible to be exact.'

Jamila looked at the rotting head that was staring sightlessly back at her from the metal trolley. She had seen plenty of dead bodies during her service, but there was something about this head that disturbed her more than usual. It reminded her of pictures she had seen of the heads called *mokomokai* that Maoris in New Zealand cut off their enemies. After they had removed the brains and the eyes, the Maoris had smoked them to preserve them, and even sell them as souvenirs. But they had always looked as if they were asleep, these heads, rather than dead, and that they were having nightmares, and were desperate to wake up.

'What about the Bishop of Southwark?' she asked Dr Crowe. 'Will they be bringing him here?'

'Right now, he's still being examined at Lambeth Road, because the flies covered his clothing rather than his skin and they have all the right equipment there to analyse it. But, yes – DCI Butcher called me yesterday afternoon and he'll probably be brought here in a day or so for a full postmortem.'

'Can you believe that there were enough flies actually to lift him up into the air? I find it incredible, and yet it happened.'

'This is something you need to discuss with Professor Yearling. I've heard that some insects can be given remarkable strength by feeding them on a drug rather like locamidazole, which is used as a substitute for physical exercise. This includes some varieties of flies – although I'm not sure if that includes coffin flies.'

He gave a theatrical pause, and then he said, 'I don't know, though. Perhaps their strength was given to them by something other than a drug. Some kind of force, although I can't think what it could be.'

'Let's go, then,' said Jerry. 'I could murder a coffee. Maybe with a shot of brandy in it.'

Dr Crowe sat down at his desk and started to dictate a report about the state of the torso and the severed head on his audio recorder, while Zahir picked up the sheet so that he could cover the torso up again. But as Jerry opened the laboratory door to leave, a blurry voice said, '*Clown*.'

Jamila turned back and said, 'Pardon?'

Zahir shrugged. 'I didn't say anything.'

'Oh, I thought you did. Dr Crowe, did I hear you say something?'

Dr Crowe swivelled round in his chair. 'No, sorry. I thought it was DS Pardoe.'

'Someone said something that sounded like "clown".'

'Yes. I heard it too. It must have been that noisy plastic sheet.'

For a long moment, they all stood in silence, in case the voice spoke again. Jamila looked back at the old man's head on the metal tray. His blackened tongue was still hanging out, as if he were threatening her, or showing his contempt, like a Maori rugby player performing the *haka*. Because of that, he reminded her even more of a *mokomokai*.

'All right, let's go for that coffee,' she said. 'Maybe I'll forget the coffee and just have the brandy instead.'

The rest of their day was exhausting. They drove round to seventeen different addresses in Clapham to interview more than twenty of the congregation at St Gratus church who had seen the Right Reverend Christopher Knight being covered with a mass of flies and raised up almost to the rafters. At least half a dozen of them were convinced that it was God giving them a demonstration of what could happen if you dared to believe that you were as holy as Him.

With a solemn frown, one of the vergers even quoted Proverbs 16 to them, 'Pride goeth before destruction. And a haughty spirit before a fall.'

Apart from their theories about divine punishment, however, none of these witnesses were able to give them any information that helped them to understand any more clearly why the Right Reverend Knight had been attacked and killed by so many flies.

It was dark by the time they returned to the station. They went to the canteen for a coffee and a lemon tea, which they took up to the communications room. DC Mallett was waiting for them, so that he could play back for them all the videos that had been sent to him by members of the congregation. These videos featured a lot of jostling and screaming and cries of 'My God!' but again they showed them nothing that they didn't know already.

'I think I've had it for today,' said Jerry, leaning back in his chair. 'My spots are starting to itch.'

'There's one more video to go,' said Edge.

'Oh, forget it. I've seen enough of that flying bishop to last me a lifetime. I think I'll go home and watch a Superman film.'

All the same, Edge switched on the last video. Unlike the previous sequences, it had been taken outside the church, showing the members of the congregation as they pushed each other in their panic to escape out of the doors and into the graveyard.

Although the video was jerky and tilted and lasted for

only a few seconds, it caught a man standing between the gravestones, watching the terrified worshippers as they came jostling outside. He was wearing a wide-brimmed hat and a light brown overcoat.

Jerry sat up straight. 'Play that again,' he told Edge. 'Now freeze it there. That's right. Back a little. That geezer next to that gravestone – you can't see his mush very well, but he's wearing exactly the same as that teacher from St Juliana's told me the geezer who brought all those flies into his classroom was wearing. Trilby titfer and a camel-coloured coat.'

Jamila nodded. 'The same man we recognised from his EvoFIT as Vincent Narrow.'

'For real?' said Edge. 'That's Vincent Bloody Narrow? When my old man was serving in the Met, he was part of the team that arrested Narrow. He led them a right old dance for years, that's what he told me. Nobody would ever squeal on him, and he knew so many people in Lambeth and Wandsworth that he could knock on almost any door if my old man was breathing down his neck, and they'd let him in.'

'If it *is* Narrow,' said Jamila, 'we have to ask ourselves again what a serial housebreaker is doing causing all kinds of mayhem with a massive swarm of flies? Especially a serial housebreaker who is out on parole.'

'Well, his mush is going to be all over the media,' said Jerry. 'Let's hope someone clocks him and tells us where he is, so that we can nail him before he has the Archbishop of Canterbury doing a barrel roll over Buckingham Palace.'

It was past ten o'clock when Ashish came to collect Jamila and take her back to Redbridge. Jerry climbed into his own car and sat behind the steering wheel for a while, feeling chilly and drained. Watching the lights of Ashish's BMW turn out of the station car park and disappear up Lavender Hill had made him feel lonelier than ever. He knew that Jamila didn't fancy him, but that didn't stop him from feeling jealous.

He had tried phoning and texting Maureen in the few spare moments that he had managed to snatch during the day, but she still didn't answer and she still hadn't texted him back. Although he felt so tired, he decided to drive to Clapham Common on his way back home and call on her. He found it hard to imagine this day ending up any worse than it had been already, but maybe he would find her with another man. At least that would explain why she hadn't been answering him.

He parked outside her block of flats and pressed the bell for her third-floor apartment. He waited and waited, chafing his hands together, but there was no buzz to open the front door. He tried phoning her and texting her again, but there was still no response. He was about to give up and leave when the front door opened and a young woman came out with a small Pekingese on a lead. She held the door open for him and he said, 'Thanks, love, brilliant,' and stepped inside.

There was no lift in this block of flats so by the time he had climbed up to the third floor he was panting, and he had to stop for a moment, holding on to the banister rail. Once he had got his breath back, he knocked on Maureen's door, but to his surprise he found that it was slightly ajar, and that when he knocked it opened even wider.

'Maureen?' he called out. 'Mo – it's me, Jerry! Are you there?'

He entered her narrow hallway and switched on the light. Three of Maureen's coats were hanging on pegs, and he recognised the pink hooded Puffa jacket that she had been wearing when she came round to see him. It was cold outside, almost down to zero, so he found it hard to believe that she had gone out without it.

'Maureen?' he called again.

He brushed past the coats and went towards the living-room door, which was closed. Before he reached it, though, he thought he could hear a buzzing sound. Like flies. Like a whole swarm of flies.

Cautiously, he opened the door. It was dark inside, although the hallway light behind him was enough to show him that the whole living room was glittering with wings. He reached inside and found the light switch, and when he clicked on the light, thousands of flies rose up into the air, whirling around and around and pattering against the walls. Some of them flew towards the door and Jerry had to flap them away to stop them flying into his face.

'Jesus Christ,' he said, out loud. And then, 'Mo? You're not in here, are you, Mo?'

The flies began to settle again, and when the air was clear, Jerry stepped into the room, his shoes crunching on all the flies that covered the carpet. He looked towards the window. The curtains were still open, but there was no light coming in from the street outside because the windowpane was black with flies, and they were speckled all over the curtains, too.

In front of the window stood a three-seater sofa, and as he came crunching closer, Jerry realised that it was not only the scatter cushions on it that were crawling with flies. A body was lying on it, and like everything else in the room, this body was completely clustered with flies, layer upon layer of them, all buzzing and struggling against each other as if they were fighting for a space where they could cling with their sticky pulvilli to the body underneath.

He whacked at the flies with his hand, backwards and forwards. A few of them flew up off the body, although they buzzed in irritation and tried to settle again almost immediately, so that he had to keep on whacking at them. All the same, he was able to keep them away for long enough to expose the body's face.

It was Maureen, and she was staring at him, but she was plainly dead. Flies were creeping in and out of her nostrils and walking all over her eyes, while even more flies were struggling to climb over her lips and into her mouth.

Jerry stopped flapping at the flies. All he could do was stand there and watch as they covered up her face again. Some of them started to buzz around his head, and one of them landed in his ear, so that he had to pinch it out between finger and thumb, and squash it.

He quickly left the living room, crunching on more flies as he walked out, and slammed the door shut behind him. Then he took out his phone and called the station for backup, and Lambeth Road for forensics, with an ambulance to take away Maureen's body.

Finally, he called Jamila. She and Ashish had driven as far as Hackney Marshes, so she was only a little over fifteen minutes away from home.

'Sorry, guv,' he told her. 'I'm afraid you'll have to ask Ashish to do a U-ey and come back.'

'What's happened? You sound terrible.'

'It's those bloody flies again. They've taken my Maureen.'

Jerry found himself unable to say any more, and he had to squeeze his eyes tight shut to stop them filling up with tears. There was a moment's silence, and then he heard Jamila say, 'Ashish. We have to turn back.'

'Are you kidding me?'

'It's my job, Ashish. I'm sorry.'
'I thought I was dating *you*, Jamila, not the Met.'
Jamila said something that Jerry couldn't hear clearly, and then her phone went dead.

15

The forensic team arrived just under an hour later, led by the Martian, Derek Grant. It took them over three more hours to take pictures of Maureen's living room with her body still lying on the sofa. At the same time, they were lifting fingerprints from the door handles and using ultraviolet lamps to detect shoe impressions in the hallway carpet.

Ashish had driven Jamila back to Clapham to join Jerry – grumbling all the way, according to Jamila. While the forensic team were making sure that they had examined every angle of the fly-infested room, she and Jerry sat together at Maureen's kitchen table.

A few flies had strayed into the kitchen, too, and were crawling over the hob and the work surfaces and clinging to the lights. Whenever they tried to land on his sleeve, Jerry swatted at them with a wooden spatula.

Jamila and Jerry said very little. They were both tired and perplexed by this investigation, and Jamila knew how much Jerry must be grieving for Maureen, even if she hadn't been the love of his life. Every now and then she glanced at him sympathetically across the kitchen table, and each time he would give her a quick tight smile in return.

Once the forensic investigators had completed their survey, they brought up a stretcher and lifted Maureen's body on to it.

She was still covered from head to foot in a living mass of flies, and no matter how much they tried to clear them off, the flies kept buzzing persistently back. Eventually, they wrapped a clear plastic sheet around her before they carried her downstairs to their ambulance. They would take her first to Lambeth Road, and then send her on to Dr Crowe, although they gave Jamila a sample jar of several flies so that she could take them to Dr Crowe for this afternoon's meeting with Professor Yearling.

The Martian had called a local pest control company, and two of their technicians had been waiting outside for the past half-hour. Now that Maureen's body had been removed, they came trudging upstairs with all their equipment to clear the flat of flies. They looked like a comedy duo – one tall and thin with a ponytail, the other short and stocky and bald. They both wore dark-green overalls with *GJ Pest Control* emblazoned on their backs.

They heard the chorus of buzzing as soon as they entered the hallway, and the tall one let out a '*Wow* – is someone using a chainsaw in there?'

But then the Martian opened the door and when they saw how many thousands of sparkling flies were crawling all over the living room, they both stopped and stared in disbelief. The short one turned to the Martian and said, 'Holy shit, Del. When you said you had a serious fly problem, I never thought you meant a fucking plague. This is like something out of the Old Testament.'

'There's been some kind of an outbreak, Gary,' the Martian told him. 'We don't know what's caused it yet, and I can't give you all the gory details, because it's still under investigation. But we've been in constant contact with a bug expert from Oxford University, and we're hoping that he's going to be able to tell us more.'

'Bloody hell. I've never seen a cluster like this, not nowhere. We'll have to smoke them, I reckon. Steve, mate, did you pack them smoke bombs?'

The tall one opened up his heavy carry-all and lifted out a CritterKill smoke bomb. 'I've got three of them here, but I reckon one's going to be enough, even with this lot.'

'Right,' said the Martian. 'We'll let you crack on. How long is this going to take?'

'At least a couple of hours, and then we'll have to ventilate the room and clear away the bodies, so allow four to be on the safe side. We don't want you breathing none of this stuff in. It can not only choke you, it can give you the runs something rotten.'

It was nearly six o'clock in the morning by the time Jamila and Jerry left Maureen's flat. They went back to Lavender Hill station and sat in the canteen with a strong black coffee with four sugars for Jerry and a lemon tea for Jamila.

'I don't know what to say to you,' Jamila told Jerry, very gently. 'It's distressing enough finding anyone who has had their lives taken away from them before their time, let alone someone you knew and for whom you had feelings.'

'What I'm asking myself is why *her*?' said Jerry. 'All the other victims of this fly massacre have been connected in some way to religion, but Maureen didn't even believe in Father Christmas, let alone God.'

'Yes, but think about it, Jerry. She may not have been connected to religion, but she was connected to *you*. And that could tell us something interesting. It seems as if someone is controlling or directing these flies, doesn't it, and if that's the case, it's very likely to be Vincent Narrow. But whoever it is, they could easily have found out from the media that you are one of the investigating team. And somehow they discovered that you and Maureen were involved together.'

Jerry said, 'You could well be right. Maybe they infected her with anthrax so that she could pass it on to me.'

'Nothing in this investigation surprises me,' said Jamila. 'That man from the pest company said it was like something out of the Old Testament, and I couldn't agree with him more. The next thing we know we'll be showered with locusts and lice and frogs and ashes, and all the firstborn will die, and the Thames will turn into a river of blood.'

'Always so bloody upbeat, the Bible, don't you think?'

'Oh, the plagues are described in the Quran, too. But now you're feeling a bit better, maybe we should think about going to see Father Devine.'

'Your exorcist mate?'

'That's right. It's possible that he could give us some idea of why these flies have suddenly started swarming. By the way, I asked DS Watkins to get in touch with St George's to see if Miriam Rosen or Gerald Bridger were fit to be interviewed yet. Apparently, both of them are still comatose. They've been given CT scans and it looks as if they both have a form of encephalitis.'

'I don't know what we need most. An exorcist or a bloody great tanker full of fly spray.'

When they had finished their drinks, they went upstairs and wrote an outline report together. It was past eight thirty by the time they had completed it, and DCS Chance had turned up, so they were able to give him a first-hand summary of what had happened to Maureen. He sat behind his desk with his hands clasped tightly together, which was always a sign that he was finding it difficult to understand the investigation that they were briefing him about.

Jamila finished by telling him that Jerry and Maureen had been in a relationship, and he closed his eyes for a moment and shook his head from side to side.

'This mustn't get out. Not yet, anyhow. Not until we know the full implications. You can just imagine what the headlines would be.'

'We'll be checking all the CCTV footage around Clapham Common to see if we can find out how so many flies got into Maureen's flat,' Jerry told him. 'And we've still got an APB out for Vincent Narrow. We've posted a twenty-four-hour watch on his home address but there's been no sign of him yet.'

'How about this Professor Yearling? Do you think he might be able to give us some idea where all these flies are coming from?'

'He'll be coming down from Oxford later today,' said Jamila. 'He's arranged with Dr Crowe to examine the flies that lifted up the bishop, but now he'll have many more specimens to look at too. At the very least he'll be able to tell us if they're all the same kind of fly.'

DCS Chance stood up and cleared his throat. When he spoke, he sounded as if he were giving a sermon.

'As of this morning, within a three-mile radius, we have five stabbings to look into – two fatal and three with life-threatening injuries. On top of that we have two rapes and four sexual assaults, a major haul of heroin and fentanyl, eleven car thefts, seven complaints of domestic abuse, a serious case of vandalism at Clapham Junction mosque, and twenty-three complaints of shoplifting.'

He paused and looked at Jamila, and then at Jerry. 'I think you'll agree that the last thing we need is a load of effing flies.'

Jamila tried ringing Dr Crowe to find out what time he expected Professor Yearling to arrive at Falcon Road, but Dr Crowe didn't answer his mobile nor the phone in his laboratory. Instead, she called the main coroners' office number.

'Sorry, we haven't seen Dr Crowe this morning. He's usually in bright and early, but not today.'

'Has he contacted you, to tell you that he's going to be late?'

'No, sorry.'

'What about his assistant? Is he there?'

'Zahir? No, we haven't seen him today either.'

Jamila looked across at Jerry. She had been hoping that Professor Yearling had arranged to visit Dr Crowe around three or four o'clock, so that she and Jerry could have at least two hours' rest after their exhausting night at Maureen's flat. But it worried her that Dr Crowe had not showed up at all, and neither had his assistant. It was critical to their investigation that Professor Yearling could examine the flies that had been taken from the Right Reverend Christopher Knight, and now from Maureen. They needed urgently to know if they were the same variety of fly, and how old they were, and whether they had any distinguishing characteristics that might give them a clue where they had been hatched.

Professor Yearling had told them that it should be possible to identify what surfaces they had landed on from the chemical composition of the sticky adhesive on their feet. Analysing the contents of their stomachs should also reveal if someone had been breeding them by feeding them an artificial diet of sugary foods, or if they had been living off a natural diet of rotten flesh and faeces.

'Dr Crowe's not there,' she told Jerry. 'I have a bad feeling about this.'

'Come on, maybe he's simply knackered, like we are, and he's taken a morning off. I wouldn't blame him. Imagine what it's like, poking around with a lot of smelly dead bodies, day after day.'

'I think we should go round to Falcon Road in any case. Ever since I saw that head and that torso, I've had a creepy feeling about it.'

'What, and heard somebody saying "*clown*"?'

Jamila didn't respond to that, but shrugged on her coat and buttoned it up.

'Are you coming?' she asked Jerry.

'Can't we just wait until Dr Crowe calls us?'

'Something's wrong, Jerry. I am sure of it. I feel it in my water. My mother always used to say that I was a female Kuda Bux.'

'What's that?' said Jerry, zipping up his anorak. 'Someone who can't stop talking?'

'No, Kuda Bux was a famous Pakistani mystic. He could read books and ride a bicycle through the middle of London even though he was completely blindfolded with lumps of pastry dough stuck over his eyes and bandages wound round his head.'

'Oh, yeah? I reckon there's a few officers here at Lavender Hill who are blindfolded like that, but they can't read or ride bikes. They can't even hit the urinals.'

They drove across to Falcon Road and parked outside. Kirsty must have been having a day off, because a sour-faced woman in a baggy lavender cardigan was sitting behind the reception desk, and she insisted on seeing their ID before she allowed them to take the lift upstairs.

The door to Dr Crowe's laboratory was closed, and Jamila knocked, and waited, but there was no reply. She tried the handle and the door opened, so they both stepped inside.

It looked as if the laboratory had been ransacked. One of the trolleys was lying on its side on the floor and all the drawers of the refrigerator had been left open. In one of the drawers, the body of Sister Teresa still lay, covered with a green sheet, but all the other drawers were empty, although they knew that the Reverend Wymarsh's body had been taken away yesterday morning in preparation for his funeral. Papers and folders were scattered everywhere, as well as shattered glass flasks and broken test tubes.

Flies were crawling everywhere, too, although not nearly as many as the thousands that had been teeming all over the floor and the walls and the windows of Maureen's flat.

'Jesus Christ,' said Jerry. 'How the hell did somebody get in here to do all this? And why didn't anybody see them, or stop them? That old witch on reception even wanted to see our IDs.'

Jamila already had her phone to her ear, calling for DCI Butcher, as well as backup and forensics. She pointed to the refrigerator in the far corner of the laboratory. Its door was wide open and there was nothing inside except bottles. 'Look, Jerry. That head and that torso have gone. Whoever did all this damage must have taken them.'

'Yes, but *why*, for Christ's sake? And where's Dr Crowe and that assistant of his? Don't tell me they've been taken too.'

'Let's leave this laboratory as it is,' said Jamila. 'Nobody could have done this much damage without leaving plenty of circumstantial. I want to find out if anyone else here heard or saw anything unusual. And if anyone has any idea where Dr Crowe might be.'

'What about Professor Yearling? We still need him to take a look at these bloody flies, don't we? He's not going to be able to do it in here, though, is he?'

'I'll see if I can get in touch with him and ask him what he wants to do. There are other laboratories here he could use.'

They went outside and closed the door behind them. When they looked along the corridor, they saw an emergency fire door right at the end, and that it was slightly ajar. They walked quickly along to it and Jerry opened it wider. It gave out on to a metal fire escape that led down into the small private car park at the back of the building. They could see three cars parked there: a Honda Civic, a Vauxhall Astra and a silver Mercedes S-Class.

'Right, so there's at least three people here,' said Jerry. 'Let's go and find them.'

They knocked on all the doors on the first floor, next to Dr Crowe's laboratory, but there was no response. Next, they went up in the lift to the second floor, and there they found a library where a bald bespectacled man and a woman in a tweed suit were both sitting in front of their respective laptops with matching frowns on their faces.

Jamila took out her ID card. 'I'm sorry to disturb you. My name is Detective Inspector Jamila Patel and this is Detective Sergeant Jerry Pardoe. May I ask if those are your cars parked outside, and if so, which is whose?'

'Mine's the Honda,' said the bald man. 'And Megan's – that's the Astra.'

'Do you know who owns the Mercedes?'

'Of course, yes, that's Dr Crowe's.'

'Dr Crowe doesn't appear to be here today. Have you seen him?'

The woman pulled a face. 'Not today, no. I was supposed to, though. We were meant to be going over the results of his latest autopsies, ready for filing. He's usually frightfully punctual but I expect he's been held up.'

'His car's here, though. So where is he?'

'He might have left it overnight,' said the bald man. 'I believe there was some sort of old fellows' get-together at the Royal Society of Medicine yesterday evening.'

Jerry said, 'How about his assistant – have you seen him?'

Both the bald man and the woman shook their heads.

'And can we ask if you've seen anything unusual in this building today?'

'Such as what, for instance?'

'Any unfamiliar people? Anything at all that caught your attention as being out of the ordinary? Or maybe you've heard some strange noises, like banging or crashing or breaking glass?'

'No, nothing like that.'

'What about flies?' asked Jamila.

'Now you come to mention it, there have been a few flies buzzing around, which is odd, isn't it, when you think that it's November.'

'But apart from that, you're sure that you've seen nothing and that you've heard nothing?'

'Sorry. Not a sausage. We've been sitting here all morning preparing a report on stethoscope incisions.'

'Stethoscope incisions give *much* better post-autopsy reconstruction for grieving relatives,' the woman put in. 'Why, you'd hardly know that some of the corpses were actually dead.'

Jamila and Jerry went back down to Dr Crowe's laboratory and took another look around, just to make sure there was no obvious evidence that they might have missed. Because Sister Teresa had been pulled out of her refrigerated compartment, she was beginning to smell unpleasantly fetid, and Jamila kept her handkerchief pressed over her nose and her mouth.

They were about to leave when Jerry saw a sharp glint of light underneath the tipped-over trolley. When he bent down to look at it more closely, he realised that it was a silver signet ring. He took out his phone and took a picture of it where it was lying, and then he pulled a tissue out of the box on Dr Crowe's desk and picked it up. The ring had leaf-engraved shoulders and bore the initials *DW*.

'Maybe this was dropped by whoever smashed this place up. It's not Dr Crowe's, is it, his initials are JC, same as Our Lord, and it's not Zahir's.'

'We can post a picture of it on social media, and on the news,' said Jamila. 'Perhaps someone will recognise it.'

Her phone warbled, and it was Professor Yearling, answering her voice message.

'I'm afraid we have a bit of a situation down here at Falcon Road,' she told him. 'Someone's broken into Dr Crowe's lab and wrecked it, and removed some of the remains that he was examining. Not only that, we haven't been able to find Dr Crowe himself. As I told you in my message, though, we still need you to examine these flies to see if you can give us any idea where they might have come from.'

'His laboratory's been vandalised?' said Professor Yearling.

'Who on earth could have done that? I've been trying to call John Crowe myself without any luck, because I wanted to ask him if we could meet a little earlier. I'm coming down to London anyway for a meeting this evening, so yes, I will be able to examine those flies for you. I've prepared all the necessary chemicals for the tests that I'll be carrying out. If it's all right with you, I'll see you about half-past three.'

Jamila and Jerry went downstairs to the front desk to wait for DCI Butcher and backup officers to arrive. The receptionist in the baggy lavender cardigan grudgingly gave them a contact number for Zahir, but although Jamila rang and rang, she could get no answer out of him either.

'I am sure that something really bad has happened to those two,' she told Jerry, frowning. 'I have never felt such a sense of misgiving. I don't know what we are up against here, but I'm sure that it's much more powerful than flies alone. The flies are only the symptom of what it is. You remember what Dr Crowe said – it could be a force of some sort giving them such extraordinary strength, rather than a drug.'

'I'll nip out and take a look at his motor,' said Jerry. 'Maybe he's left something inside that might give us a clue where he is – a parking ticket or something like that. It's well strange that he's left it parked here all day but he's not here himself.'

He went out of the fire door at the back of the coroner's office, with the receptionist staring after him disapprovingly. It had been slightly foggy this morning, but now the car park was beginning to be spotted with rain, and so the fog was clearing.

He went across to Dr Crowe's Mercedes and peered into the windows, but they appeared to have a dark silvery tint, so that he was unable to see anything inside. Almost at once, though, he saw that the tint was rippling, and that it wasn't a tint at all. It was thousands of flies, completely smothering the windscreen and all the side windows.

He tugged at the driver's door handle, and it opened. With an angry chorus of zizzing, the flies inside the car rose up into the air, and scores of them came flying out, so that Jerry had to raise his hand to prevent them from pattering into his face. Some of them circled around and around the Mercedes, while others clung to the roof and the bonnet, and others flew back inside.

A man was sitting behind the steering wheel – a man so thickly coated in sparkling flies that he looked as if he were made out of crystal. From the top of his head, tangled grey hair was sprouting out through the struggling layers of insects. Apart from the fact that this was Dr Crowe's car, this was confirmation enough for Jerry that he had found Dr Crowe.

16

When Ronnie Gibbs pushed his way through the swing doors of The Waker pub on Lavender Hill, he saw that his three gang members were already sitting at their usual table in the corner. Their beer glasses were almost empty and so he went up to the landlord, Jim Fellowes, behind the bar and gave him a circular twiddle of his finger that meant 'more drinks all round and one for me'.

'How's it going, Ronnie?' asked Jim Fellowes, as he pulled back the beer pump. 'Manage to find a buyer for all them bicycles, did you?'

'What bicycles?'

Jim Fellowes placed a foaming pint glass on the counter and as he did so he could see that Ronnie's expression was utterly blank. He knew what *that* meant. It meant that whatever you thought you knew about Ronnie's wheeling and dealing, you didn't know, so keep your gob shut.

'I've seen how you could make yourself a nice bit of dosh, though,' he persisted, as he poured a second pint. 'Did you see that *Crimewatch Live* on the telly yesterday morning?'

'No, I didn't, mate. I had a late night and I didn't wake up till lunchtime.'

'The rozzers are looking for Vince Narrow, and they're

offering ten thousand notes to anyone who can put the finger on him.'

'Vince Narrow? If I knew where Vince Narrow was, I wouldn't tell the filth, no matter how much they was offering. I'd blow his bloody brains out. But come to think of it, I ain't seen him for at least a couple of weeks, and he ain't done no jobs that I've heard of.'

'You still ain't forgiven him for robbing your uncle's gaff, have you?'

'Yeah, that – and all the other ways he's gone out to piss me off over the years, like nicking the catalytic converter from under my Beamer. He said it was never him, but I knew damn well that it was, and I knew damn well that he done it on purpose, just to get up my nose.'

'Here, you go and sit down and I'll bring your drinks over,' said Jim Fellowes.

Ronnie went over to the corner and sat down next to his three gang members. They always sat here, next to a stained-glass window depicting the woman after whom The Waker had been named. In Victorian times, she was paid sixpence a week to go around the streets of Clapham in the morning, blowing dried peas out of a peashooter to hit people's bedroom windows and wake them up in time for work.

The stained glass was scarlet and green and purple, and when the sun shone through it the faces of the men sitting there looked as if they were suffering from some mottled skin disease.

Ronnie squeezed into his seat. 'Jim's just told me that the filth are offering a ten grand reward to anyone who can tell them where Vince Narrow's holed up.'

'I ain't seen him in a while,' said Nick, who was Ronnie's driver whenever they were out on a job together, or simply cruising the streets to show the locals that he was still around, and still had his thumb on Clapham's underworld. 'He used to have his breakfast in Hoppers every morning and I'd see him in there when I went in to fetch a coffee. But not for what— four or five days now.'

'Maybe he's retired,' put in Jock, picking up his fresh pint with his heavily tattooed hand. 'Or maybe he's snuffed it.'

'I wish,' said Ronnie. 'I'd dance on his fucking grave.'

'So – did you get to see that Akbas last night?' Frank asked him. Ronnie's gang had been involved in increasingly violent skirmishes with a Turkish drug dealer. Earlier this year, Murad Akbas had set up a takeaway pizza business in Camberwell that was a front for selling heroin and cocaine. He had been so successful that he had started to encroach on Ronnie's territory.

'Yes, Murad and me had a bit of a chat,' said Ronnie. 'Quite friendly, as it happened. We met in the Ali Baba kebab shop. Nice tasty lamb kebabs they do in there. Murad said that it's a free country, which means that he's got the right to sell his shit anywhere he wants, so I said that yes, it's a free country, which means that if I catch any of his pushers on my turf I'm not going to hesitate to cut their nuts off. He said in that case he'd better start using women, and we had a good old laugh about that.'

'How did you leave it?' asked Frank.

'I drew a line down the Stockwell Road and Murad agreed that he'd stay on his side of it. No exceptions.'

Frank nodded. He hadn't doubted for a moment that Ronnie would be able to warn Akbas off. Ronnie had a look about him – he was podgy, with wavy blond hair, a double chin and a nose like a piglet, a sort of cockney Donald Trump – but it was his colourless eyes that disturbed people the most, not only his enemies, but his gang members too. You never could tell if Ronnie was pleased with you or if he felt like slicing your ears off.

'You think he'll stick to it? Akbas?' said Nick.

'He'll be a damn fool if he don't. If we chop the goolies off of one of his pushers and the poor bloke has to go to the A & E, the hospital's bound to notify the filth, aren't they, and then the filth are going to find out that Akbas has been flogging a whole lot more than pepperoni pizzas and that's his two-million-quid drug business straight down the Swanee.'

Jock swallowed almost half of his fresh pint of beer in three gulps. Then he slapped the table with both hands and said, in his strong Glasgow accent, 'Right! I'm bustin' for a widdle. Does anyone feel like a packet of crips while I'm up?'

'You can get us some porky scratchings,' said Nick.

Jock went off to the men's toilet. It was cramped and dark in there, because the lightbulb had burned out and there was only a small grimy skylight, and it smelled of stale urine and cherry fragrance toilet blocks. The single stall had a notice on the door saying 'out of order' so Jock stood in front of the urinal and unbuttoned his jeans.

He was still halfway through urinating when he heard the door open.

'Nearly finished, pal,' he said. 'I've three-and-a-half pints to empty out, God forgive me.'

The newcomer said nothing in reply, but Jock could hear a soft buzzing noise, as if the man were shaving himself with an electric razor.

'Nearly finished,' he said. 'The wifey used to moan that I had a bladder the size of Loch Ness.'

He was shaking himself when he became aware that the buzzing was coming up closer behind him. Before he could tuck himself into his underpants and start to button up his jeans, he was suddenly gripped around the throat by two powerful hands. Two sharp thumbnails dug painfully into the back of his neck and eight fingers wrapped themselves in a double chokehold around his Adam's apple. The hands felt as if they had a crunchy texture, and about six or seven dark specks flew into his eyes, catching themselves in his eyelashes and almost blinding him.

'*Gaah!*' was all Jock could manage to say. He flailed his arms, trying to hit the man behind him, but he couldn't reach him. Then he tried to swing his left leg backwards, to kick the man in the crotch, but when he did that, the man slammed him forward so that his forehead cracked against the tiles on the wall. He felt warm blood streaming down his face and he dropped to his knees, stunned. The man carried on choking him, and now he knocked Jock's face twice against the ceramic rim of the urinal, snapping the bridge of his nose.

Jock made one last desperate effort to twist himself around and break the man's strangulating grip. All he could hear was this furious buzzing, and when he managed to turn his head halfway to the left, he saw that the man was covered from head to foot in flies. Even his face was crawling all over with flies, and Jock couldn't even see any eyes.

Jock tried to turn his head further, but the man squeezed his neck so much tighter that he felt as if his lungs were going to explode. After a few agonising seconds, he blacked out. The man then smashed his head against the urinal again and again, until his skull cracked apart and lumps of his beige-coloured brains were splattered all over the cherry-pink toilet block.

He fell down on to his knees as if he were praying, with his head resting against the waste pipe. The man stood over him for a while, but then the buzzing grew louder, and the flies' wings began to ripple and glitter. As if they had been summoned by some silent command, they all rose into the air.

Ronnie looked at his Rolex watch. 'Jock's taking his fucking time. Not constipated, is he?'

'I shouldn't think so,' said Frank. 'Him and me, we had a vindaloo at the Maharani last night. When I went this morning, it felt like half of Clapham was falling out me arse.'

'How much has he drunk? I want him to pick up all that red diesel that Billy Albu's got for us, and I don't want him getting nicked for DUI.'

Frank stood up. 'I'll give him a shout. I could do with a wizz meself.'

He went across to the men's toilet, blowing a kiss to Jim Fellowes' wife, Margaret, who was drying glasses behind the bar. She jabbed her finger into her open mouth to show him that he made her feel sick.

As soon as he pushed open the toilet door, though, the smell that came billowing out made him feel as if he wanted to retch too. This was more than the reek of urine and faeces and toilet blocks. Frank knew what this was, because he had served in the army in Afghanistan. This was the smell of a rotting human body.

He stepped cautiously into the gloomy toilet, cupping his hand over his nose and his mouth. At first, he was unable to understand what he was looking at. But then he realised that Jock was crouching face down on the floor and that another man was lying face down on top of him. This other man, though, was wearing only a pair of padded white plastic pants, like a diaper, and apart from that he was naked. His ribcage had collapsed, so that he looked weirdly flat, and his skin had turned black and greasy, with bubbly yellow patches. He smelled suffocatingly sweet, with a strong hint of cheese.

A few flies were crawling over the man's shoulders and back, and some were droning around in the air.

It was obvious that Jock was dead, too, with his skull split open and blobs of his brains lying in the urinal. Totally shocked, Frank took two stumbling steps backwards out of the toilet and slammed the door shut. Ronnie and the rest of the gang heard the door slam and looked across the pub at him.

'What's up, Frank?' Ronnie called out. 'Jock stunk the khazi out?'

Frank came back over. 'He's brown bread, Ronnie,' he said, in a shaky whisper. 'He's lying on the floor with his bonce cracked open. And there's another dead geezer in there with him, only this geezer smells like he's been dead for nearly a month.'

Ronnie stared at him. 'What do you mean, he's brown bread? He only went for a slash. Are you joking, or what?'

'Go and see for yourself if you don't believe me. We need to call the Old Bill, and right now.'

There was a long pause, and then Ronnie said, 'You're serious, aren't you?'

'Jock hasn't come out, has he? And I've only fucking wet meself.'

Ronnie took out his phone. 'Look at the date. The twenty-third. They always say that twenty-three's an unlucky number. I should of fucking stayed in bed.'

Nick leaned across the table. He also spoke quietly, so that Jim and Margaret Fellowes wouldn't hear him. 'Who's this other geezer? This one that's been dead for nearly a month?'

'God knows, Nick. But he couldn't have walked in there by

himself, could he? Somebody must have carted him in there, but God knows why.'

'Well, God may know, Frank, but He ain't going to tell us, is He? That's the trouble with God, if you ask me. Always keeps Himself to Himself. Miserable bastard.'

DI Simon Fairbrother came out of the toilet and peeled off his face mask.

'My God,' he said. 'I cannot imagine what the hell went on inside there.'

DS Morrison shook her head. 'Someone bashed him to death against the urinal. I mean, he's one of Ronnie Gibbs's gang, so I can understand that the member of another gang could have had a score to settle with him. Maybe one of the Tooting Bec Terrors. But why leave him with a corpse on top of him? What's that about?'

The Martian came out of the toilet, too, pulling back the rustling hood of his polypropylene hazmat suit so that his pointed ears sprang out.

'So, what do you reckon, Derek?' DI Fairbrother asked him.

'Me? I'm only paid to collect and analyse the evidence,' said the Martian. 'Not to have inspired hunches like you lot.'

'But supposing we *did* pay you to have inspired hunches?'

'I'd still be stumped. The victim was strangled, we can see that from the contusions around his throat. He was strangled and then his head was struck against the wall and the toilet fittings with sufficient force to shatter his nasal septum and break apart the frontal plate of his skull. After that, for some reason, a dead male was laid on top of him. I'd estimate that this deceased gentleman probably passed away about twenty to twenty-five days ago, because he's already started butyric fermentation. This gives the body a strong Stilton smell. Butyric acid helps our digestion, but it also makes our vomit smell the way it does.'

'Oh, my Lord,' said DS Morrison. 'I wish I hadn't had that cheese sandwich for lunch now.'

'Sorry about that,' the Martian told her. 'But the mystery isn't so much why the perp would have wanted to leave the deceased gentleman on top of the victim. It's how the perp managed to do it.'

'Not at all easy to carry a dead body into a pub at lunchtime, I would have thought,' said DI Fairbrother. 'Not without being noticed.'

'The thing is – did anyone actually do that?' asked the Martian.

'I don't understand you. How else did the body get into the toilet?'

'Well, we lifted some footprints from the tiles and some of them are bare footprints that match the deceased gentleman's feet, as if he had actually walked across the toilet floor unaided.'

'You what?'

'Yes, and we also lifted some fingerprints from the toilet door and the handle of the back door that leads out to the yard at the rear of the pub. And here's what's really stumping us. A preliminary test showed us that they appear to match the deceased gentleman's fingerprints. Not only do they feature the same whorls and loops, but they also carry traces of butyric acid. And the fingerprints on the back door handle were the last fingerprints that anyone left there.'

'So what are you suggesting?' DI Fairbrother asked him. 'That this dead man opened the back door and walked into the toilet by himself?'

The Martian pulled a face. 'I'm only telling you what circumstantial evidence we've come across – so far, anyway. We'll be testing it all more thoroughly in the lab, and we haven't finished yet, so we're bound to find more. But I'm afraid it's up to you to work out what actually happened.'

'Bloody hell, Derek! This is even weirder than that bloke who was supposed to have dug his way out of his grave in Wandsworth Cemetery!'

'Well, I have to agree with you. But there's one more thing I should tell you. The deceased gentleman had a number of flies caught in his eyelashes. They may mean nothing. I mean, dead bodies attract flies, don't they? But we've bottled them up and we'll hand them over to DI Patel and DS Pardoe, because they've been investigating all these incidents that involve flies. Maybe this is going to be a case for them, rather than you.'

DI Fairbrother turned to DS Morrison. 'That would be a relief, I can tell you. I'll give them a bell now. I'm beginning to feel like the zombie-hunter-in-chief.'

17

Professor Yearling came hurrying in through the doors of the coroner's building as if he were late for an appointment. He crossed the reception area and shook Jamila and Jerry's hands with both of his.

'This is such a tragedy,' he told them. 'John Crowe was one in a million. He had only to take one sniff of a corpse and he could tell you to the day how long it had been dead.'

'It was those flies again,' said Jamila. 'We really need to know more about them. You are becoming very important to our investigation, professor, believe me.'

They went upstairs in the lift together to a small laboratory two doors along the corridor from the pathology laboratory in which Dr Crowe had been working.

The flies that Dr Crowe had collected from every one of the victims had been transferred to this laboratory. Most of them were dead now, but Dr Crowe had kept some of them alive by feeding them with apple cider vinegar and sugar.

Dr Crowe's Mercedes saloon had been taken to Lambeth Road on a car transporter with his body still inside it, covered in a blue sheet. Before he was taken away, though, one of the forensic technicians who had attended the scene had given Jamila and Jerry a test tube containing five of the flies that he had picked off Dr Crowe himself.

'It'll obviously take me some considerable time to test all these samples,' said Professor Yearling, taking off his overcoat and hanging it up. 'But I can tell you from just a first glance that they are all coffin flies, *Conicera tibialis*, although I can see some slight variations in their eyes and their wings. Normally, you would expect to find flies only on a dead body – blowflies, houseflies or flesh flies – *sarcophagidae* – but it seems that these flies swarmed all over their victims while they were still alive, or certainly before they had been dead long enough to start to decompose.'

'Do you think that you'll be able to give us at least some idea where they might have come from?' asked Jamila.

'If they fed on any distinctive foodstuff and if they clung to any distinctive type of surface, then it's certainly possible. But I have to admit that I have never in the whole of my career as an entomologist come across a massive swarm of coffin flies like these. And what's even more unusual about them is that they appear to have selected particular individuals to settle on.'

'You're right, they have,' said Jerry. 'And apart from that, they also seem to have this incredible strength. Like, how the hell could a bunch of flies have lifted the Bishop of Southwark fifty feet up into the air – even a couple of thousand of them?'

'I've been looking into that since you first told me about it,' said Professor Yearling. 'I discovered that some experiments were carried out in the mid-1970s in Argentina – not with flies but with bees, because Argentina produces more honey than any other country in the world. They found that they could direct a swarm of bees to fly together in a particular direction by means of ultrasonic signals. Not only that, they could make them cluster together more tightly, which could conceivably have given them greater combined strength.'

'Could flies be directed like that, do you think?' asked Jamila.

'It's possible. There was another experiment in Croatia in 1989 with female horseflies. Horseflies normally feed on nectar, but in order to develop their fertilised eggs the females go searching for blood, both animal and human, and as you know they can give you a very nasty bite. Entomologists in Croatia found that specific sounds attracted female horseflies and other sounds repelled them. These sounds were too high-pitched to be audible to humans.

'I'm not saying that this is what we're dealing with in these investigations, but it shows that it's possible for flies to be controlled in some way.'

'Very well then, we'll leave you to get on with your analysis,' said Jamila. 'You have our numbers for when you're ready to contact us. But the sooner the better, if you can.'

Professor Yearling opened the green metal box of chemicals that he had brought with him.

'I will, of course. I'm wondering, though. If these flies *are* being deliberately directed, do you have any idea at all what the motive could be?'

'It could be religious,' Jamila told him. 'Apart from DS Pardoe's friend Maureen Glover, all the victims so far have had some religious connection, although they didn't all belong to the same faith. Maybe we're looking for a homicidal atheist.'

Jamila and Jerry had only just sat back in their car when Jamila's phone warbled.

'Oh. Simon. What's up?'

Jerry started the engine and began to drive back towards the station, but Jamila laid a hand on his arm and said, 'Hold on, Jerry. There might be another one. Do you know a pub called The Waker?'

'Yes. It's on Tipthorpe Road. Right dump. Warm beer and cold fish and chips.'

'Simon Fairbrother says there's been a murder. One of Ronnie Gibbs's gang. But a decomposed body was found on top of him. And there were flies in his eyes.'

'Ronnie Gibbs? That fat lump of leftover lard? Why would those flies go after one of his lot? He's about as far from religious as Satan on his day off.'

'Simon said it was only a few flies, but there's some really unusual evidence that he can't explain and he thinks you and me should at least take a look.'

'Do you know something? If I was religious, and I wasn't driving, I'd cross myself.'

The Waker was less than half a mile away from Lavender Hill police station. When Jamila and Jerry arrived there, they found that Tipthorpe Road was jammed with squad cars and forensic vans and two ambulances, and that the pavement on both sides of Lavender Hill had been cordoned off. When Jerry climbed out of his car, he recognised several TV and newspaper reporters on the other side of the street. They shouted questions at him and Jamila, which he couldn't hear, so he simply waved to them.

Inside the pub, they found DI Fairbrother and DS Morrison sitting at one of the tables, talking to Ronnie Gibbs and his gang members Frank and Nick. The Martian and two other forensic technicians were coming in and out of the men's toilet, accompanied by the lightning flicker of electronic flash cameras. The bar smelled of stale beer, but it was also permeated with the distinctive smell of human decomposition.

DI Fairbrother stood up. 'Hey – glad you could get here so quickly, you two. I think you'd better come and see the deceased for yourselves. Deceased plural, that is.'

'Hi there, Gibbsy,' said Jerry to Ronnie Gibbs. 'How's the diet coming along?'

Ronnie Gibbs discreetly lifted his middle finger.

'Which one of your lot's snuffed it?' Jerry persisted.

'Jock. Jock Maclean.'

'Any idea who might have had it in for him?'

'Half of Clapham, probably, plus a few Scottish psychos.'

'We'll have a chat in a minute, okay?'

'I've got nothing to tell you, Pardoe. Even if I had, I wouldn't.'

'That's what I always liked about you, Gibbsy. Mr Co-operative, that's what we call you at the station. Not because you've ever been helpful. It just looks like you've eaten your way through the whole of the Co-operative supermarket.'

'Fuck off, Pardoe.'

Jamila and Jerry put on face masks and went into the gents' toilet. The Martian described how Jock had been strangled and how his head had been smashed against the wall and the urinal. But Jamila and Jerry couldn't take their eyes off the man's decomposing body that was lying on top of him, especially when the Martian told them about his footprints and his fingerprints.

'Could somebody have held his hand in such a way that they could have used it to open the door handle without touching it themselves?' asked Jamila.

'I can't see how,' said the Martian. 'The prints were

sufficiently clear to have been made by the application of firm pressure, and they were curled around the handle in the way that you or I would have opened it. And the footprints have all the clarity of somebody walking evenly across the floor with their full weight, not a dead body being dragged. But both the fingerprints and the footprints are undoubtedly his.'

DI Fairbrother was standing in the toilet doorway behind them. 'He's a zombie,' he said. 'That's the only explanation I could think of. But we did find a few flies sticking to the Scotsman's eyes, so maybe you can tell us different.'

They left the toilet and went back into the bar. 'Here,' said the Martian, and he handed Jamila a clear plastic evidence jar containing the flies. Jamila held them up to the light so that she could see them more clearly, and Jerry peered at them too.

'Coffin flies, unless I'm mistaken,' she said to Jerry.

Jerry nodded. 'I was hoping they wouldn't be. Yippee. It looks like we've got another fly murder to deal with, doesn't it? And this one certainly wasn't a vicar or a priest, either.'

He went back across the bar to the table where Ronnie Gibbs and Frank were sitting.

'This is dead serious, Gibbsy. We really need to know who might have wanted to merk your Jock. We're not just talking about a one-off hit here, we're talking about a serial killer. He's already done for too many and we're pretty sure he's going to go after some more.'

He paused, and then he said, very quietly, 'If you can give us some idea who did it, we might be able to turn a blind eye to some of your own little shenanigans.'

Ronnie Gibbs spread his hands. 'I'd appreciate the favour, Pardoe, my old son. But the genuine truth is that I haven't got a fucking clue.'

'Jock hadn't told you about any threats that he might have received? How about you? Have you had any threats lately?'

'Are you having a laugh? I get twenty threats a day, and twice that on Sundays.'

'Was Jock religious at all? Like, did he go to church or anything like that? There's a Church of Scotland on Garratt Lane, isn't there?'

'He was always asking Jesus to help him out. But, no, he never went to church. Not so far as I know, anyhow. I reckon he would have been struck by lightning if he'd so much as stepped into a church.'

'All right, Gibbsy, we'll leave it for now, but we'll probably want to talk to you again after the autopsy. And meanwhile, if you can think of any reason why anybody should have gone after Jock, you'll contact us, won't you?'

Jerry turned to leave, but then he stopped. 'Oh – and one more thing, while you're here. DS Watkins wants a word with you about some bicycles. You couldn't give her a bell at the station, could you?'

Ronnie Gibbs gave him his colourless death stare. 'Bicycles? Do I look like the kind of bloke who'd have anything to do with bicycles?'

'Well, I can't imagine you wobbling along on one, Gibbsy, but I know that quite a few have gone missing and they're Treks, which sell for nearly fifteen grand each.'

Ronnie Gibbs shook his head. 'Don't mean nothing to me, Pardoe. Sounds more up Vincent Narrow's street. Maybe you should have a word with him.'

'I would, if I knew where he was. You don't have any ideas, do you?'

'No. We ain't seen him neither. It could be that somebody

else has caught up with him. The Devil himself, with any luck.'

When they returned to the station, they went up to the communications room to see if there was any CCTV footage that might show who had entered the back yard of The Waker before Jock Maclean was murdered.

Edge was up there, standing behind the chair of PC Sadza. They were both looking at three screens, which gradually became speckled with scores of dark-grey dots, one after the other, until all three of them were totally blank.

'Oh, don't tell me,' said Jamila. 'You're looking for the suspect who entered The Waker but the cameras were covered in flies.'

'It has to be deliberate,' said PC Sadza, turning around in her chair. 'Mallett was telling me the same thing happened when those bodies were taken from Lettice & Pray. But how can you order a whole lot of flies to go and cover up a CCTV camera? And it was only for less than three minutes – look, this is the same scene now.'

She switched over the left-hand screen to show them the back yard of The Waker as it was now, stacked with beer crates and cordoned off with blue police tapes.

'So we can't see who entered the back door of the pub?' said Jamila. 'Derek Grant told us that the last person to leave their fingerprints on the handle was the corpse they found lying on top of the murder victim.'

'Jock the Shock, the victim, wasn't it?' Edge asked her. 'One of the worst of Ronnie Biggs's bunch of thugs. I always reckon it was him who burned down that BP petrol station on

Clapham North Side. I'm surprised someone didn't top him years ago.'

'I'll prepare you a full report on which cameras were obscured, and for how long,' said PC Sadza. 'That might at least give you some idea where the suspect came from.'

'Thank you,' said Jamila, and both she and Jerry went downstairs to Jerry's office. DS Watkins was there, eating a takeaway McDonald's and prodding at her PC, and she gave them a salute.

'I am really at a loss what to do next,' said Jamila. 'Professor Yearling may be able to tell us where all those flies came from, and if they were breeding naturally or if somebody has been breeding them artificially. Hopefully, he will also have a clearer understanding of how they can be directed where to go. But until we hear from him – and until we are given a full forensic report from The Waker and an autopsy on Jock Maclean – I have no idea how to progress this investigation at all.'

Jerry snapped his fingers. He reached into the pocket of his coat and took out the small plastic evidence bag that he had tucked in there when they had been looking around Dr Crowe's vandalised laboratory. He had been so distracted by the sight of the two bodies at The Waker that it had slipped his mind.

'Maybe this'll give us a lead. Whoever DW is, or was, they must have left some DNA on this ring. I'll send it over to the Martian so that he can test it.'

'Jerry, there must be at least ten thousand people in London with the initials DW.'

'Okay, maybe it's clutching at straws. But what else have we got?'

'We could go and see Father Devine.'

'Your exorcist chum? Why not? Better than sitting around twiddling our thumbs.'

'I'll call him,' said Jamila. 'I just hope he hasn't gone to Rome. They have a kind of exorcists' get-together at this time of year to discuss what demons they've managed to get rid of since the last time they met.'

'Jesus. And they call *us* the Ghostbusters.'

18

It was raining again, and the traffic was so heavy it took them well over an hour to reach the church of Our Lady Help of Christians in Ilford. By the time they arrived, it was dark.

The church was halfway down Albert Road, a Victorian redbrick building with narrow stained-glass windows and four needlepoint spires, one at each corner, surrounded by overgrown laurel hedges. Jerry managed to park in a tight space right outside, and they entered the church through the double oak doors and walked up the echoing aisle. They found Father Devine waiting for them in his sacristy, printing out orders of service for Sunday's communion.

'Jamila – so good to see you!' he said, standing up. He was not much taller than Jamila, with fraying white hair and rimless spectacles, and a large mole on his chin. He was wearing a black cassock, buttoned all the way down to his ankles. 'And this is—?'

'Jerry Pardoe. Detective Sergeant Jerry Pardoe.'

Father Devine shook Jerry's hand as enthusiastically as if he were congratulating him for winning first prize in the church lottery.

'We're sorry to disturb you so late, father,' said Jamila. 'Unfortunately, this case is becoming increasingly urgent, and we're worried that more people are going to be targeted. As I told you on the phone, Jerry and I tend to be assigned to investigations that appear to have some element of the supernatural – or at least, which our superior officers can't understand. They call us the Ghostbusters – but not to our faces.'

'You mentioned something about flies.'

'Yes. We've been investigating several murders and assaults that have involved huge numbers of flies. And I'm talking about thousands of them – tens of thousands.'

'Goodness me. I've seen some mention of them on the television news.'

'Yes, but fortunately our media people have been able to keep the press releases pretty low-key. In actual fact, the murders have been not only mystifying but absolutely devastating. But we've been doing our best not to start a mass panic.'

'Do sit down,' said Father Devine. 'Would you care for a cup of tea? I'm afraid I don't have anything stronger – only communion wine.'

'I'm afraid I'm an atheist,' said Jerry. 'And I'm driving.'

Jamila described to Father Devine all the murders and assaults involving flies. She told him that the murder victims had either been clergy or had some connection to religion, with the exception of Jerry's girlfriend, Maureen Glover, and Nadia Green from the funeral director's, and Dr Crowe, and of course Jock Maclean.

She also told him about the invasion of flies at St Juliana's school.

Father Devine sat with the tips of his fingers pressed thoughtfully together against his lips. When Jamila had finished, he opened a drawer in his desk, took out a candle, fitted it into a brass candle holder and lit it.

'I'm lighting this to ask the Lord for understanding about

what I'm going to say next,' he told them. 'I may be utterly wrong, and what I'm suggesting may be blasphemy. However, I'm sure that you both know what it says in the Bible about swarms of flies, and who threatened to let them loose on anyone who failed to obey His will. It was the Lord God Himself.'

'Blimey,' said Jerry. 'That's what I said to that schoolteacher bloke, but it was only a joke, believe me.'

'Are you serious?' asked Jamila. 'You're saying that *God* might be responsible for killing people with all these flies? But the victims included a bishop and vicars and a nun. Why would God want to sacrifice His own representatives here on Earth?'

'Ah, you see, that only makes them more liable to divine punishment should they have done wrong. And of course God will have known if they had committed some mortal sin, even if they had succeeded in concealing it from everyone else.'

'But what about Dr Crowe? And those two women, Maureen and Nadia? And that gangster Jock Maclean?'

'God may have intervened because He was concerned that Dr Crowe might reveal His true purpose. From what you have told me, it was possible that he could have done, given time. As for the women, He may have wanted Maureen to infect Jerry to deter him from finding out who was responsible for these murders, but Nadia – who knows? She may have been only a collateral victim.'

'And all those children from the Church of England school? What about them? Don't tell me that God wanted to do any harm to them?'

'I don't know, Jamila. Perhaps he wanted to warn them to be obedient and follow His teachings, and that He would punish them if they didn't. Perhaps he wanted to show them that He's not some figment of our collective imagination, but that He's real.'

'I'm in a fix here, father,' said Jerry. 'A genuine fix. I don't believe in God, so how am I supposed to arrest someone I don't believe in? And where do I find Him? Third cloud from the left and straight on till morning?'

Father Devine gave him a wry smile. 'I'm afraid you couldn't arrest Him. And even if you could, where would you put Him? He created the whole world. I don't think a police cell could hold Him, and I don't think you'd find a magistrate who would be prepared to sentence Him.'

'So what are Jamila and I supposed to do? Just let Him carry on murdering people if He reckons they've committed some sin, and even people who haven't, and turn a blind eye?'

'I have a suggestion,' said Jamila. 'Why don't you come with us, father, to the coroner's laboratory where Dr Crowe was carrying out his autopsies? Professor Yearling – the entomologist – is still there, testing the flies that were taken from the victims' bodies. Perhaps if you carry out an exorcism there, you'll be able to confirm if the flies are really under the command of God, or if they're being directed by somebody or something else?'

Father Devine took off his spectacles and stared at her short-sightedly. 'You realise you're asking me to risk my life, confronting God?'

'It's up to you. But if we can find out for certain that it really *is* God who's behind all these flies, then we may be able to save the lives of many more people. We could pray to Him for absolution.'

'Even if it isn't God, which personally I very much doubt, maybe you can tip us off to who actually *is* responsible,' put in Jerry. 'Then with any luck we can find him and bang him up.'

'We will have to do it tonight,' said Father Devine. 'I am expected in Cardiff tomorrow to give a talk to the National Synthesis Team.'

'Very well, let's do it tonight,' said Jamila. 'I know it's getting late, but if you're up for it.'

Father Devine thought for a moment, and then he said, 'Very well. Give me a few minutes to pack the necessary things.'

He went over to his large mahogany wardrobe and took out a burgundy leather case. Jamila and Jerry watched him as he opened it up and carefully arranged in it a worn-looking Bible, a bottle of holy water, a conical incense burner, a rosary, a candle holder and six red candles, a crucifix with an effigy of Jesus on it, and what looked like a human jawbone.

'What's the bone?' Jerry asked him.

'It's a holy relic. The jaw of St Stephen, who was stoned to death in Jerusalem in AD 36 for converting Jews to Christianity and speaking out against the Sanhedrin, the supreme rabbinical court. It was with this actual jaw that he spoke the word of Christ.'

Jerry nodded. He was tempted to say, *Maybe he should have kept his cakehole shut*, but he stayed silent.

It was still raining as they drove back to Falcon Road. It was nearly eight thirty by the time they arrived and the coroner's office was closed, but inside the reception area the lights were on, and they could see the night watchman sitting at the reception desk watching *Ramsay's Kitchen Nightmares*.

Jerry knocked on the glass door and the watchman came over to let them in.

Jamila showed him her ID, and then she said, 'Is Professor Yearling still here?'

'Yes – yes, he is. He said he'd be another hour or so. I offered him one of my corned beef sandwiches, but he said he was messing around with dead flies so he didn't really fancy it.'

They went upstairs and along to the laboratory, where Professor Yearling was sitting at a table with a row of glass flasks and petri dishes in front of him, as well as a microscope.

'How's it going, professor?' said Jerry.

Professor Yearling sat back in his chair and stretched. 'Quite promising so far, as a matter of fact. Dr Crowe has a high-performance liquid chromatograph and that's made my analysis much easier. The tests I've completed up until now show that all these flies have been artificially bred on a diet of sugar and rotten peaches or nectarines. Actually, a diet of sugar shortens their lives by causing a build-up of uric acid in their digestive systems, but whoever has been breeding them obviously didn't seem to care.'

Jamila looked across at Father Devine. If God had been responsible for breeding the flies, would He really not have cared how long they lived?

'Any idea yet *where* they were bred?' she asked Professor Yearling.

'Not yet. But I'm still analysing the oils from their feet. So far, I've come across traces of something quite interesting, but I've a lot more flies to test and I'll need to come back tomorrow. Of course, I'll let you know if and when I'm able to give you any indication of where they might have come from.'

'Thanks,' said Jamila. 'Actually, the reason we've come here this evening is to take another look at Dr Crowe's laboratory. If you hear any funny noises coming from out of there, don't worry. It will only be us.'

'Oh – okay,' said Professor Yearling, although he looked over at Father Devine standing by the doorway with his burgundy leather case and he raised his eyebrows.

Jamila and Jerry led Father Devine back along the corridor to Dr Crowe's laboratory. They switched on the flickering fluorescent lights and looked around. The Martian's forensic technicians still had examinations to complete, so the laboratory had not yet been cleared up, except that Sister Teresa's body had been removed to the morgue at St George's Hospital. The trolley was still lying on its side and broken glass and crumpled papers were still strewn across the floor.

'I don't reckon it was God who smashed this place up,' said Jerry. 'He wouldn't have nicked a torso and a severed head, neither. Like, what would He have done with them?'

'"God moves in mysterious ways, His wonders to perform",' quoted Father Devine.

'If He did this, father, then I can only agree with you.'

Father Devine set down his case on Dr Crowe's workbench, where four glass jars with labels on them were still arranged in a row, half filled with dead flies. He set up the candle holder and lit his six red candles, although it took him a little time to light the incense cone. Once he had done so, though, the laboratory began to fill with the sweet, woody, citrussy smell of frankincense. Jerry sneezed, but pinched his nose to stop himself from sneezing again.

Now Father Devine picked up the crucifix in his right hand and his Bible in his left, and he said to Jerry, 'Would you mind turning off the lights? Spirits of all kinds are very reluctant to appear in fluorescent light, whether they're good or malevolent. It's the ultraviolet. They find it blinding.'

Jerry went over and flicked the switches, and now the only illumination was the six red candles, with their flames dancing together in the faint chilly draught from the air-conditioning. The candles lit up the curling smoke from the incense cone, and cast tall, distorted shadows of Jamila and Jerry and Father Devine on the laboratory walls.

Father Devine raised the Bible and the crucifix and spoke in a high, clear voice, almost singing.

'In the name of Jesus Christ we drive you from us, whoever you may be, unclean spirits, all satanic powers, all infernal invaders, all wicked legions, assemblies and sects. In the name and by the power of Our Lord Jesus Christ, may you be snatched away and driven from the Church of God and from the souls made in the image and likeness of God and redeemed by the precious blood of the Divine Lamb.'

As he said these words, one of the candles went out, and then another, but he continued with his incantation.

'Most cunning serpent, you shall no more dare to deceive the human race, persecute the Church, torment God's elect and sift them as wheat.'

One by one, the remaining four candles flickered out, and they were left in total darkness.

'Jesus, this is spooky,' said Jerry. 'Okay if I turn the lights back on?'

'No, wait,' Father Devine told him. 'I think I hear something. Can you?'

Jerry listened. At first, he could hear nothing at all, but then he heard a soft, persistent buzzing noise, like flies tapping against a window.

'I can hear that too,' said Jamila. 'But it can't be the flies in those jars... they're all dead.'

'Hush,' said Father Devine.

The buzzing grew steadily louder, and as it did so, a faint green light appeared, just above the small trolley that Zahir had used to wheel the severed head across the laboratory. The light gradually took on the same shape as the head, with its tongue hanging down, and it was reflected in the stainless-steel surface of the trolley, so that it looked like two heads, one on top of the other, one upside down, so that their tongues were joined.

'Holy crap,' said Jerry. 'What the hell is that?'

Father Devine was silent, and for a moment Jerry thought that he might not answer him. After a while, though, he said, '*That* is what we call a spiritual resonance. If a strong spiritual force has manifested itself in any location, it can leave behind an audible echo and sometimes even a visible image of itself. Could this be the head you were telling me about?'

'It certainly looks like it,' Jamila managed to tell him, although her voice was tight with stress. 'I've heard of such things in Pakistan, with dead relatives appearing during Eid-ul-Adha, but I've never actually seen anything like it before.'

'It proves to me anyway that I was wrong,' said Father Devine. 'This is not God's work. I have no idea who it might be, or what, but it is not inspired by Our Lord.'

He paused. The shimmering green head remained where it was, and although its features were indistinct, it was possible for Jamila and Jerry to see that it was badly decomposed, as the real head had been.

Father Devine took a step towards it. 'Who are you?' he demanded. 'Are you able to speak, and tell me who your master might be?'

There was no answer – only the repetitive buzzing of the flies that weren't there.

'Who are you?' Father Devine repeated. 'If you tell me your name, perhaps I can ask the Lord to grant you peace for all eternity.'

The green-lit head began to flicker and fade.

'Who are you?' Father Devine begged it. 'Don't go before telling me who you are. You could save the lives of many others.'

Over the buzzing noise, Jerry was sure he heard the blurry word '*clown*', spoken in the same voice that he had heard it before. Then the head was swallowed up by the darkness, and there was silence.

'That's it,' said Father Devine. 'I doubt if I'll ever be able to raise him again. One manifestation is about as much as most spirits can manage, whatever people tell you about repeated hauntings. Let there be light, please, Jerry.'

Jerry groped his way across the laboratory and flicked the switches back on. When he looked around, the only flies he could see were the dead flies in Dr Crowe's sample jars, and there was no sign of an illuminated head floating over the stainless-steel trolley.

'Did you hear "clown" again?' he asked Jamila.

'I thought I heard something, just before it disappeared, but I couldn't be sure what it was.'

'How about you, father? Did you hear anything?'

'Not really. But then there was so much buzzing, and I'm a little deaf.'

'I'm sure I heard "clown",' said Jerry. 'But don't ask me what it means. There's nothing remotely funny going on here.'

Father Devine took out his bottle of holy water and swung his arm from side to side to sprinkle it all around the laboratory.

'In the name of Jesus, I command right now every spirit that is not of God to leave this room. We humbly beseech Thee to bless and sanctify it, and all who may enter into it, amen.'

'Does that include us?' asked Jerry.

19

Jamila and Jerry left the coroner's office and started to drive back to Lavender Hill. At the same time, the wedding party for Terry and Christine Adam at the Palette Hotel in Battersea, only two miles away, was becoming increasingly noisy.

The Palette Hotel's decorative venue room was crowded with over two hundred guests. Nearly half of them were vicars and curates and members of church societies, and there was even a Belgian pastor, but they were all drinking and dancing and singing raucously along to 'Sweet Caroline'.

Terry and Christine had been dancing with their aunts and uncles, but now they came back to dance together again. Terry was tall with a ginger beard and was occasionally mistaken for Prince Harry, while Christine was short and plump with curly brunette hair and rosebud lips. Terry was a finance manager for Southwark Council, while Christine was the daughter of the Reverend Victor Plume, the vicar of St Peter's.

'What an amazing day,' said Christine. 'But I still can't believe I'm Mrs Adam.'

'I bet Eve couldn't believe it either,' grinned Terry.

'I'm absolutely knackered, though. Do you think we could go to bed soon?'

'Well, it's legal now, isn't it? But I think your dad's got a few more words he wants to say.'

'Oh, no. He's already given one speech.'

'He told me he's got a surprise for us.'

'I think I know what it is. I heard him on the phone to the travel agents.'

'Sweet Caroline' finished and the DJ put on 'I Wanna Dance With Somebody'.

'Come on, Chrissy. Last dance of the evening,' said Terry.

'My feet are killing me. These shoes!'

'Take them off, then.'

As Christine bent down to prise off her new high-heeled shoes, a fly landed on her bottom lip. She spat it away in disgust, but then a fly landed on her cheek and another on her eyelid.

She brushed those away too, but when she looked up she saw that flies were crawling on Terry's shoulder, and that flies were buzzing everywhere in the venue room and clustered all over the chandeliers. The music kept playing, but the guests had stopped dancing and were flapping their hands to keep the flies away from their faces.

'Stop! Stop! Stop!' called out the Reverend Plume, striding across the dance floor to the plinth where the DJ was playing.

As soon as the music was switched off, Terry and Christine could hear all the hoarse cries of revulsion from the men and the petrified squeals from the women. Even more flies were pouring in from the bar area, thousands of them, and they were circling around and landing everywhere – on the walls and the curtains and the tables and the plates of wedding cake. They pattered against the guests' faces like a shower of dry raindrops and clung to their hair.

'We need to get out of here!' shouted Christine's father. 'Everybody out! I don't know where these flies are coming from, but everybody out!'

The swarm of flies was so thick now that many of the guests had their faces covered in shimmering grey masks, and they had dropped to their knees on the dance floor, choking and coughing up the flies that were crawling into their nostrils. The chorus of buzzing was deafening.

Christine's white satin wedding dress was spotted all over with flies, and her Princess Leia braids looked as if they had come alive. Terry was leaning over, one hand against the wall to support himself, vomiting up a half-digested mixture of salmon and asparagus and wedding cake and struggling flies.

The Reverend Plume was unable to shout out again, because he too was trying to beat off the dozens of flies that kept landing on his lips and catching in his eyelashes. Squinting, he looked around for Christine, and saw her close behind him, her entire face now covered in a mass of flies. He couldn't speak, but he went over and seized her plump right arm and started to tug her towards the archway that led to the bar. Beyond the bar was the hotel's reception area, and if they could reach that, they would hopefully be able to escape to the fresh air outside. He could only pray that Terry and the rest of the guests could see him clearly enough to follow him.

He had not even reached the archway, though, before he saw three figures walking towards him. Although he was half blinded by flies, he could make out that two of them were glittering from head to foot, as if they were encrusted with diamonds. The third was a bulky-looking man in a camel-coloured overcoat and a brown trilby hat.

As they approached, the man in the camel overcoat went over to the sliding door on the left-hand side and dragged it across to the centre of the archway. Then he went over to the right-hand door and dragged that across, too, so that access to the bar was blocked off.

HOUSE OF FLIES

The Reverend Plume reached his hand up to crush the flies that were crawling all over his chin. 'Who are you?' he croaked. 'Open up those doors at once!'

The man in the camel overcoat came stalking right up to him, while the two glittering figures circled around behind him. The venue room was filled not only with that relentless buzzing but with choking and retching noises and pitiful cries of distress, so that it was almost impossible for the Reverend Plume to hear what the man was saying to him.

'Who are you?' he repeated angrily. '*What* are you? In the name of God, open up those doors! Everybody in this room needs to escape from these terrible flies!'

The man came in closer, and leaned so close to the Reverend Plume's ear that the brim of his trilby hat scraped against the side of his head.

'I'm here to bring you your nemesis, holy man,' he said, in a voice as harsh as sandpaper. 'You and all the other holy men and women what have been stinking this place out since your daughter got herself hitched.'

'What are you talking about? We're celebrating my daughter's marriage, that's all!'

Now that the man was close, the Reverend Plume noticed that not a single fly was crawling on him – not even on his hat.

'I'm talking about you people who think you're all so righteous that you can rule the world and tell the rest of us what to do and what to think. That's what I'm talking about. And what have you done all over the centuries but torture and kill any poor sods who refused to believe in your guff.

'So I'm here to bring you your nemesis, governor, long overdue. And I've chosen your daughter's wedding day to make sure she don't produce no more of you stinking hypocrites.'

'Open up those doors!' the Reverend Plume shouted at him.

'Open up those doors and get out of my way! I'm calling the police!'

'You're not calling nobody. You never gave a chance to nobody who didn't kowtow to you and your imaginary god since time immemorial, so why do you think we're going to give you a chance now?'

Christine collapsed on to the floor on her hands and knees. 'Daddy!' she spluttered, blowing flies from her lips. 'Daddy, save me!'

The Reverend Plume swatted more flies away from his face, and then he reached into the inside pocket of his jacket for his phone. As he lifted it up to prod out 999, though, one of the glittering men stepped up behind him and seized him by the neck, crunching the flies that clung to his fingers. The Reverend Plume gagged and dropped his phone, and the man in the camel coat bent down and picked it up.

'Oh, shit. The screen's cracked. Pity.'

The glittering man gripped the Reverend Plume's neck tighter and tighter, and kept him standing upright, wheezing desperately for breath. His eyes were bloodshot and bulging and his tongue was lolling out, and his face was clustered with more and more flies.

'So tell me, governor, where's your God now?' the man in the camel coat mocked him. 'I don't hear Him banging at the doors, trying to get in here to save you! All your life spent praying to Him, and singing to Him, and drinking His wine and eating His biscuits, what was it all for? Where is He, now that you really need Him?'

The man looked around the venue room. Almost all the two hundred guests were either kneeling or lying on the floor in their dinner jackets and their evening dresses, coughing and choking with their throats crammed with flies. He turned to the second glittering man, snapped his fingers and pointed to one of the vicars lying halfway underneath a wooden chair, kicking his legs and struggling to breathe. The glittering man went over and tossed the chair to one side with a clatter before lifting the vicar into a sitting position. Flies were already crawling into the vicar's lungs, so he didn't even look round to see the fly-covered creature who had picked him up.

Without any hesitation, the glittering man pressed one knee against the vicar's back. Then he grasped his head in both hands and twisted it around with a crackle of muscles and cartilage and vertebrae until the vicar was facing backwards, with an expression of sheer horror on his face. The glittering man then let him fall back down, with his chest upwards but his nose pressed against the floorboards.

The first glittering man, who had been strangling the Reverend Plume, now loosened his grip and let him sag. He shook the reverend's head from side to side like a rag doll to make sure that he was dead, and then he let him collapse on to the floor.

Now the man in the camel coat led the two glittering men between the gasping guests, stepping over those who were lying down. Every time he came across one of them wearing a clerical collar, he beckoned to the glittering men and one of them would either kneel on his chest and strangle him or twist his head round like the first vicar they had killed, snapping his neck.

Once they had finished, they had left over seventy clergy dead, including the pastor from Belgium. Many of the rest of the guests had already been choked by flies, and those who were still living were spewing up blood.

Before he walked back to open the sliding doors, the man in the camel coat went over to Christine, who was lying on her side, her face puffed up and her lips purple, her wedding dress spotted all over with fly excrement. Her hazel eyes were open, but she was clearly dead.

'Sorry to spoil your big day, love,' the man said quietly. 'It wasn't your fault your dad was a vicar. But it's way past time that we ended this Christianity lark. Time to get real, do you know what I mean?'

Not far away, Terry was lying against the wall, and he was dead, too. The man in the camel coat went across and spat on him. 'Serves you right for getting married in church, mate. No rumpy-pumpy for you tonight, wedding night or not.'

He slid back the doors, and then he and the two glittering men walked together back through the bar and out through the reception. The phone was ringing but the night receptionist couldn't answer it because she was lying with her head resting against her desk, strangled.

The man in the camel coat and the two glittering men pushed their way through the front doors of the Palette Hotel and out into the darkness and the rain.

Jerry was lying on his bed in his T-shirt and his shorts watching *Mission Impossible – Dead Reckoning* when his phone rang.

Please don't let this be anything urgent, he thought, as he reached across to his bedside table.

'Jerry – it's DCS Chance. You know where the Palette Hotel is, don't you?'

'Of course. Battersea Power Station. *Très* classy. What's the problem? Someone complaining the caviar was past its sell-by date?'

'It's a major incident, Jerry. There could be as many as a hundred fatalities. And it looks like your flies might have been responsible. I've already contacted DI Patel and she'll be on her way over. Thirty-two uniforms too. Plus paramedics, of course, and forensics.'

'Not those bloody flies again? Jesus.'

'We have to keep a tight lid on this one, Jerry. None of the media have been notified, and all personnel have strict instructions to keep their traps shut. I'll be getting in touch with the mayor and the deputy commissioner in a minute to let them know what's going on. But if there's any press outside the Palette when you get there, you don't have any comment to make – none whatsoever.'

'Okay, guv. Got you. My lips will be zipped. We don't want your mass hysteria, do we?'

Jerry rolled off his bed, switched off his television and hurriedly tugged on his jeans and a thick black Aran sweater that Maureen had given him for his last birthday.

Whenever he was working on a case, it was constantly churning over in his mind, like shuffling through a pack of Tarot cards. He could never stop thinking about who might have committed it, and why, even if it appeared to have some supernatural element. Was there some obvious clue that he and Jamila might have missed?

But as far as these fly murders and assaults were concerned, the cards in his mind were blank. Granted, there might be some religious motive for most of them, but how on earth could anyone breed such overwhelming swarms of flies? How could they possibly direct them to cling in their thousands to disinterred dead bodies, so that these bodies could actually walk around, and strangle people? How could they make sure that they covered over the lenses of any CCTV cameras that might give some indication of where they were going?

Jerry had absolutely no idea where he and Jamila could

start building a case. It seemed that Vincent Narrow might be involved somehow, but Vincent Narrow was a notorious East End housebreaker, not some vengeful religious terrorist.

And now what? Over a hundred fatalities. He was already exhausted after Father Devine's attempted exorcism, and baffled by the appearance of the green fluorescent head. Yet it looked as if he would not be getting any sleep tonight, or during the day tomorrow, or even the night after.

He left his flat and drove to Battersea Power Station, with its four commanding chimneys. It was no longer a power station, but the original building had been preserved and was now surrounded by expensive apartments and high-class restaurants and shops. Jerry found it almost impossible to park there, because every one of its curving streets was jammed with police patrol cars and vans and scores of ambulances, as well as forensic vans and vans from the BBC and ITV and Sky News. Clearly, the attempt by DCS Chance to keep the media in the dark about what had happened had proved futile. There were too many high-rise private apartments overlooking the entrance to the Palette Hotel.

Eventually, Jerry managed to park on the grass in the children's playground, next to the slide, sticking his notice that said *Metropolitan Police* behind his windscreen. He walked across to the Palette Hotel and into the reception area, which was crowded with uniformed police officers in yellow high-viz jackets and forensic technicians in white Tyvek suits and paramedics. He found Jamila and DCI Butcher in the hotel manager's office at the far end of the reception area.

'Here,' said Jamila, and she handed Jerry a face mask. 'You'd better come and see what's happened, and there are still a few flies buzzing around. How are you feeling, by the way? Do you think you'll be up to this? You said you needed a good night's sleep.'

'I still feel like I'm getting over the flu, but I'm not too bad. The old doxycycline seems to be working.'

Jamila led him through the bar until they reached the venue room. It looked like a battleground, with dead bodies in evening dress strewn all over the floor, while survivors were being treated with oxygen and CPR by paramedics. The whole room flickered with flashlights as forensic technicians carefully stepped their way between the bodies, taking pictures. Uniformed police officers were kneeling down beside the dead, lifting out their wallets to identify them and labelling their mobile phones.

A few flies were still clinging to the chandeliers, and occasionally one or two of them droned closely around Jamila and Jerry as if they were trying to overhear what they were saying.

'It was a wedding party,' said Jamila. 'The bride was the daughter of the vicar of St Peter's, and so many of the guests were clergy and people associated with the church. So far, we've counted one hundred and seven dead and another thirty-three who may not survive or may suffer from permanent brain damage, even if they do.'

'Any coherent witnesses?'

'I've managed to talk to two of them, including the disc jockey. They said that the whole room suddenly filled up with flies, and as soon as it did, three men came marching in. One of them shut the sliding doors that lead through to the bar, so that nobody could get out.'

Jerry could see only Jamila's large brown eyes over her face mask, but he could tell how serious she was.

'One of the men was wearing a trilby hat and a camel-coloured coat,' she told him.

'I don't believe it. A hundred to one it was Vince bloody Narrow. What about the other two?'

'Glittering, that's what the disc jockey said. He said they looked like two mirror balls in a disco. It was only when they came closer that he realised the reason they were glittering was that they were covered all over in flies.'

Jerry stood aside as a woman in a flouncy pink dress was carried past him on a stretcher by two paramedics, with an oxygen mask over her face.

'Dead men walking,' he said. 'Or rather, dead men *flying*.'

20

Jamila and Jerry were still at the Palette Hotel when they heard the clock in the reception area strike six. By then, all the survivors had been carried off to hospital, and at least thirty of the dead had been removed. The uniformed officers were taking great care to make sure that all the dead were correctly identified and that the positions in which they were lying were accurately marked, so that they could eventually put together a comprehensive map of who had died, and where.

DCI Butcher came up to Jamila and Jerry, looking at his watch. 'I reckon you two can go and grab yourselves some breakfast and a couple of hours of kip,' he told them. 'Simon Fairbrother's going to be rocking up here in a minute and he can keep his beady eye on things.'

'I don't know about breakfast,' said Jerry. 'I could certainly use a few zees.'

As they walked back through the reception area, though, the hotel doors opened and the Minister for Policing came in, the Rt Hon. Tristan Bagnold, MP, accompanied by the deputy mayor, Phyllis Abimbola, and six or seven senior members of staff from both the Home Office and City Hall.

'I've been told to find Detective Inspector Patel,' said the minister loudly, looking around above everybody's heads as if he were on the seashore, trying to catch sight of a distant ship. 'I was informed that she might be able to bring me up to speed on what was going on.'

'That is me, sir,' said Jamila. 'And this is my partner on this case, Detective Sergeant Pardoe.'

'Oh. I see. Well, I've already been given some pretty comprehensive background information by Sir Brian Blakely at Scotland Yard. Apparently, we're looking at a body count of well over a hundred. Tragic.'

'Yes, sir. Some of the deceased guests from the wedding party have yet to be taken away. Do you want to come through and see them?'

The minister came up closer to Jamila and Jerry so that nobody else in the crowded reception area could clearly overhear what he was saying. He was at least six foot three, and Jerry found himself on an eye level with the knot on his Old Etonian tie.

'Sir Brian wised me up about the flies,' he said quietly. 'He also told me why you and your partner here had been specially brought in to investigate.'

Jamila said nothing, but waited to hear what the minister would say next. Jerry knew that she was always reluctant to admit that they could be dealing with something supernatural. She had told him how differently the British regarded ghosts and spirits and demons, compared with Pakistanis. Her grandmother had sworn that she had seen only the top half of a woman in a hijab sliding along the corridor of her house, and her cousin believed that her dead sister came into her bedroom every night to complain about the pneumonia that had killed her.

The minister looked around again, and then he said, 'The thing is, it's absolutely crucial that we prevent news about this damn fly thing from getting out and causing widespread alarm. We have a general election coming up in less than six weeks, as you're well aware, and the Prime Minister doesn't want to give the impression that we've allowed some rampant infestation to develop in the same way that we allowed Covid to spread.'

'It's not going to be easy,' said Jamila. 'I expect the commissioner told you that there have been whole swarms of flies, thousands of them. And how do we explain what happened to the guests at this wedding party? One hundred and seven dead so far, and more not expected to survive.'

'Food poisoning, that's how we explain it,' said the minister. 'Undercooked chicken, for the wedding feast, or contaminated oysters. E. coli or salmonella or vibriosis, or something else equally nasty.'

'There are still quite a few flies around, even outside,' put in Jamila. 'The press must have seen them, and it's not exactly the time of year for flies, is it?'

'They feast on dead bodies, don't they? And there were more than a hundred here. There's your explanation.'

That's one thing you have to admit about politicians, thought Jerry, although he remembered what DCS Chance had told him, and kept his mouth shut. *They're experts at telling porkies.*

Jerry drove home, although Jamila waited for another twenty minutes for Ashish to come and collect her. She appreciated the lifts that he was giving her while her own car was being repaired, but at the same time it made her feel dependent on him, and she had never been dependent on any man, not for money nor promotion nor physical protection.

She loved Ashish. He was handsome and most of the time he was charming and funny, but he could be impatient sometimes, and haughty. She supposed that haughtiness came naturally to a surgeon, who had power over the life and death of other people.

He stopped his grey BMW outside the Palette Hotel and remained behind the wheel as Jamila crossed over the street and climbed in.

He leaned over and kissed her and said, 'Goodness, what's going on here? All these ambulances! There must have been a massacre!'

'Something like that. A lot of people dead. It was a wedding party, and we think they all might have gone down with food poisoning.'

Ashish steered his way smoothly between the ambulances and the police vans. His car, being electric, was almost completely silent.

'That's terrible. How many dead altogether?'

'We don't have a final figure yet, but well over a hundred.'

'So why did they call on you? Surely this was just a case for food safety inspectors. Is there any suggestion that the poisoning might have been deliberate?'

'I'm afraid that I can't really discuss it with you, Ashish. Not while the case is ongoing.'

Ashish laughed. 'What? You don't trust me? You allow me to take off your knickers, but you won't tell me if some people I don't even know might have been poisoned on purpose?'

'If any details were to get out, I would be in trouble, that's all.'

'Oh, yes? And who do you think I would tell? Most of the people I meet during the day are under general anaesthesia.'

'Very funny, Ashish. But it's been a really distressing night and I haven't had any sleep, and I can't tell you anything – any more than you could give me any private details about your patients.'

'I told you about that man who had a champagne bottle stuck up his rectum.'

'Yes, but you didn't tell me his name and quite frankly I don't want to know who he was.'

'I told you the bottle was Dom Pérignon.'

'Ha ha. Do you have a cold coming? You sound as if you have a sore throat.'

'No. I just haven't had my coffee yet.'

They drove the rest of the way to Redbridge without speaking. Jamila was so tired that she rested her head against the car window and kept nodding off. When they arrived at her block of flats on Wanstead Lane, she opened her eyes, surprised that she was home so soon. This time, Ashish opened the passenger door for her, and helped her out, and came with her to the porch while she searched through her pockets for her keys.

'Can I come up?' he asked her.

'Okay, for a while. Do you want that coffee? I'm absolutely gagging for one. Unfortunately, we can't stand around drinking coffee while we're looking at dead people.'

They went upstairs to Jamila's flat. It was decorated in a rich Pakistani style, with curtains in the block-printed ajrak pattern and dark blue velvet on the sofa. The living room was filled with Qamar perfume, which was advertised as making women feel that they were trying to hide their passionate feelings behind a veil, but their fragrance was giving them away.

Jamila kicked off her shoes and went through to her bedroom to take off her jacket. When she came back, Ashish was standing in the middle of the living room, still in his short black overcoat, and he looked serious.

Jamila went up to him and placed her hands on his hips. 'What's the matter, darling? You look as if you found a beetle in your balti.'

'I've been joking with you, Jamila,' Ashish told her. 'But this is not a joke.'

'I'm sorry. What is not a joke?'

'This investigation that you're involved in. It's time for you to resign from it.'

'What? I don't understand. You don't *know* what investigation I'm involved in. I've never said a word to you about it, have I? And no matter what I'm investigating, you can't tell me to resign from it. It's my job, Ashish. I don't tell you who you can cut open or who you can't, do I?'

'As a matter of fact, I *do* know what investigation you're working on. And I do know what happened to all those people who died last night. It's essential that you resign from it, so that the people who deserve to die get what's coming to them, and so that nothing unpleasant happens to you.'

Jamila took a step back, and looked up at Ashish in bewilderment.

'Is that a threat?'

'No, my sweet. It's only a caution. I wouldn't tell you to go out in a thunderstorm without an umbrella, would I?'

'How do you know anything about the investigation I'm working on? Have you been sneaking a look at my phone or something?'

Ashish gave a little grunt of amusement. 'A little fly told me.'

'Ashish, why are you talking to me like this? Do you really know what case I'm working on? Even if you do, why should you care? It's no business of yours.'

'Ah, but it is. If your chief superintendent gives you instructions, you obey him, don't you? In the same way, I'm doing nothing more than I've been instructed to do.'

'I still don't understand what you mean. What have you been instructed to do? And who by?'

'That would be telling, wouldn't it? In the same way that you've been told to keep quiet about this, so have I.'

Jamila was breathing hard. For the first time in a long time, she actually felt frightened. She even thought about her gun, locked in the safe in her bedroom.

'I think it would be a good idea if you left,' she told Ashish.

'What? No coffee?'

'Ashish, please go. I have no idea what you're talking about, but it sounds very threatening, and you're upsetting me.'

'Don't you love me?'

'Not when you talk to me like this.'

'If you loved me, you'd resign from this investigation, and never speak to anyone about it, ever again.'

Jamila turned her back on him. She was about to go and open the front door of her flat and demand that Ashish leave at once. Ashish, though, took two steps forward and seized her shoulders, pulling her round to face him again. She had never seen such an expression on his face before. He was staring at her as if he were furious, but it was a cold, mystical fury, without expression, like a wolf.

'Ashish, what's got into you?'

Still gripping her shoulders, Ashish opened his mouth. Jamila was shocked when three or four flies came crawling out over his lower lip. They buzzed around between them and then they settled on her hair.

'*Ashish!*' she screamed, and she twisted herself around in one of the capoeira moves that she had practised, so that he lost his hold on her. She backed quickly away, batting the flies out of her hair, but she had only retreated a few steps before Ashish stretched his mouth open even wider. He was still staring at her with that cold furious look in his eyes when a whole black stream of flies came gushing out of his throat, hundreds of them, with an angry, high-pitched zizzing sound. They came swarming towards her, clinging on to her hair and her sweater and pelting against her face.

Jamila didn't hesitate. All her capoeira teachers had told her that the best defence is to run away, as fast as possible. She turned around and rushed along her hallway between the coats that were hanging on either side, wrenching open her front door and then jumping down the stairs to the ground floor, three and four at a time.

She didn't look back, but she could still hear that angry zizzing behind her and several flies were still whirling around her, keeping up with her. She went out through the entrance lobby of her block of flats and into the street, and started to run, as fast as she could. Even after she had covered more than two hundred metres, though, she could still hear the swarm of flies close behind her. She stopped on the corner of Blenheim Avenue, panting, and immediately she was bombarded with flies, all over her face and her clothes and trying to crawl into her ears.

She started to run again, smacking the flies off her as she ran. She made her way to the end of the avenue, and then crossed over Cranbrook Road, with two cars blowing their horns at her as she ran in front of them. Swinging open the wrought-iron gates of Valentines Park, she half ran and half slid down the slope that led to the long canal in the middle of the park. She could feel the flies pattering against the back of her neck, and their relentless zizzing was even louder than the traffic noise.

Without breaking her stride, she took a deep breath and threw herself into the canal, startling a family of ducks that were circling around nearby. The water was freezing, and it took all her strength not to gasp and let out the air in her lungs. She sank slowly downwards until she felt the floor of the canal on her stockinged feet, and she kept waving her arms to keep herself from rising up to the surface.

It was dark down there, dark and green. She could feel every muscle in her body becoming numb with cold, but she was able to hold her breath for nearly a minute and a half before she had to come up for air. Her head broke the surface and her throat squeaked as she breathed in again. She shook her wet hair out of her eyes and then she paddled herself around in a circle to see if the flies had gone. There was no sign of them anywhere, and she whispered a prayer of thanks. '*Mujhe bachanay ka shukriya.*'

An elderly man who was walking his cocker spaniel nearby came over to the side of the canal.

'You all right, love? Fall in, did you? Bit chilly for a swim.'

He reached down and helped Jamila to climb out of the water. She shivered and said, 'Thank you so much. Yes. I tripped and fell in.'

'You weren't trying to end it all, if you don't mind my asking?'

'Oh no, sir. Life is too precious. And if I did want to

end it, I would do it in private. Not with an audience of ducks.'

She walked quickly back to her flat, shivering all the way. The elderly man had offered to lend her his donkey jacket, but she had told him that she didn't have far to go.

She didn't have her key, so she pressed the bell for her downstairs neighbour, Mrs Cooper, and she let her in.

'You've been out dressed like that?' asked Mrs Cooper.

'I was running, and my tracksuit's in the wash.'

Mrs Cooper stared at Jamila's feet. 'What about your trainers? Are they in the wash too?'

Jamila didn't answer, but gave her a fleeting smile and climbed back up the stairs to her flat. She kept a spare key stuck under the mat, but the door was ajar. She pushed it open wider and called out, 'Ashish? Are you still there, Ashish?'

There was no reply, so she stepped cautiously inside. A few dead flies were scattered on the carpet, but she couldn't see any living ones still flying around. She could only assume that as soon as she had run out of the flat with all those flies swarming after her, Ashish had left. But how he had stored all those flies in his stomach, she couldn't begin to imagine. No wonder he had been speaking to her with a catch in his throat.

She picked up her phone and called Jerry. It took him so long to answer that she was about to leave him a message, when he eventually picked up.

'Sorry, guv. I was having a bit of a kip. What's the SP?'

'More flies, Jerry,' she said. Despite her determination to sound calm, she couldn't stop her voice from shaking. 'I can hardly find the words to explain to you what has happened.'

'You all right, guv? You sound a bit wobbly.'

Jamila went into her bedroom. Once she had tugged off her damp sweater, she tucked her phone under her chin and started to tell Jerry how Ashish had opened up his mouth and hundreds of flies had poured out.

'Bloody hell. If I hadn't seen all those flies already, I would have thought you were pulling my leg.'

Jamila managed to peel off her straight-fit trousers and her knickers and her socks, and now she wrapped herself in her fluffy pink dressing gown.

She was describing to Jerry how she had escaped from the flies by jumping into the Valentines Park canal when she went into her kitchen to make herself a mug of lemon tea.

'I couldn't think of any other way to—' she began, and then she stopped dead.

After nearly ten long seconds of silence had passed, Jerry said, 'Sorry? You couldn't think of any other way to what, exactly?'

'Ashish is here,' Jamila told him, and she sounded as if she were still underwater.

'Do you want me to come round?. He's not threatening you, is he?'

'No, Jerry. He's not threatening me. He's never going to threaten anybody, ever again. He's dead.'

Ashish was sitting at the kitchen table. Both of his hands were flat on the decorative mat in front of him, except that underneath his right hand there was ten-inch carving knife.

Ashish had cut his throat right through to his spine. His head was tilted so far back that his face was upside down, staring with his eyes open at the kitchen counter behind him.

The shoulders of his coat and his shirt collar were drenched in blood, and there was blood spattered all over the floor.

While Jamila stood staring at him in shock, a single fly crawled out of his windpipe and flew towards the window, where it tapped and buzzed, trying to escape.

21

'You can come and stay with me if you like,' said Jerry. 'My settee turns into a bed. Well, it does if you give it a good kick.'

'Thank you for the offer, but no,' Jamila told him. 'It would not be appropriate. I will book myself a room at the Premier Inn until the forensics have finished at my flat, and it has been cleaned.'

'You're welcome, and it would be free. And I could rustle up a mean vegetarian breakfast. I've got more tins of baked beans than you could count.'

Jamila smiled and shook her head. Before she had dressed and left her flat, she had called DCS Chance to inform him that Ashish had released a vicious swarm of flies on her, and that she had returned to find that he had taken his own life.

'You're all right, are you, Jamila?' DCS Chance had asked her. 'Not injured at all?'

She had been surprised how readily he had believed her. He was usually so sceptical about anything that appeared to be remotely supernatural. But now there had been so many incidents involving flies, with so many fatalities, that he was obviously prepared to accept that every attack had been organised. As weird as they were, they needed to be treated as seriously as protection rackets or drug dealing or armed robbery.

After she had spoken to DCS Chance, she had contacted Derek Grant at Lambeth Road. He had assured her that he would immediately send a team of forensic technicians to remove Ashish's body. They would then conduct a thorough examination not only of her flat and Ashish's house, but his BMW, too, which was still parked in Wanstead Lane.

'And I'm really, really sorry for you,' the Martian had told her. 'You must be shattered.'

'I am numb, Derek, to tell you the truth. I am simply numb.'

Once the forensic team had completed their work, Jamila would call in Matrix, the crime scene cleaners, who would remove any trace of blood and flies and disinfect the whole flat. All the same, she was not at all sure if she would be able to continue living there. She already had the feeling that every time she walked into the kitchen she would picture Ashish with his throat slit wide open and his head hanging backwards.

Now she was sitting with Jerry in the office that he shared with Ruth Watkins. They were speaking quietly because DS Watkins was on the phone, investigating the killing and disembowelling of more than fifteen dogs in Brockwell Park. The killer had posted on Facebook that he was taking systematic revenge for all the times that he had stepped in dogs' faeces, or found it hung up by their owners in plastic bags from the trees in the park. He called himself 'God's Pooper Scooper'.

'Fancy a sandwich or anything?' Jerry asked Jamila. 'I don't suppose you've got much of an appetite.'

Jamila was trying hard not to listen to what Ruth Watkins was saying on the phone.

'I might have a cup of lemon tea. I don't know why, but

after jumping into that canal I still feel frozen inside. It's like my stomach's filled up with ice cubes.'

Jerry stood up, but at that moment his phone rang. It was DI Fairbrother, and he was calling from the morgue at St George's Hospital.

'Jerry? We've managed to identify the body that was lying on top of Jock Maclean at The Waker. His name was Donald Wills, and he was interred at the Strayfield Road extension to Lavender Hill Cemetery on the second of April this year.'

'Donald Wills?' said Jerry. 'That's DW. The same initials on the ring I found in Dr Crowe's laboratory.'

'Well, whether it was the same bloke or not, his grave was dug up three days ago. The trouble was, the cemetery staff didn't think anything of it. His widow had passed away at the beginning of this month and her funeral was booked in for next Sunday, so they assumed that it was dug up because she was going to be interred on top of him. The lid of his coffin was closed, so they didn't realise that he was no longer inside it.'

'Did anybody see who dug him up?'

'Not as far as we know, and there's no CCTV in the graveyard. They don't expect the dead to rise out of their graves at night and start dancing. But forensics will be taking a look. Maybe he dug himself out, like that Philip Harris.'

'Bloody hell. That was one thing they never trained us for at Hendon – chasing after dead bodies.'

'Forensics are testing that ring to see if the DNA matches Donald Wills. If it does, we can only conclude that in one form or another, he was present when Dr Crowe's laboratory was wrecked. Or maybe somebody else was wearing it, and it dropped off their finger because it didn't fit. But then you have to ask yourself, where did *they* get it from?'

Jerry closed his eyes. 'I think we need to stop asking ourselves hypothetical questions, guv, and wait for the evidence. Otherwise, we're all going to go doolally.'

He and Jamila went down to the canteen. Jerry chose a rare roast beef sandwich, although when he unwrapped it and looked at it he found that he had completely lost his appetite. A sneaky voice in the back of his head had whispered, *slices of dead body*.

It reminded him of the time that he and Edge had gone for dinner at a seafood restaurant in the East End. He had just lifted an oyster to his lips when Edge had leaned over and frowned at it and said, 'That's not *snot* in that shell, is it?'

'When do you think we might get some pathology results?' he asked Jamila, watching her poke with her spoon at the lemon slice in her tea, as if she were making sure that it was dead.

'I'm not sure, Jerry. Perhaps by the end of the week or early next week. There are so many of them – what with all those victims from the Palette Hotel. They've sent quite a few of them to other hospitals. Some of them have gone to Ipswich and at least thirty of them have gone to Broomfield, where they examined all those Vietnamese immigrants who were found dead in that lorry, do you remember? But Dr Crowe and your Maureen are both being examined at St George's, so we should have their results quite quickly.'

'After what you've been through today, you should take some time off. I mean it.'

Jamila shook her head. 'No, I can't. What would I do?

Sit in my hotel room trying not to think about Ashish? I need to keep myself busy. And I am more determined than ever to discover who is doing this, and where all these flies are coming from. I am still wondering why your Maureen infected you with anthrax and why Ashish released those flies on me. Perhaps it's because whoever is responsible for these murders knows that you and I have been assigned to find them.'

'I was kind of toying with the same idea.'

'Our identities are hardly a secret. Every police station has more leaks than a kitchen colander. And I'm sure we've been seen in more than one TV news report.'

Jerry finished his coffee and Jamila finished her tea, although Jerry wrapped up his sandwich for later. They were about to leave the canteen when Edge appeared.

'Ah, I'm glad I caught you. Ruth told me you were here. I've got that audio bloke Neal Ferguson up in communications.'

'Oh, Neal Ferguson – he's brilliant,' Jerry told Jamila. 'He's probably the best forensic audio scientist in the country. He can make out what somebody's been saying even if they've got the massed bands of the Welsh Guards playing in the background and a Fair Isle sweater pulled over their head. Not only that – he can usually tell you *who* was talking, too.'

Edge said, 'He's been enhancing the recording that Dr Crowe was making, the last time you saw him. You said you heard somebody saying "clown", but you were sure it wasn't Dr Crowe, and it wasn't his assistant either.'

'And Neal reckons he knows who it was, and what they were saying?'

'Come up and see him. He'll tell you.'

They went upstairs to the communications room, lit up as usual with CCTV screens all around it. Neal Ferguson was sitting at the far end, wearing a large pair of headphones. What was left of his frizzy brown hair was sticking up as if he had been electrocuted, and his spectacles were balanced on the very tip of his nose.

'DC Pardoe!' he greeted Jerry. 'Haven't seen you since that nasty abduction case in Streatham!'

'It's DS now,' said Jerry. 'Twice as much work but a bit more dosh. What have you got for us?'

'It's a pretty clear audio that didn't need a lot of enhancement, except for the signal-to-noise ratio, because there's some persistent rustling in the background. It's mostly Dr Crowe describing his results, until it gets to the point when I assume you were leaving the lab because I can hear the door open. That's when this different voice says just one word. I can understand perfectly well why you thought it was "clown".'

Neal Ferguson played back a few seconds of his enhanced recording. They heard Dr Crowe saying '— *head detached between C_4 and C_5* —' and then that strange voice saying what sounded like '*a crown*', rather than '*clown*'.

'A crown?' asked Jerry. 'That still doesn't make any sense.'

'I've played it over and over,' said Neal Ferguson. 'I'm not at all sure it's "a crown". Listen again. That's more of an "eh" than an "a".'

'So it's "eh crown" and not "a crown"? That still doesn't mean anything.'

'I've run it through my complete compendium of sounds, in all different languages, and it does sound like one word, although it's a place rather than a word – Ekron.'

'Ekron? Never heard of it,' said Jerry. 'Where's that?'

'It was one of five Philistine cities in central Israel. It was called Accaron originally. Today it's called Tel Miqne. It was destroyed in 603 BC by the Babylonians. Some historians even doubted that it ever existed, but in the 1990s a team of archaeologists dug up a stone inscription that proved that it had, as well as a whole lot of other artefacts, like jugs and drinking bowls and olive oil presses, and even some human bones.'

'Well, that is all most interesting,' said Jamila. 'But how sure can you be that the word was "Ekron", and not "a crown" or "clown"? Or maybe some other word from another language? It seems very strange to me that in a pathology laboratory in England, some disembodied voice should come out and say the name of an ancient city that has not existed for over two thousand years. I mean, why?'

'I'm afraid it's up to you to find out "why",' said Neal Ferguson. 'All I can do is tell you that I've tested this recording again and again, with automatic gain control and spectral subtraction, and I will stake my reputation on that voice saying "Ekron". There is no word in any known language that sounds like that, and no other place on the planet with that name.'

Jamila turned to Jerry with her eyebrows raised. He thought she still looked shocked and unwell and that she ought to go off to her hotel and rest, but he knew from experience that the more he insisted, the more stubbornly she would resist.

'I cannot imagine where this information takes us,' she said. 'Thank you, anyway, Mr Ferguson, for your services. If you are eventually needed to testify to this enhancement in court, will you be prepared to do so?'

Neal Ferguson took off his headphones. 'I'd testify to it in front of God.'

'Well,' said Jamila. 'We hope that won't be necessary.'

While Jamila went to check in to the Premier Inn, Jerry tried to contact more of the survivors from the Palette Hotel massacre to see if they had recovered sufficiently to describe what they had seen. Also, with the help of the registry office, he managed to find Donald Wills's sister in a care home in Tunbridge Wells, and get in touch with her on the phone. In a thin and reedy voice, she was able to confirm that he used to wear a signet ring with the initials DW engraved on it, which had been given to him by his wife, Hilda. As far as she knew, he had never lost it, and he was still wearing it when he was buried.

So good old Donald Wills was probably there at Falcon Road, thought Jerry. Although he was eight months dead, he was ransacking the pathology laboratory and taking away the head and the torso that Dr Crowe was examining. As bizarre and unbelievable as it sounded, it was the only logical explanation, and he must have had a motive for doing it – the most obvious being that he was helping to prevent anybody from finding out who the remains belonged to.

Perhaps Dr Crowe had already identified the remains and that was why the flies had attacked and killed him. And there was still no sign of his assistant, Zahir. He had not returned to his digs in Battersea that night and nobody had seen him since.

Jerry zipped up his anorak. He was about to go out to Nine Elms to interview one of the survivors from the Palette Hotel, a young waitress who had been serving at the wedding breakfast. He had reached the door of his office when he heard a pattering against the window.

'Oh, shit,' he said. 'Why is it that every time I decide to go out, it starts raining?'

'Don't talk to me about shit,' Ruth Watkins retorted. 'I've been talking about it ever since I got in this morning. Do you know many dog owners got fined last year for fouling the streets?'

'I'd have to guess,' said Jerry. 'Thirty-three and a turd?'

'Jerry, for God's sake!' Ruth turned back to her computer, but as she did so, three or four flies came circling around her and one of them started to crawl across her screen.

'I can't believe it!' she said, flicking it away. 'Where did these come from?'

But then the pattering on the window grew louder and more persistent, and flies started to struggle in through the gaps in the ventilator, hundreds of them, until the air in the office was filled with them, buzzing and tapping against the walls and the furniture. Some of them settled on the desks and the chairs, while others clung to the coats that were hanging up by the door. Still more of them crawled across the floor and in and out of the wastepaper baskets, as if they were searching for incriminating evidence.

'Oh my God! Oh my God!' Ruth screamed, standing up and batting flies out of her hair and off the front of her sweater. They were even crawling up her shiny black tights, underneath her skirt.

'Come on, Ruthie,' said Jerry. 'Let's get the hell out of here. We need to call those pest control geezers.'

They left their office and Jerry slammed the door behind them, so that only a few flies were able to follow them. As they hurried along the corridor to the lift, though, they could hear more doors slamming around the whole police station, and shouting on every floor.

Before they could reach the lift, DCs Okeke and Battersby came bursting out of their common room, with a cloud of black glittering flies buzzing noisily all around them. None of the officers said anything to each other, they simply ran towards the lift together, beating the flies away from their faces.

Jerry jabbed the down button and the four of them stood hopping and flapping their arms as they waited for the lift to arrive. When it pinged, though, and the door slid open, even more flies came pouring out, and they could see DS Morrison kneeling in the corner, her hands held on top of her head, and she was covered in a mass of flies.

Jerry and DC Okeke entered the lift, and each of them took hold of one of DS Morrison's arms, so that they could help up on to her feet. Ruth stuck her foot into the lift door to prevent it from closing, and they dragged DS Morrison out of the lift and back along the corridor towards the stairs.

Flies were everywhere. Not only were they flying around the stairwell, they were covering the banister rails and the light fittings and crawling all over the framed pictures of decorated senior officers that hung on the walls.

Jerry and DC Okeke helped DS Morrison to climb down the stairs, with Ruth and DC Battersby following close behind them. They could hear panicky cries of distress rising from the floors below, and more doors slamming. When they reached the first floor, the fire alarm went off, jangling so loudly that they could barely hear themselves think.

As they passed the interview room, the door flew open

and DCS Chance appeared, along with two newspaper reporters, and they too were surrounded by whirling clouds of flies.

'*Clear the building!*' screamed DCS Chance, over the deafening ringing of the fire alarm. '*Everybody out! Everybody out!*'

They clattered down to the reception area. The front door was wide open, and the officers and staff from the station were already gathering in the narrow street outside, still smacking at the flies that were clinging to their clothing.

DCS Chance came up to Jerry and his face was flushed. 'This is insane! The whole damn station's out of commission! You have to track down who's behind this! And as soon as you possibly can! I mean, like yesterday!'

'We're trying, sir, believe me. I think we've made a little progress, but we still don't know how it's possible for anybody to conjure up so many flies, or what their motive could be. DI Patel and me, we were both thinking that they're trying to stop us from finding out who they are, and – Jesus – this looks like we were right.'

DCS Chance stood looking back into the station. The reception area was now a glittering mass of flies, crawling all over the floor and the walls and the ceiling and the reception desk.

'All right,' he said. 'Keep at it. And if you need more professional help, don't hesitate to let me know. But this whole fly thing is going to go public now, even if that Tristan Bagnold wanted us to put a lid on it. Those two reporters I was just talking to, they came from the *Sun* and the *Telegraph*, and I was halfway through telling them that it was only a few isolated incidents – even what happened at the Palette

Hotel – when the whole damn interview room filled up with flies. I almost swallowed one, for God's sake.'

DI Fairbrother came up to them. 'I've called the pest control people, sir. They said they could be here in half an hour. Mind you, I think it might be worth calling more than one company, don't you? This is not just an infestation, is it? It's a bloody plague.'

22

During the night, three different pest control companies sealed off the police station and fumigated every floor with permethrin smoke bombs. They warned that it would take at least four hours before it was safe to return inside the building, and even then there would be heaps of dead flies to be shovelled up.

Most of the night duty staff were sent off to Wandsworth police station, which was only two miles away, while a mobile command centre with all the latest technology would be driven down from Hemel Hempstead and parked outside.

Jerry stayed in his car until it was nearly midnight, talking to Edge. He had called Jamila, and when he told her how the station had become suddenly filled up with millions of flies, she had wanted to come and see them for herself. He had said that there was no point. There was nothing that either of them could usefully do until the morning, when the insecticidal fog had finally cleared. She would be better off staying at her hotel and catching up on some sleep.

'I will,' she said, and Jerry could hear the relief in her voice. 'To tell you the truth, I feel like death.'

Jerry returned to the station at eleven o'clock the next

morning. He had seen reports on the ITV news about the whole building becoming inexplicably infested with flies. The Rt Hon. Tristan Bagnold had been interviewed, but all he had said was that health inspectors would be looking into the cause of the infestation and that it could have been the result of a cracked sewer pipe. Perhaps gristle and fat from the local meat market had built up in a sewer and that had attracted so many flies.

When Jerry arrived, the whole building was still cordoned off and the vans from the pest control companies were still parked next to the huge mobile command centre. He recognised Gary from GJ Pest Control, who was puffing away at a raspberry-flavoured vape and talking to his bookie on his phone.

'So what's the SP?' Jerry asked him, when Gary had finished placing his bets. 'Flies all dead yet?'

'No, mate,' said Gary. 'You're not going to believe this, but none of them. We've tried fogging them and spraying them and zapping them with electric fly killers on every floor. Nothing seems to affect them.'

He held up his thumb and his index finger and pressed them together. 'I think the only way we're going to kill them off is to pick them up one at a time and squash them.'

'Are you serious? That would take you the rest of your life. What about today? Can I go back into my office? I need to pick up my laptop.'

'Not for another two or three hours at least, mate, sorry. We've just let off a whole lot more smoke bombs. This time, we're using permethrin with an increased amount of piperonyl butoxide. It's not an insecticide in itself, your PBO, but it destroys the flies' central nervous system, and that makes them less able to resist the permethrin.'

While Jerry was still talking to Gary, Jamila arrived in an Uber taxi. She was wearing a white polo-neck sweater and a long navy overcoat and she smelled of Qamar, and she looked far brighter than she had yesterday. Jerry told her that the flies had so far resisted all attempts to exterminate them, but that the three pest control experts were having another try to kill them off.

'They're using – what was it?' he asked Gary.

'Piperonyl butoxide. PBO.'

'Oh, yes, I've heard of that,' said Jamila. 'It's most effective for getting rid of pubic lice.'

Jerry looked at her and thought, that's one of the things I really find attractive about her. She's a woman of the world. But he resisted the temptation to wonder what she would do for company now that Ashish was dead and she was unattached. It was far too soon.

'Can you bottle some samples of these flies for me?' Jamila asked Gary. Then she turned to Jerry. 'I've had a call from Professor Yearling and he wants to meet us at Falcon Road at two o'clock. If these flies can't be killed by the usual insecticides, I think he needs to take a look at them for us.'

'Did he tell you what he wanted to meet us for?' asked Jerry.

'Not in any detail. But he said he might have some information that could help us to find out where all these flies have been coming from.'

'The Right Honourable Bagpuss seems to think they're coming out of a broken sewer.'

'I don't think there's any chance of that, Jerry. That would be random. The way these flies have been targeting people – me included – it has to be deliberate. And the way that Vincent Narrow keeps appearing. I'm quite sure that he doesn't keep crawling out of some drain somewhere.'

They mounted the metal steps at the back of the mobile command centre. Inside, they found Edge and three female officers, surrounded by banks of CCTV screens. A large dish on the roof of the command centre could pick up signals from two different satellites, so that Edge and his team could connect to any video camera in the immediate vicinity, and beyond, as well as sending messages and receiving them from any other police station.

'Morning, guv!' said Edge. 'We've been playing back all the CCTV footage from around here, trying to track where all these flies came from before they arrived here at the station.'

'Any luck?' asked Jamila.

'Possibly. They covered up all the camera lenses in sequence like they did before, so we can't see exactly where they originated. But the first camera they covered up was on the corner of Battersea Park Road and Atherton Street. So there's a fair chance the swarm started roughly around there somewhere, or not too far away. Not all the streets around there are covered by CCTV, although quite a few of the houses have doorbell cameras.'

'Atherton Street, that's all residential,' said Jerry. 'Bloody great big Victorian mansions. Very nice place to live if you've got a million-and-a-half quid to buy yourself a gaff and another fifty grand to do it up.'

By the time Jamila and Jerry had arranged to meet Professor Yearling, the flies that were crawling over every inch of the police station had still not succumbed to the smoke that was supposed to paralyse their nervous systems and then kill them.

Gary opened up the station's front door so that he could collect at least a dozen flies in a screw-top jar. When he did so,

Jamila and Jerry could hear the frantic zizzing noise that still filled the whole building. It went on and on, like some terrible tinnitus.

'Well, this hasn't worked, has it?' said Jamila, as Gary handed her the screw-top jar. 'What are you going to try now?'

'We're giving the little buggers a bit longer, but if they don't start dying off within the next couple of hours, we'll have to think about spraying the whole place with paraquat. It's so bloody poisonous it's been banned in Britain since 2007, but we still have a few bottles left in store. If we have to use it, though, the whole place is going to need a really intensive clean afterwards. One sip of paraquat and you're on your way to join your ancestors, I can promise you.'

Jamila and Jerry looked into the reception area before Gary closed the door, and they could see that the floor and the walls and even the windows were all thickly blanketed in glittering flies, while scores more flies were circling around in the air.

'I reckon this is what hell looks like,' said Gary. 'Not flames, but flies.'

Professor Yearling appeared to be tired when they arrived at Falcon Road. The jacket of his three-piece suit was hanging over the back of his chair and his waistcoat was unbuttoned. On the desk in front of him was a sheet of paper with about fifty dead flies arranged in neat parallel lines, resembling a military parade in miniature.

'I saw the news about the flies invading your police station,' he told them. 'There's no question that we're dealing with some highly unusual force here.'

'"Unusual"?' said Jamila. 'That must be the understatement of the year.'

Professor Yearling shrugged. 'Maybe it's similar to the way that fish swim in shoals or hundreds of starlings fly together in a murmuration, although we still don't know exactly how or why they manage to do that. We suspect it's one way they protect themselves against predators. Safety in numbers, so to speak. But of course, these flies *are* the predators.'

'These flies that are filling up our nick, it seems like they're immortal,' said Jerry. 'We've had the pest control geezers in all morning, and they've tried every insecticide you can think of. So far, they haven't managed to kill even one.'

'Really? That convinces me even more that we have some form of remote control at work here. Don't ask me what it is, but we can change the channels on our televisions without getting out of our armchairs, can't we, and we can fly model aeroplanes by radio, so perhaps someone's discovered how you can fly real flies in the same sort of way. But anyhow, let me show you why I asked if you could meet me here.'

He tapped at his computer keyboard and the image of a fly's feet appeared on the screen, hugely magnified by an electron microscope.

'You can see here the glue-like substance that flies produce so that they can stick on to ceilings. It's surprising there has been so little research into it. Spiders produce an adhesive substance, too, so that they can run up walls, but it's not the same stuff. The important thing about the glue that flies have on their feet is that we can analyse it chemically and tell where they've recently landed.

'In the case of *these* flies – every one of these flies – the sugars and oils I found on their footpads contain traces of arsenic, as well as some blue and green pigment.'

Jamila stared at the screen and then shook her head. 'Arsenic? Blue and green pigment? So what does that tell us?'

'Arsenic used to be used in the manufacture of a dye called Scheele's Green, which was a very popular colour in the nineteenth century for wallpaper, as well as fabrics and wax candles and children's toys and even food colourants. The trouble with Scheele's Green was that it contained copper arsenite, and it was highly toxic. People died from sleeping in bedrooms with green wallpaper, or wearing green dresses, and a whole party of children died from inhaling the candles at their Christmas party. In Scotland, people died from eating green blancmange.'

'So what have you found out?' asked Jerry. 'These flies landed on something with this green colouring in it?'

'Specifically, wallpaper,' said Professor Yearling. 'And not just any old wallpaper. The adhesive on the flies' feet also contained a blue and green pigment produced only by a wallpaper manufacturer called Jeffrey and Company. What's more, Jeffrey and Company prepared this pigment exclusively for William Morris, who as you very well know was probably the most popular wallpaper and fabric designer of all time.'

'And that tells us what, exactly?'

'It tells us that these flies came from a house that's still decorated with original William Morris wallpaper, even after all these years. Many people kept it up because it's so attractive, but it did tend to flake or go mouldy, and it went out of fashion in the fifties and sixties, so I doubt if there are very many houses remaining that still have the original paper.

'I've checked all the patterns of William Morris wallpaper and this blue and green pigment was used only in a pattern called "Tulip and Bird", so that narrows it down a bit. You can still buy wallpaper with this pattern today, but of course it doesn't contain arsenic.'

Professor Yearling brought up the pattern on his computer

screen. It was made up of rows of stylised green tulips with blue pigeons hiding behind them.

'I'm in two minds,' said Jamila. 'We could show a picture of this on the television news tonight and ask if anyone recognises it. On the other hand, if we do that, it could well alert whoever might have been sending out all these flies, and they might leave their house or even tear down all their wallpaper. And of course we don't even know if they actually live there. It could be the wallpaper from some victim's house.'

Jerry said, 'I think we should hold our horses, guv, at least until we have a bit more information. Don't get me wrong, professor. This is valuable evidence. But it's the kind of evidence that puts the icing on the cake, do you know what I mean? First of all, we have to find the cake.'

Professor Yearling stared at Jerry for a moment as if he were speaking in a foreign language. Then he said, 'Yes. I think I follow you. You can't ice a cake you haven't got.'

Later that afternoon, when Jamila and Jerry were ready to call it a day, DCI Butcher rang Jamila and told her that they might have some important new evidence. Jamila put him on speakerphone so that Jerry could hear him too.

'That reconstruction artist Len Makepeace just called me,' said DCI Butcher. 'Okay – someone pinched the actual head that was found in Battersea Park, but Len still had all his 3D pictures of it. He said that he completed his model and ran the image of it through live facial technology. He's ninety-nine per cent sure that he's identified him.'

'And?' asked Jamila. 'Who does he think it is? Or *was*, rather?'

'Hang on, I've written it down. Humphrey Bly, that was his

name – Bly with a "y", not like Captain Bligh from the *Bounty*. He was an anthropologist, so Len told me, and quite a famous one. He studied Middle Eastern culture and published a book called *Canaanite Gods and Goddesses*.'

'Len doesn't live far away, does he?' said Jerry. 'Crystal Palace, if I remember. We could drop round and take a look at this Humphrey Bly... well, his reconstructed bonce, anyway.'

'What was an anthropologist doing on LFT?' asked Jamila. 'That's for identifying criminals.'

'According to the records, Humphrey Bly had a bit of a barney in a branch of Tesco a couple of years ago because he tried to walk out without paying for a bottle of wine. When he was stopped by the shop's security guard, Bly hit him over the head with the bottle and smashed it. In court, his solicitor said that he was drunk at the time because he was going through a very stressful time in his life, although he didn't say what was causing it, this stress. Anyway, that's why his face was on LFT.'

'Dr Crowe told us that his torso had been covered in flies, like all the other victims,' said Jerry. 'But he wasn't a clergyman and he wasn't a gangster and he wasn't a copper. So I'm wondering why the flies should have attacked him for whatever he was. Anthropoppo-whatsit.'

'Anthropologist,' Jamila put in. 'Someone who studies human culture.'

'Yes, that,' said Jerry. 'Couldn't get my mouth round it, that's all.'

It took them only twenty-five minutes to drive down to Crystal Palace, although it started to rain again and the traffic was slow. Len Makepeace lived in a large semi-detached house in Jasper Road, and they were able to park in his driveway, although Jerry had to climb out of the driver's seat into a wet laurel hedge.

Len Makepeace opened the front door for them with a smile. He had curly white hair and a beige cardigan, and he looked like someone's grandfather. He led them to the back of the house, where he had converted an extension into a large workshop. Shelves on two sides were lined with more than fifty reconstructed heads, some modelled in clay and some 3D-printed in plastic. A few of them had glass eyes and wigs and looked as if they were alive, and might speak at any moment.

On a bench in the centre of the workshop, Len Makepeace had built up a clay reconstruction of the devastated head that Jamila and Jerry had seen in Dr Crowe's laboratory. This head, though, was the head of man with a broad leonine forehead and a firm chin and the appearance of being in command.

'It wasn't easy, this one,' he told them, although his arms were folded as if he were satisfied with what he had achieved. 'The cheekbones weren't too difficult to model, but the nose was the real problem because he didn't have one. I had to guess, based on what I thought might be his ethnicity. He looked somewhat Scandinavian, so that's why I went for the smaller nose. Over the centuries, Scandinavians have developed smaller noses because they take in less cold air. Of course, there are exceptions.'

'But when you checked him out on LFT, he came up straight away?' asked Jamila. Although the clay head's eyes were still hollow, she had the uncomfortable feeling that it knew she was there, and was staring at her.

'Immediately. Humphrey Oscar Bly, MSc Anthropology – Oscar being a Norse name, of course. He spent years in the Middle East studying Canaanite and Ugaritic culture. I've looked him up on Wikipedia and there's quite a lot about him, including pictures. Here – I'll show you.'

Len Makepeace sat down in front of his computer and brought up the Wikipedia page for Humphrey Bly. Jerry could see that the clay reconstruction of his head was uncannily accurate. The main picture showed Bly in a dinner jacket, receiving an award from the Society of Cultural Anthropology for his work on Abrahamic religions. In several smaller pictures he was seen at various archaeological sites in the Middle East, wearing sunglasses and flappy khaki shorts.

As Len Makepeace scrolled down the page, he came to a picture of Bly sitting in his study at home, with an unlit pipe clenched between his teeth.

He was about to continue scrolling when Jamila leaned forward and said, 'Wait, wait – can you enlarge that? Look, Jerry – the wallpaper! Look at the wallpaper!'

Although the photograph was black-and-white, and the background was in shadow, Jerry could make out that the wall behind Bly was decorated with rows of tulips with birds nestling behind them – the same William Morris pattern that Professor Yearling had shown them.

'Tulip and Bloody Bird,' he said. 'How about that?'

'We can easily find this Humphrey Bly's address,' said Jamila. 'Then we can pay it a visit. Perhaps *this* is where all these flies have been coming from.'

She took out her phone and called DC Okeke. She asked him to go through the electoral register. If he was unable to find Humphrey Bly listed as a voter, he could check with the Society of Cultural Anthropology, to see if they had a record of his address.

'What's surprised me is that nobody reported him missing,' she said. 'Didn't he have any family or friends?'

She looked over at the clay head. If only it could talk, and tell her what secrets had been hiding inside the real head of Humphrey Bly. But for the first time since the start of this investigation, she was beginning to feel positive. It had been a more rewarding day than she could have hoped for, what with the evidence that Professor Yearling and Len Makepeace had both given them. She was sure now that they were at least one step closer to discovering who was directing these swarms of flies, and what their motive was.

Jerry was driving her back to the Premier Inn when her phone rang. It was DC Okeke.

'I found Humphrey Bly in the Wandsworth electoral register, ma'am. No bother at all. He lives on Atherton Street, in St Mary's ward. He's the only voter listed at that address. The house doesn't have a number, but it has a postcode and a name.'

'What's the name, Iniko?'

'Ekron, ma'am. Spelled E-k-r-o-n.'

23

When Jerry came to pick up Jamila from the Premier Inn at five thirty the next morning, he noticed at once that her eyes were red, as if she had been crying.

'Are you all right?' he asked her, pointing to his own eyes. He didn't call her 'guv'.

Jamila sniffed and tried to smile. 'Sorry. It just hit me, what happened to Ashish. I was totally numb about it until I woke up.'

'You really loved him, didn't you?'

They went down the steps in front of the hotel and crossed over to the car park.

'Yes, I loved him,' said Jamila. 'He could be impatient, and I am not sure I could have spent the rest of my life with him. But he always took such good care of me, and perhaps I could have tamed him.'

As they reached his car, Jerry felt a strong urge to take Jamila into his arms and give her a consoling hug. But she was a detective inspector and he was only a detective sergeant, and he knew that if they started a relationship it would be catastrophic for both their careers. Besides, she had never shown that she found him attractive. Maybe she was only interested in Pakistani men with lots of money.

They drove to Wandsworth police station. DCI Butcher had

already assembled eleven uniformed officers to assist in an early-morning entry into Humphrey Bly's house on Atherton Street. They had no idea if it would have to be a forced entry or what they might encounter inside, so they had chosen to take more officers than they would probably need, and five of them were armed.

They would be accompanied by a pest control technician who would be carrying enough permethrin sprays to treat the whole house, if necessary.

The team were all waiting for Jamila and Jerry in the operations room, drinking coffee and watching the television news.

'Any word from Lavender Hill?' Jamila asked DCI Butcher. 'Have they finally managed to kill off all those flies? If they haven't, how can we be sure that we'll be able to kill off any flies that we might come across?'

'Simon Fairbrother called me not ten minutes ago. They're dying, those flies, that's what he told me. Not all at once, but they're definitely on the way out. Dropping like flies, you might say. Maybe they had some kind of inbred resistance, like DC Mallett can drink eight pints of Carlsberg and still pick a winner at the races.'

'Oh, you're talking about last year's outing to the Epsom Derby,' said Jerry. 'But don't forget that he fell over on his way back to the bus and he didn't wake up until we'd got back to the nick.'

A slate-grey dawn was just beginning to break when they drove to Atherton Street. It was only a short street, but the late-Victorian houses on either side were all imposing, with their own gated front gardens. The house called Ekron was halfway along, and Jerry parked in front of it, with a squad car and two police vans parked up behind him.

The officers all climbed out, one of them carrying a battering ram. Ekron's garden was overgrown compared to all the others, with a sad-looking silver birch tree surrounded by dead weeds and a plastic dustbin lying on its side. Its windows were all dark, although some of them had curtains drawn, or sagging, and the attic windows were covered by broken Venetian blinds.

'Right,' said DCI Butcher. 'Let's see if there's anyone home.'

Two armed officers were the first to climb the stone steps up to the front door. When they reached it, one of them turned around and said, 'It's open, sir, believe it or not. No need for the bosher.'

Jerry and Jamila went up after them. The front door was painted a faded maroon colour, and the knocker was brass, in the shape of a grinning devilish face. One of the officers pushed the door wide open and they entered the hallway, with a floor covered by dark brown carpet. It was musty and airless in there, with a faint hint of something lemony.

'Smells like somebody pissed in here,' remarked one of the armed officers.

Four or five overcoats were still hanging on pegs on the side of the hallway. They were all shabby and old-fashioned, and one of them had a worn-out black velvet collar.

'Bly was wearing this in one of those Wikipedia pictures,' said Jerry, lifting up the sleeve.

On the wall at the end of the hallway hung a framed portrait of a sly-looking woman with a strange five-pointed hat and her hand half covering her face, as if she were laughing at them.

They went into the living room. It was furnished with a brown leather sofa and two brown armchairs, and the carpet was brown, too. There was a misted mirror over the fireplace in which they all looked as if they were standing in a London fog, and the mantelpiece was lined with an assortment of porcelain and metal figurines, three of which had wings like demons.

Jerry circled around the room, ducking down to look under the chairs and tugging at the curtains. 'Not a fly in sight. Flyless in Gaza, you might say.'

'You've impressed me,' said Jamila. 'I wouldn't have guessed you'd read Aldous Huxley.'

'We had to read it at school, *Eyeless in Gaza*. I didn't only read *Penthouse*.'

They went through to the kitchen. Its windows looked out over the overgrown back garden and a dilapidated shed. It was here that the lemony smell was strongest, and Jamila picked up a glass jar that had no lid on it, labelled *Za'atar*. She sniffed it and said, 'This is a very popular spice in Israel. It's a mixture of thyme, oregano, sesame seeds, salt and sumac. It's the sumac that smells like lemons.'

'Maybe Mr Bly got a taste for it while he was out in the Middle East,' said Jerry.

He looked around the kitchen. Three slices had been cut from a loaf of bread, but it had been left on the breadboard and now it was green with mould.

'Looks like he left in a bit of a hurry,' said DCI Butcher. 'Didn't even have time to make himself a sarnie.'

They looked in the dining room, in which stood a dusty antique dining table with six chairs and a massive mahogany sideboard with three empty decanters on it. It felt as if no dinner parties had been held in here for years, and the echoes of any conversation and laughter had long since died away. A few dead wasps lay on the windowsill that overlooked the garden, but not a single fly.

'So where's his study, with that tulip wallpaper?' asked Jerry.

'It's not down here,' said Jamila. 'Perhaps it's upstairs.'

After they had opened the doors to the downstairs toilet and the cupboard under the stairs, which had contained nothing but gas and electricity meters and several pairs of wellington boots, they climbed the stairs to the first-floor bedrooms.

On the landing hung a framed engraving of a man in a hooded robe, standing in what looked like a temple. His back was turned and both his arms were raised, as if he were praying or summoning up some spirit. In the darkness underneath the arches in front of him, two slanting eyes appeared to be staring back at him.

'That's well creepy,' said Jerry, peering at it closely. A caption on a metal plate underneath the engraving read *The messenger from Ahaziah*.

Jerry turned to Jamila. 'Any idea what that means?'

Jamila shook her head. 'Not a clue. But we can look it up. It may have some relevance.'

They could tell from the large unmade bed which room Humphrey Bly had been sleeping in. His crumpled green duvet had been thrown back as if he had just got up, and the pillow still bore the impression of his head. Five books were stacked on his bedside table, four of which were about various branches of anthropology, but there was also a copy of *The Seventh Seal*.

Jerry flipped through the pages. 'What's this about?'

'A knight who challenges Death to a game of chess,' Jamila told him. 'He hopes that as long as the game goes on, Death won't be able to take him.'

'Perfect bedtime reading, wouldn't you say? Especially if you want to have screaming nightmares.'

'But still no flies,' said Jamila, lifting up the duvet and giving it a shake.

'Are you sure we're not barking up the wrong tree here?' asked DCI Butcher from the bedroom doorway. 'Maybe this Humphrey Bly didn't have anything to do with these flies at all.'

'He must have done, somehow. Dr Crowe found sticky stuff from coffin flies all over his remains. He said that most of it may have come after his head and his torso were dumped in Battersea Park, but he was fairly sure that flies had also been settling on him while he was still alive.'

They opened the doors to the other three bedrooms. Two of them still had beds in them, although they had no duvets or blankets. The third was bare, with nothing in it but suitcases and a golfing bag with only two clubs in it.

They went up to the two attic bedrooms, but they had no beds either, and had simply been used for storing books and chairs and a bicycle with no wheels.

'Forensics are going to be testing the whole house top to bottom for any trace of flies,' said Jamila, as they all went back downstairs. 'I have to say that I'm more than a bit mystified that we couldn't find Humphrey Bly's study here, with that William Morris wallpaper. That picture was taken five years ago, and according to the electoral register he's been living here at this address for at least seventeen years. It must have been taken at some other location that he was using.'

'Funny this house doesn't have a cellar,' said Jerry. 'I thought all these big gaffs had cellars.'

DCI Butcher and the rest of the officers left the house, leaving Jamila and Jerry standing in silence in the living room. They could still smell that faint lemony aroma.

'Something's not right here,' said Jamila, after a while.

'What do you mean?'

She sat down in one of the armchairs. 'I don't usually credit myself with having a sixth sense, although it runs in my family. My granny, as I've told you, could see people that weren't there, and my Aunt Inaya could tell fortunes that always came true.'

'So what's wrong about this place?'

'It's very hard to describe, but I have the feeling that the house that we're seeing here is not what it's really like.'

'Sorry, you've lost me.'

'Perhaps I'm overtired. Perhaps I need some breakfast. But I look around these rooms and for some reason I can't quite believe what I'm seeing.'

Jerry went across and picked up one of the bronze figurines from the mantelpiece. He took it over to Jamila and said, 'Guv, just feel this. It's heavy. And it's real.'

'Yes, and it's a demon. You know as well as I do that demons can play tricks with your senses. They can make you go blind and they can make you feel sick and they can make you feel like you're freezing to death, even though you're not.'

'I think I need to take you to Sendero's and buy you a cup of strong coffee.'

'Well, you can do that, Jerry, but for some reason I believe we're being tricked in some way. I think I'm going to call Father Devine and ask him to come here and see if he can sense anything unusual.'

'Father Devine? He's an exorcist, isn't he, not a medium? If that's the way you feel, maybe we should ask that Madam Fortuna to come and have a sniff around.'

'I'm not at all sure Madam Fortuna isn't a fake. You remember the time we asked her if she could contact any of the five dead women that Bryan Goody had murdered?'

'She managed to get in touch with all of them, didn't she? And we actually heard them speak. Although none of them told us where their bodies were buried.'

'That's because Madam Fortuna is quite an accomplished ventriloquist. At least, that's what I think. And the reason they didn't tell us where their bodies were buried was because she didn't know.'

'Well, whatever. But maybe the women themselves didn't know.'

They went out into the hallway. As Jamila opened up the front door, Jerry turned around to take another look at the portrait of the sly woman in the five-pointed hat, as if to give her the finger. He was disturbed to see that it was a completely different portrait. Somehow it had been changed for a woman in a headscarf with tears in her eyes, holding up the lifeless body of a white dog, its jaw slack and its legs splayed upwards. Behind her, the sky was crowded with crows, almost as thick as flies.

'Here, guv – take a shufti at this picture! Either you're right and this whole place isn't what it looks like, or else some pranky bastard has nipped in and changed it while we've been upstairs.'

Jamila came back from the front door. She slowly approached the portrait and then stood and stared at it for almost half a minute.

'Now I am convinced even more that we are being tricked,' she said. 'That dog is a Bully Kutta, which is native to Pakistan. And that woman looks so much like my dead cousin Anabia. My family used to say that when we were younger, she and I could have been twins.'

'You're having a laugh, aren't you? How can anybody have changed this picture to look like your cousin?'

'There's even more to it than that, Jerry. There is a saying in Pakistan, *Bohat saarey sawalaaf poucheen aur aap ka jawab sirf aik murda kutta hoga.*'

'What does that mean? "I could murder a curry"?'

'No. It means: "Ask too many questions and your answer will be a dead dog." It is a warning not to be nosy.'

Jerry couldn't take his eyes off the weeping woman in the picture. He began to feel like Jamila, as if the rug of reality had been pulled out from under their feet.

'Okay then,' he said, 'let's give Father Devine a bell. At least he might be able to tell us if we can believe what we're seeing here. Or not, as the case may be.'

24

Ronnie Gibbs dipped the last chip in tomato ketchup and popped it into his mouth. Then he crumpled up the fish-and-chip wrapper, scraped back his chair and went across to drop it into the bin.

Eating cod and chips out of the paper was a luxury that he gave himself almost every time his wife, Megs, went to spend the night with her sister in Southend-on-Sea. As much as he intimidated his own gang and anybody else who crossed him, he could never intimidate Megs, and when it was mealtime she always insisted on plates, and knives and forks, and napkins.

As he was crossing the hallway towards his bedroom, his phone rang. It was Nick, his driver.

'Sorry to disturb you, Ronnie. You haven't heard from Frank, by any chance?'

'What do you mean, have I heard from him?'

'Him and me, we was supposed to go bowling down at Strike. But when I went to pick him up round at his gaff, there wasn't nobody in. I called him on his phone but he never answered.'

'Have you tried The Waker? Maybe he went there for a snifter and had five too many. You know what Frank's like.'

'I've been round The Waker. And The Crown. And The Four Thieves. He weren't in none of them, neither.'

'Maybe he's got lucky and picked up some brass.'

'Leave it out. *Frank?* The last time he picked up a woman was when he threw his old lady down the stairs.'

'Oh well, Nick. Don't worry about it. He'll turn up. I want him tomorrow afternoon because we're going round Panahar's and a couple of other Indian restaurants. We need to collect our monthly insurance payments.'

'After what happened to Jock, though—' said Nick.

'For Christ's sake, don't get your knickers in a twist. You don't seriously think that anything as weird as that could ever happen again? A dead body beating him up in a khazi?'

'I suppose you're right. But I might go round his gaff one more time, like, to see if he's made it home.'

Ronnie went into the bedroom. Megs had straightened the shiny red quilt and propped up three of her pink teddy-bears on the pillows. Ronnie sat down on the bed and took off his trousers and his socks and unbuttoned his shirt.

Once he had undressed, he wrestled himself into a black Arsenal T-shirt and pulled on a baggy pair of boxer shorts. Before he went back to the kitchen, he was careful to hang up his trousers and drop his shirt, socks and pants into the laundry basket. He may have beaten a man so badly with a hammer that he would never be able to speak again, and he may have used a Stanley knife to cut the finger and thumb off a poker player he suspected of cheating, but he didn't want to make Megs angry by leaving his dirty clothes lying on the floor.

He picked up the can of Carlsberg that he had been drinking with his supper and took out a cigarette from the olive-green packet on the table, which warned 'Smoking Causes Blindness'. Then he slid open the glass door that gave out on to the balcony.

His flat was on the eleventh floor of a high-rise block on Palmer Road in Battersea. The evening was cold but clear, although the lights of London blotted out the stars. The endless sound of traffic was like a great beast groaning in its sleep.

Ronnie lit his cigarette and blew out smoke. This was something else of which Megs disapproved: smoking inside the flat. But he liked her bossing him around. After spending his days bullying and threatening other people, it was a relief to come home and be told what to do – even down to putting the lid back on the toothpaste after he had finished brushing. Years ago, when they had first got together, he used to enjoy her caning his bare bottom and scolding him for being a naughty boy.

He had not told Megs or anyone else how he really felt about the way in which Jock had been killed. But it had deeply disturbed him – mostly because of the dead body that had been lying on top of Jock in the toilet. Ronnie couldn't help wondering if somebody Jock had beaten up or tortured sometime in the past had come back from the grave to take his revenge on him. He knew that such a thought was nothing more than a load of old nonsense, but he couldn't shake it out of his mind.

He went up to the railing around the balcony and blew out smoke. Although it was so cold, and he was wearing only his T-shirt and boxer shorts, there was enough warmth wafting out from the kitchen door behind him. He came out here almost every night, not only for a smoke but because it always gave him a great sense of satisfaction, looking out over the skyline of London at night – the sparkling lights of the river and the four tall chimneys of Battersea Power Station and the London Eye – and thinking how successful he had been. Back in the 80s he used to be a skinny snivelling punk, but a gym owner had taken him under his wing and said, 'You want to get anywhere in life, Ron? Build up your muscles and never take shit from no one.'

He took a last drag from his cigarette and tossed it into the darkness. As he did so, though, he caught sight of something glittering – something that seemed to be rising up the side of the block of flats from the car park below. He frowned, trying to work out what it was. It was rising higher and higher, and it appeared to be coming up towards him. At the same time, he started to hear a buzzing noise, which grew louder and louder, until he could hear it quite distinctly over the grumbling of the traffic.

The glittering object reached the same height as Ronnie's flat, and then it stopped rising upwards and hovered in the air, only about two metres away from his balcony. When he realised what it was, Ronnie shuddered with shock and disbelief, and squirted a little pee into his boxer shorts.

It was the figure of a man, but he was covered all over with a mass of flies, thousands of flies, all of which were furiously beating their wings. He simply floated there, sometimes going up and down a little, with the flies buzzing in chorus.

'I'm fucking dreaming,' said Ronnie, out loud. Then he gripped the balcony's handrail and leaned forward and screamed at the figure, 'I'm dreaming! I'm fucking dreaming! So fuck off, because you're not real!'

In response, instantly, the buzzing rose to a pitch that was almost as high as Ronnie's scream. The glittering figure raised both its arms and came rushing towards him. It collided with the side of the balcony, with flies bursting in every direction like shrapnel. It seized Ronnie around the neck with both hands and then it threw itself backwards and downwards, dragging him after it. Ronnie let out a strangled cry and tried to snatch at the railing to stop himself from being pulled over it, but all the flies had exploded into the air around them, and now the figure of a man was covered in nothing but a filthy white shroud. He was bulky, and at least as heavy as Ronnie, and the two of them fell nearly thirty metres together into the car park.

As they plummeted downward, there was a moment when all Ronnie could hear was the rippling of the man's shroud. Then they hit the roof of a silver Land Rover with a deafening bang and ended up lying together in the deep dent that they had created. They were face to face, and the man's hands were still clasped tightly around Ronnie's neck.

Lights were switched on all over the block of flats and windows opened, with residents leaning out to see what had happened. After less than twenty minutes, the evening air was filled with the sound of police and ambulance sirens, and the car park was lit up with blue flashing lights.

Jerry had only just dropped off to sleep when his phone rang.

'Jerry? It's DI Fairbrother.'

'Am I dreaming this?'

'No, Jerry, sorry, I'm afraid not, although I'll forgive you for thinking that you are dreaming when I tell you what's just gone down. Actually, it's your mate Ronnie Gibbs who's just gone down. He's fallen off the balcony of his block of flats in Battersea.'

'Oh, shit. El Snuffo?'

'He fell eleven floors and landed on some poor bastard's Discovery. But here's the thing. He's got a decomposed dead body lying next to him, almost the same as that gang member of his, Jock Maclean, and this time the body's got its mitts around his throat, like he's trying to strangle him.'

Jerry threw back his duvet and sat up, scruffing up his hair. 'I don't believe this. Have you told DI Patel?'

'Yes. I've already sent someone to pick her up from the Premier.'

'All right. I'll be with you as soon as I can. What's the address?'

The two bodies were still lying together on top of the Land Rover when Jerry arrived. They were brightly lit with LED lamps, although a blue forensic tent had been put up over them to prevent the residents from the flats above from taking pictures. Not only that, it was beginning to drizzle.

Jamila was already there, talking to Simon Fairbrother. She was wearing a mulberry-coloured waterproof jacket with the hood up, probably because her hair was messy. She looked extremely tired, and as DI Fairbrother was explaining something to her, she kept nodding and closing her eyes as if she were quite ready to go back to sleep standing up.

'Ah, Jerry,' said DI Fairbrother. 'I thought you'd like to know that we've been able to identify this dead bloke. We had his image on file and we were able to match it, even though his face is a bit squashed.'

He held up his phone and showed Jerry the picture on it. The caption read *Henry Maybury, 67, retired floor manager, Debenhams department store*. The man in the photo had thinning white hair and bushy white eyebrows and had one eye closed against the sunlight, as if he were winking.

'He was the second deceased who was taken from Lettice & Pray – the one who died in a traffic accident along with his grandson. That may be why his face is so squashed. Or maybe it's squashed from falling nearly a hundred feet. Or a bit of both.'

Jerry opened the tent flap and looked up at the block of flats. Almost all the windows were lit up, and an even brighter light was shining from the eleventh-floor flat, where the Martian and his team were examining Ronnie Gibbs's balcony.

'We're sure that's where they fell from?'

'The woman who lives directly underneath Ronnie Gibbs heard him screaming his head off. Then a couple of seconds later she heard a bang when they landed down here on this Land Rover. But what we still can't work out is where Henry Maybury's body came from. The front door of Ronnie Gibbs's flat was locked from the inside and we had to bust it open. And Gibbs's missus is away at the moment, in Southend. We managed to contact her using Gibbs's phone and she's on her way back.'

'Maybe this Maybury geezer simply rang the doorbell and Gibbs let him in.'

'Oh. You think someone like Ronnie Gibbs would invite a decomposing body into his flat?'

Jamila came out to join them. 'Is there any sign of flies?' she asked.

'Forensics are going to test their bodies for that fly residue when they get them into the morgue. But otherwise, no.'

'I was trying to think how Henry Maybury could have entered Ronnie Gibbs's flat,' said Jamila. 'If the door was locked, perhaps he gained access from the outside.'

'That's eleven floors up,' said DI Fairbrother. 'Not only was he dead, but there's nothing to hold on to – even if you were alive and you had the strength to climb up.'

'I was thinking of the Bishop of Southwark.'

Jerry and DI Fairbrother turned and looked at each other, and then turned back to Jamila. 'What are you suggesting?'

asked DI Fairbrother. 'That he might have been covered in flies and, like, *flown* up there?'

'Perhaps it's a mad idea. But what happened to the bishop was mad. The bishop flew right up to the ceiling before he fell. This Henry Maybury could have done the same, but taken Ronnie Gibbs back down with him.'

'Well, forensics will be able to tell us if he was covered all over in flies, like the bishop. But eleven floors up?'

'In this investigation, Simon, I am ruling out nothing as impossible.'

They went back inside the tent. It was filled with a strong pickle-like odour from the embalming fluid leaking out of Henry Maybury's body, as well as an underlying smell of faeces because Ronnie Gibbs had emptied his bowels.

'Let's hope that whoever owns this Land Rover is insured against dead bodies dropping on top of it in the middle of the night,' said Jerry.

DI Fairbrother said, 'It's extraordinary. Look how tight Maybury's clutching Gibbs's neck. They fell all that way and he still didn't let go, as if he really had it in for him. But why would a retired floor manager from Debenhams want to strangle a local gangster?'

'We'll be talking to Maybury's relatives,' said Jamila. 'But judging by what happened to Jock Maclean, I'm inclined to think that his body was simply being used by someone who bore a grudge against Ronnie Gibbs, and that he never even knew him.'

'I think I need some fresh air,' said Jerry. He lifted the tent flap just as DS Morrison appeared. She was wearing blue nitrile gloves and holding up a pair of binoculars.

'I've just found these on the ground down by one of the dustbins.'

She turned the binoculars this way and that. Jerry could see that one of the wire D-clips holding its woven strap had been twisted and opened up, so that the strap had slipped out.

'Maybe they're a bit of circumstantial and maybe they're not,' said DI Fairbrother. 'What are they? Nikon? They're not cheap, they're not, Nikons. At least a hundred and fifty quid. Bit strange to drop them and leave them behind.'

Jamila said, 'They could have been accidentally dropped from one of the flats. They're very tough, aren't they, so I'm not surprised they're not broken. But give them to forensics. Whoever they belonged to, they will have left plenty of their DNA on the eye cups.'

As they were talking, the forensic ambulance came reversing slowly into the car park. At the same time, the Martian appeared from the side entrance to the flats. He came over to Jamila and Jerry, tugging down his face mask and pulling off his gloves.

'Another weird one,' he said. 'We haven't found any flies, though. Not one. It could be they've all flown off.'

'Where are you taking them?' asked Jamila, nodding back towards the tent.

'St George's mortuary, for a start. Then we may have to move Mr Maybury's remains to Falcon Road for more specialist examination. I'm only glad that I don't have the job of explaining what's happened to his nearest and dearest. "Oh yes, Mrs Maybury, after your husband's body was nicked from the funeral home he fell eleven floors out of a block of flats. But don't worry. We'll make sure that his remains are treated with the greatest respect. No, we still don't know what's happened to your dead grandson. Perhaps he'll turn up later."'

Jamila and Jerry walked back to Jerry's car.

'Sometimes I seriously wonder why I chose this job,' said

Jerry, as he opened the passenger door for Jamila to climb in. 'Every day's more effing tragic than the day before.'

As he sat down behind the steering wheel, Jamila's phone rang again. She listened, and then she said, 'That was Simon Fairbrother. Almost all the flies at the station are dead now. He said they're ankle-deep in some of the corridors, but they're going to call in some cleaners to have them cleared away.'

'So – I wonder what that was all about?' said Jerry, turning his head to back out of the car park. 'Maybe we were being warned. I really get the feeling that whoever's controlling these bloody flies knows exactly what we're doing to track him down. Or her, of course. It wouldn't surprise me if it's a woman. My granny used to scream at any fly that dared come into her kitchen and they'd do a U-turn and fly back out again. She never needed fly spray.'

'I'm tired,' said Jamila.

25

The next morning, Jamila and Jerry met at Jack's at the Junction café. Jamila ordered the veggie platter, and Jerry went for his favourite chorizo benedict.

Neither of them had slept well and they hardly spoke as they ate their breakfasts and drank their tea and their coffee. Three council workers were sitting next to them and kept exploding into loud laughter, which made their morning feel even more surreal. Jerry thought: *This is a world in which dead bodies can rise from the grave and swarms of flies can hunt down living people, and you can find something to laugh at?*

Jamila's phone rang. She answered it and said, 'Very well. Very well. We'll see you there at nine thirty.' When she had put down her phone, she explained to Jerry, 'That was Father Devine. He's running a little late. But he can meet us at Atherton Street.'

'I'm sorry, guv, but I still don't understand what you think he can do for us.'

'Perhaps nothing, Jerry. But inside that house I had such a strong feeling that something was wrong. Something otherworldly. I mean, think of that picture in the hallway and the way it changed. If Father Devine gives me nothing else, he can at least give me reassurance that there is nothing sinister going on there.

'By the way,' she added, 'we should be receiving the final autopsy results on your Maureen and Dr Crowe sometime today. Perhaps they'll give us another clue to what's behind all these fly attacks.'

'Maybe they've found out how Maureen gave me anthrax – that's if it *was* her. At least most of my spots have pretty much faded away.'

After they had finished their breakfast, they drove to Lavender Hill. Over a dozen professional cleaners had been drafted in overnight to suck up the heaps of dead flies with Mammoth vacuum cleaners, which could each hold eighty litres of insect corpses. After that, they had disinfected every floor, wall, window, door handle and desk. When Jamila and Jerry arrived, they had almost finished, and the whole station smelled of Jantex surface cleaner.

DI Fairbrother had gone home, but DCI Butcher was there. He had been attending a right-wing anti-Islam demonstration outside the Masjid mosque in Battersea. The protest had started off peaceful, but a group of drunken thugs had arrived and after that it had degenerated into a riot. Five police officers had been seriously injured and windows in the mosque had been smashed with bricks taken from nearby garden walls. The police had been unable to disperse the rioters until well past three in the morning.

'Public order's totally breaking down these days,' said DCI Butcher. 'We're holding two of the English-only mob in the cells downstairs, and I'll be giving them a grilling later, when they've sobered up. But honestly. Someone only has to post a grievance on social media, whether it's true or false, and the next minute it's stirred up a major disturbance – hundreds of yobbos throwing stones and looting shops and setting fire to police vans. And it doesn't matter what kicked it off, it's always our people who get hurt trying to control it.'

'Do you have any idea what started this one off?' asked Jamila.

'Not yet, but since it's the English-only mob I can safely assume it's something racist. Maybe some Muslim lad tried to chat up some local girl, who knows? This lot don't need much of an excuse to start a riot.'

Jamila and Jerry went up to Jerry's office to collect Jerry's laptop and to see if they had received any messages. Jerry had received a reminder that he had an overdue dental appointment, while Jamila had been informed that an autopsy of Ashish's body had already been carried out, so that the Muslim practice of holding a funeral immediately after death had been respected as much as possible. His funeral would be held tomorrow morning at the al-Falah mosque in Ilford, followed by burial at Elmbridge Gardens of Peace. As a woman, Jamila would be allowed to attend the prayers, provided she sat in the back of the mosque, but she would not be allowed to attend the burial.

In his confidential report, the pathologist who had carried out the autopsy said that he taken samples from Ashish's oesophagus and stomach lining, although Muslims would regard this as desecration of his body. These samples would be sent to Professor Yearling to see if he could determine what kind of flies had come pouring out of his mouth.

'Three guesses,' said Jerry. 'If they weren't coffin flies then I'll eat my shorts, with or without ketchup.'

★★★

Father Devine was waiting for them on the corner of Atherton Street, carrying his exorcism case in one hand and a large black umbrella in the other.

'I think the Lord has decided that we need a good wash,' he said, as they came up to him.

'Aren't there any prayers to stop it raining?' asked Jerry.

Father Devine closed his eyes and said, 'Lord our God, who in times past withheld rain at the word of your righteous prophet Elijah, hear the humble pleas of us unworthy sinners during this season of constant precipitation. Do not hand us over to well-deserved chastisement for our many and manifold sins, but have mercy on us and spare us from the unpredictable elements of nature, so that we may lead lives of peace and repentance for the rest of our days.'

He opened his eyes, and as he did so there was a deep grumble of thunder from the north side of the river.

Jerry looked up at the rolling grey clouds from under the hood of his anorak. 'Well, either God's saying "okay, give me a minute and I'll go and turn off the taps", or else He's asking if you're having a laugh.'

'I have never known the Lord to mock me,' replied Father Devine. He sounded impatient today, as if he had come here only as a favour to Jamila.

'Sorry,' said Jerry. 'Just acting the atheist, as usual.'

'So where is this house you wish me to investigate?' Father Devine asked them. 'Does it have any history of strange noises or inexplicable manifestations? Have any of its residents ever claimed to have been taken over or possessed by spirits, either good or evil? Do you know if anyone has ever conducted an exorcism here before?'

'All we know is that it was occupied for the past seventeen years by an anthropologist called Humphrey Bly,' said Jamila, as they walked together along the street. 'It was Humphrey Bly whose remains were found in Battersea Park, and who was being examined by Dr Crowe. When we held that exorcism in Dr Crowe's laboratory, we're pretty sure now that the head we saw and the voice we heard belonged to Humphrey Bly.'

'It's certainly possible,' said Father Devine. 'It's what we call spiritual resonance. Or, less specifically, what are popularly known as "ghosts".'

'Anyway, we carried out technical checks of the voice recordings, and it seems that Humphrey Bly didn't say "clown" but "Ekron". And here we are – this is his house, Ekron.'

Father Devine tilted back his umbrella so that he could look up at the dark brick frontage of Humphrey Bly's house. Jamila took out a bunch of skeleton keys and said, 'Shall we?'

Father Devine hesitated, with the raindrops from his umbrella dripping down his back. Then he said, 'Very well,' and all three of them climbed the steps to the porch.

They reached the front door and Jamila inserted one of the keys. She had to jiggle it a little, but the lock clicked and the door opened up. They could immediately smell that lemony sumac coming from the kitchen, and they could see that the picture hanging at the end of the gloomy hallway was still the weeping woman in the headscarf holding up the dead dog.

'Something's different,' said Jamila, as she entered the hallway. 'Look – the floor's only parquet. I'm sure it was carpeted before.'

Instead of following her, Father Devine took a step back, almost treading on Jerry's shoe.

'Father?' said Jamila. 'Come on inside and take a look around.'

'No,' said Father Devine, shaking his head. 'I'm sorry, Jamila, but I can't go in there.'

'What's wrong?' Jerry asked him, but Father Devine said nothing and continued to shake his head. Jerry had to stand to one side to let him pass because he turned around and retreated down the steps until he was standing on the front garden path. He looked up at Jamila and Jerry with a tortured expression, like some medieval martyr who was being burned at the stake and trying not to regret his faith in God. It was still drizzling but he made no attempt to open his umbrella.

'Father, why can't you come in?' called Jamila.

Father Devine tucked his rolled-up umbrella under his arm, lifted his hand and made the sign of the cross in the air.

'There is evil inside this house. A great, great evil.'

'Can't you exorcise it?' said Jerry. 'You've got all your gubbins with you, haven't you? Candles, and incense, and St Stephen's chin, and all that.'

'I wouldn't stand a chance. What is inside this house is too powerful for me. Far too powerful. I am faithful, and I have God on my side, but I am but a single feeble pilgrim faced with a force so dark and of such terrible magnitude that I have no doubt at all that it would overwhelm me. You can call me a coward if you like, but this is an evil that I simply do not have the strength or the knowledge to dismiss.'

He was panting, as if he had been running, and Jerry could see that his face was wet not only with raindrops, but with tears.

'Do you know how powerful this evil is? I can feel it from here. Actually feel it, like an animal's breath. It is aware that I have arrived here, and it can sense why I have come here, and that I come in the name of the Lord. It is mocking me – challenging me to come inside. But if I do, I will be lucky to have the swiftest of deaths. My bowels would be draped from the lights on the ceiling, one to the other, and my heart would be nailed to the door.'

'It's actually telling you what it's going to do to you, in *that* much detail?' said Jerry. 'I mean – Jesus.'

Father Devine said nothing more, but opened the front garden gate and rushed off along the road with his raincoat flapping. They saw him climb into his Honda, which he had parked on the corner of Battersea Park Road, start up his engine and drive off with a squeal of tyres.

'Well – there goes one chicken cleric,' said Jerry.

Jamila looked back into the hallway. 'Do you think he could have had a genuine reason for being so scared?'

'I don't know. Did you hear what he was saying about having his insides wrapped around the lights on the ceiling and his heart nailed into the door? It sounded to me as if he'd been helping himself to the old communion wine. Fifteen per cent proof, that stuff is. Two bottles of that and you could sing the "Hallelujah Chorus" backwards.'

'You know that I have a bad feeling about this house myself. And it's not only that picture in the hallway. I'm sure the hallway floor was carpeted when we first came. I can't believe that someone came here and lifted the carpet overnight. Even if they did, why would they?'

'Do you want to go back in and take another look at it?'

'I'm not sure. You and I, Jerry, we've witnessed some very strange and frightening things together, haven't we? We know they exist. Supposing there really is an evil force of some kind in this house? An evil force that's strong enough to scare away an exorcist before he's even set foot in the place?'

'Father Devine said he could feel it, even out here. But I can't. Can you? Maybe we should give it a quick once-over, just to see if there's anything else different, apart from the picture, and the carpet.'

'I'm not armed.'

'I don't think that makes any difference. Evil forces are generally bulletproof, I imagine. Otherwise, Father Devine would have been packing a Glock along with his incense and his holy water, wouldn't he?'

Jamila said, 'Very well. Let's take a look around. Then we'll have to sit down and plan what we're going to do next. Perhaps Humphrey Bly had nothing whatsoever to do with all these flies. Perhaps his head and his torso simply attracted them, the way that all flies are attracted to rotting meat. Perhaps that green head that Father Devine was able to raise up was simply his spiritual resonance – his ghost – and we've been led up a blind alley.'

They stepped into the hallway. Jerry had brought a flashlight with him, but when he clicked the light switch the overhead lights came on.

Jamila was right. The first time they had entered the house, the hallway had been carpeted, but now it was parquet – oak, in a herringbone pattern. There were other differences, too. The coats had been hanging on the left-hand side of the hallway, but now they were hanging from a coat stand just behind the front door.

'There's a door there, at the end,' said Jerry. 'I'm sure that wasn't there before. Maybe this place does have a cellar after all. Or at least, it does now.'

'This is too weird,' said Jamila. 'This is like a completely different house.'

'We are sure it's the same house?'

'It said "Ekron" on the gate, didn't it? And it had that same silver birch in the garden. And it smells the same, of that *za'atar*.'

Jerry went along the hallway and tried to open the door that might lead to a cellar, but it was locked.

'You think one of your keys might open this up?' he asked Jamila, but Jamila was staring open-mouthed at the living room.

'I can't believe this,' she said, walking into the room and turning around and around. Yesterday, the walls had been papered with brown chrysanthemums and the room had been furnished with a brown leather sofa and brown chairs. A foggy mirror had hung over the fireplace and the mantelpiece had been lined with figurines.

Today, the walls were painted pale green and cluttered with dozens of framed oil paintings and watercolours of Middle Eastern markets and street scenes and deserted landscapes. Instead of a brown sofa there was a chaise longue upholstered in faded green velvet and two Victorian spoon-back armchairs. There was no mirror and no fireplace, only a radiator under the bay window.

Jerry went over to take a closer look at the paintings. A few of them bore plaques, and one next to the window was inscribed *Stone Well, Tel Miqne*.

'Tel Miqne, that's Ekron. So we haven't got the wrong house. But how the hell can it all be so different? It's like a total scene change when you go to the theatre.'

Jamila paused and took a deep breath. 'Perhaps Father Devine was right, and there is a powerful force here. I can sense that something's strange, but not in the way that he could. He said it was like an animal breathing on him.'

'Let's see if that lemony stuff is still there.'

When they went through to the kitchen, they found that it was fitted out completely differently from yesterday, with dark teak cabinets topped with streaky white marble. The mouldy slices of bread had disappeared, although the *za'atar* had been left on one of the worktops at the side. This was not a glass jar, though, but a ceramic pot decorated with small blue flowers.

'Made in Hebron,' said Jamila, picking up the pot and sniffing it. 'I have an Israeli friend who gave me a whole set of side plates in a very similar pattern.'

Jerry looked out at the garden. Yesterday, it had been overgrown with unkempt bushes and weeds. Today, it was paved, with a life-size bronze statue standing by the end wall, a woman with her face hidden under a hood.

'This is giving me the right heebie-jeebies,' he said. 'Perhaps we should call it a day.'

'Come on, Jerry, we've seen scarier things than this.'

'Oh, really? Like what? Those clothes that ran around, screaming? Those children with no arms? This is a whole entire house that's changed into another house in the space of a few hours, and we're in it.'

Jamila led the way out of the kitchen and across the hallway, where the dining room had been. Jerry reluctantly followed her. But when they opened the door, they were confronted not with the dining room but with Humphrey Bly's study.

'This was definitely not here yesterday,' said Jerry. 'This

was a dining room with a bloody great dining table and eight chairs.'

Humphrey Bly's briar pipe was still lying on his desk, next to his keyboard, along with two open textbooks. His swivel chair had been pushed backwards as if he had suddenly stood up.

One wall of the study was hung with more paintings and engravings of deserts and mountains and Middle Eastern forts. On the opposite wall, Bly's various lifetime awards were arranged, including the Huxley Memorial Medal and the Margaret Mead Award plaque, two of the highest prizes for anthropology. But Jamila and Jerry were looking at the wallpaper. It was the William Morris pattern with tulips, yellowed with tobacco smoke and faded with time – but the same wallpaper that tainted the feet of the flies that had landed on it with arsenic.

'Looks like we *have* got the right house,' said Jerry. 'Second time lucky.'

He reached out towards the wallpaper, but Jamila said, 'Jerry! For goodness' sake don't touch it! I don't suppose it'll kill you if you do, but you're still recovering from that anthrax, so your resistance is probably low. Remember what Professor Yearling said about all the people who had died from arsenic poisoning.'

Jerry lowered his hand. 'Yes, you might be right. I'm not entirely sure I want "RIP – Killed By Wallpaper" engraved on my headstone. So what's the plan?'

'First, we'll bring in forensics. They need to examine the whole house, but they can start with this study. Meanwhile, we can finish searching everywhere else, including the cellar – if that door actually leads to a cellar, and isn't just a cupboard.

I think we ought to stay here until forensics arrive. I don't want to leave and come back and find that it's reverted to what it was yesterday, or something else totally different.'

'Well, it seems like we might be getting somewhere. But the way it's changed – I can't even begin to imagine how that was done. If I knew, I'd convert my crabby old flat into a luxury penthouse.'

'For the moment, Jerry, let's not beat our brains out worrying about that. Let's be thankful that we've found this study and it's taken us a step forward in what we can only hope is the right direction.'

They left the study, closing the door behind them, and Jamila called the Martian. While she was talking to him, Jerry went to the bottom of the staircase. Yesterday, the banisters had been plain, painted white. Today, there was a carved finial on the newel post in the shape of a lion's head, and all the banisters were elaborately shaped.

He looked up to the first-floor landing, and he jolted in shock when he saw that a man was standing there, staring down at him. The man was wearing a brown trilby hat and a camel-coloured overcoat, and even though the ceiling light was behind him, so that his face was partly in shadow, Jerry recognised him at once.

'Vince Bloody Narrow!' he shouted up at him. 'What the hell are you doing here?'

Vincent Narrow said nothing, but continued to stare down at Jerry as if he hadn't heard him.

'Come down here, Narrow!' Jerry demanded, gripping the lion's head. 'Hands up where I can see them, nice and slow!'

Jamila had finished talking to the Martian now, and she came to join Jerry at the foot of the stairs. When she looked up and saw Vincent Narrow, she said, 'I can't believe it!' and pressed her hand over her mouth.

'Are you going to come down here, or what?' Jerry repeated. 'If you don't come down here, I'm coming up to get you!'

Vincent Narrow still said nothing, and stepped back from the banisters so that they could no longer see him. Jerry said, 'Right, that's it!' and bounded up the stairs.

Vincent Narrow had disappeared from the landing, and all four doors to the bedrooms and bathroom were closed. Jerry flung open the first door. Yesterday, it had been the master bedroom, but now it was a small guest bedroom stacked with cardboard boxes. He went to the next door and opened it, and then the next. On first sight, he could find Vincent Narrow in none of them, so he went back and looked in all the large walnut wardrobes, behind the curtains and under the beds.

'Jerry?' Jamila called up to him.

'I reckon he's scarpered up in the attic,' Jerry told her.

'Be careful. Do you want me to call for backup?'

'I'm okay. I'll risk it. Narrow's a housebreaker, not a serial killer.'

Jerry climbed the stairs to the attic. The door was closed, and he had to push it hard. It felt as if nobody had opened it for years, and it made a grating sound on the floorboards as he swung it open. He stepped cautiously inside and switched on his flashlight. The attic contained only the water tank and three wooden storage chests. The chests were probably too small for Vincent Narrow to be hiding in, but Jerry opened the lids of each of them to make sure. He had once discovered a seventeen-stone assault suspect who had managed to squash himself inside the dumb waiter at the restaurant where he worked, in the hope that nobody would find him.

Jerry shone his flashlight into every crevice in the attic, and he even lifted up the thick brown loft insulation in case Vincent Narrow was lying underneath. There was no sign of him. Somehow, like a stage magician, he had vanished.

Jerry went back downstairs to the hallway.

'Where is he?' asked Jamila.

'I've looked in every bedroom and up in the attic and I can't find him.'

'He must be up there somewhere. I saw him myself.'

'I don't know how he's managed to get away, but he has. I even checked the windows to see if he might have climbed out, but the stay bars are all in place.'

Jamila looked around. 'I'm going to have nightmares about this house tonight. It's bad enough trying to sleep in that hotel, with drunken people shouting in the corridors at one in the morning.'

'What time did the Martian say he'd get here?'

'He said they needed at least an hour.'

'Great,' said Jerry. He tried the handle of the door in the hallway for a second time, in case it had been stiff from lack of use, like the attic door, rather than locked, but it still refused to open.

'We might as well have a shufti in here while we're waiting for them. Have you got the old lock-picks?'

Jamila took out her bunch of skeleton keys. She tried three of them without a result, but when she inserted the fourth key and turned it, they could hear the wards clicking as they were unlocked. As Jamila reached out to open the door, though, Jerry took hold of her hand and said, 'Hold on a sec, guv. Listen.'

Jamila frowned. They both stood in the hallway in complete

silence. Behind the door, something was softly tapping, and there was a droning noise too.

'Flies,' said Jamila. 'That sounds like flies.'

'Oh Jesus,' said Jerry. 'This gets worse by the minute.'

'Let's leave this door closed. I'll call those pest control people again.'

'Do you think it's worth it? A fat lot of good they were – trying to kill those flies in the nick.'

'Perhaps they had more resistance than normal flies, but they all died after a while, didn't they? We could try the same thing here. If the pest control people spray them, and then we leave this door closed for long enough, they might well drop dead, given time.'

'Listen,' said Jerry. 'They're even louder. And it sounds like they're busting to get out.'

Even though the door was solid oak, the droning was clearly audible now, and the pattering against the panels on the other side was like a furious hailstorm.

Jamila picked up her phone and prodded out the number for GJ Pest Control. But she had only managed to say, 'Is Gary there, by any chance?' when both she and Jerry were startled by the door swinging wide open.

Hundreds of flies came pouring out into the hallway. Jamila and Jerry stumbled backwards, trying to beat them off, but they settled all over their hair and their faces and their clothes. They even clung to the backs of their hands.

'Christ almighty, let's get out of here!' Jerry shouted, spitting flies away from his lips.

It was then, though, that Vincent Narrow appeared in the open doorway. Flies were circling around him, but none of them were settling on his face or his coat. He was staring at them in a strange emotionless way, as if he were trying to hypnotise them.

Even though he was half blind, batting flies away from his eyes, Jerry could see that the door didn't open on to the top of a cellar staircase, as he had expected, but into a library. It was dark in there, because the curtains were drawn, but he could make out shelf after shelf of leather-bound books, maroon and brown, all the way up to the ceiling. In the centre of the room stood what looked like a long table – shiny and black, as if it were made out of ebony.

'Get the fuck out,' said Vincent Narrow, in a voice as rasping as glasspaper. 'Get the fuck out and don't come back. Ever. This is sacred, this house. Nobody's allowed through that front door but me. I'm the guardian. Got it? I'm the guardian and you're not welcome here. So sling your hook.'

Jerry pulled the front door open, took Jamila's arm and almost dragged her outside into the porch. He followed her and slammed the door shut behind him. Once they had reached the bottom of the steps, though, the front door opened again and Vincent Narrow stepped out.

'Hey, coppers!' he shouted at them, standing on the top step and pointing his finger at them. 'Don't kid yourself that you've got away with coming in here today! You'll pay for it, I can promise you that. You'll fucking pay for it!'

'Go! Go! Go!' Jerry urged Jamila, after they had opened the front garden gate and stepped out on to the pavement.

Jamila hesitated. 'But what if we go and when we come back the house is all different again?'

Jerry gave her a push towards the end of Atherton Street, where he had parked his car. 'Let's worry about that when we come back. First of all, we have to find out what the hell's going on here. I think we should go and ask your Father Devine. There's no way he would have gone shooting off like that if he hadn't had at least some idea of what it was – this evil force that was going to wrap his guts round the lightbulbs.'

'I'll call him,' said Jamila, and when they climbed back into the car she took out her phone. Jerry checked his rear-view mirror and he was unsettled to see Vincent Narrow standing outside Ekron, his arms folded, as if he were saying good riddance and don't come back.

26

Father Devine had not returned to his church, but was visiting a care home in Ilford for elderly people with dementia. It was a huge Edwardian house half hidden behind a high laurel hedge, which was dripping in the endless rain.

Father Devine took Jamila and Jerry into a stuffy side room that overlooked the garden. As he talked to them, he constantly glanced out of the window as if he were remembering a past life, or as if he were expecting some strange person to come up to the rain-beaded window to press their face against the glass.

Both Jamila and Jerry could tell that whatever the 'animal breath' was that he had felt coming out of Ekron had deeply disturbed him. He didn't smile once, and he had pulled up the left sleeve of his dark-grey sweater and kept scratching his arm.

Between them, Jamila and Jerry described how the house had totally changed from their first visit, and how it had probably looked more like Humphrey Bly's original house, complete with his study and his library. Then they told him how Vincent Narrow had appeared – upstairs on the landing, first of all, and then in the library doorway, surrounded by a torrent of flies.

'How he got from upstairs to downstairs without us seeing him, we haven't an effing clue,' said Jerry. 'There's only one staircase and no home lift and as far as we can tell he didn't climb out of any of the windows. Maybe there's a trapdoor that we didn't see, or maybe he slid down the cavity between the walls.'

Although Father Devine repeatedly looked out of the window, they could tell that he was listening to them intently. After they had finished, though, and Jamila had asked him 'What do you think, father?', he was silent for nearly a minute.

Eventually, he said, 'You are trying to solve this mystery in the way that police detectives would solve it.'

'We *are* police detectives,' said Jerry. 'At least we *were*, the last time we got our pay cheques.'

'But from what Jamila has told me, you two have considerable experience in much more than everyday detective procedures. You've investigated some events that have been extremely unusual, to say the least. Events that one can only categorise as "supernatural" – although you'll agree that "supernatural" includes a multitude of possibilities. Everything from poltergeists to angels.'

Jerry was tempted to ask Father Devine if he had ever seen an angel, but decided to keep his mouth shut.

'You said that you could feel a strong dark force inside that house,' said Jamila gently. 'Do you have any idea what it could be? And do you think it was responsible for changing the whole house?'

Father Devine scratched his arm even more furiously. 'I don't think there's any doubt about it. Spiritual forces as powerful as this one can alter your entire perception of the world around you. Yesterday it led you to believe that you were looking around one kind of house, but in fact you were dreaming it. Perhaps the house you visited today was Humphrey Bly's real house – it sounded as if it could have been. But then again – how did this Vincent Narrow disappear from the top of the stairs and then reappear downstairs, if you weren't dreaming again, or hallucinating?'

'So what kind of spirits are able to do this?' asked Jamila. 'We have many spirits in Pakistan that can make you believe you can see something that isn't really there, such as a gwat, or that one of your dead relatives is still alive and talking to you, like a ghoul.'

'The force in this house is much more powerful and much more malevolent than any of those,' said Father Devine. 'All the same, it would not surprise me at all if it was some spirit that Humphrey Bly had brought back from his time in the Middle East, or possibly conjured up from some ritual that he had learned while he was studying Canaanite culture.'

'You really think that spirits can be conjured up?' Jerry asked him.

'Where do you think all the stories about genies in bottles came from? Behind every folk story, there's always an element of truth.'

'Can you put a name to it – this spirit, or this force, or whatever it is?'

'Most spirits have many different names, as you know.'

'So you don't know exactly what this one's called? You felt its force, and you smelled its breath, and we've told you what it can do, like changing that house around. But you can't even guess what it could be?'

Father Devine didn't answer, but tugged down his sleeve.

'And what about Vincent Narrow?' Jerry persisted. 'He's a housebreaker, and he hasn't been long out of Wandsworth nick. What's he up to? He's been seen several times when these swarms of flies have attacked people, and it's almost like he's directing them.'

'In that case, Jerry, he probably is, but it's more than likely that he's only doing what he's been directed to do, by this spirit. Almost all powerful spirits have minions to carry out their dirty work for them, like human dictators. In Hebrew, a man like Vincent Narrow would be called a *vd rvch*, a spirit slave.'

'You know what it is, don't you, father?' said Jamila quietly. 'You know its name but for some reason you're not going to tell us.'

Father Devine gave an involuntary shudder. Jerry's grandmother would have said that a goose had walked over his grave.

'I'm afraid I can't,' he told her. 'It knows that I've recognised it for what it is. I'm sure that when you took me to Humphrey Bly's house, it changed it back to what it was really like, to see if I had the courage to come inside and confront it. It even knows that I'm thinking and talking about it now. I can't escape it.'

'So you're telling us that it was able to change our perception of the house? Every single room? I mean, how? Is it some form of hypnotism?'

'I cannot even begin to describe to you the power that it has. And it's a malevolent power, believe me. It can make the dearest of friends turn on each other. It can fill a man with so much anger that he murders his own daughters. It's the power of pestilence and war and cruelty and endless discontent.

It's the reason that the world is unhappy, and always will be.'

'So what's its name? You can whisper it, can't you? Atherton Street's a good fifteen miles away.'

'It makes no difference. It will be aware that I have spoken its name, and because I am a man of the cloth, it will punish me, one way or another, in the most horrible way that it can devise.'

Jamila took her notebook out of her bag and held up a ballpoint pen. 'How about writing it down?'

Father Devine shook his head. 'It will still know that I have told you what it is.'

'What about the flies?' asked Jerry. 'Is that what you're afraid of? Those dead people covered in flies coming to get you?'

Father Devine pressed his finger to his lips. 'Please – say no more!'

'But it's this force or this spirit or whatever its name is – this is the one who's been sending all the flies out?'

'Please!' Father Devine suddenly stood up, and now he was shaking as if he were starting to suffer an epileptic fit.

'Father, we have no choice,' said Jamila. 'We have to find a way of getting rid of it, whether we know what its name is or not. Otherwise, it's going to continue to raise dead bodies out of their graves and use them to murder more clerics and more criminals.'

Father Devine sat down again. 'I believe I understand why it's been killing both. Like most evil spirits, it has an intense hatred of any religious faith, and I mean *any*. You can tell that because it has been murdering Anglicans and Catholics and Jews without discrimination. In this spirit's eyes, they are equally guilty of believing in a higher power, in one manifestation of God or another. It wouldn't surprise me at all if it attacks an imam next.'

'But why did it go after Ronnie Gibbs and that Scottish geezer who worked for him – Jock Macwhatsit? You couldn't exactly call them holy.'

'It killed them as a reward for Vincent Narrow, that's my opinion. A bonus for its faithful servant. It sounds to me as if it has Narrow completely under its influence. How it achieved that, I couldn't guess. But it is probably eliminating his enemies to make sure that he remains loyal.'

'Thank you for your help, father,' said Jamila. 'But now we need to go back to the station and plan how we're going to break into the house and exterminate it, whatever it is. I have to ask you one thing, though. If you don't come with us, will it look like Humphrey Bly's house, or will it seem to be different, like it did yesterday? You said that it was challenging you to come inside – taunting you, with that smell of animal breath – and that's why the house appeared the way it really was.'

Jerry said, 'Was it challenging *you*, specifically, father, or would any priest do? Maybe we can find another one who wouldn't mind having a crack at exorcising it, or whatever you'd have to do to get rid of it.'

'I don't know,' said Father Devine. 'Are you calling me a coward?'

'Did I say that? All I know is that it's urgent that we enter the house and deal with whatever we find in there – spirit or bogeyman or whatever it turns out to be. But I think it goes without saying that we need it to be the right house, not some fucking mirage. We'd look a right load of twats if we couldn't find this spirit and we couldn't find Vincent Narrow, but after we'd left the house these flies kept on killing people.'

'I understand, and I apologise.'

'It's mocking us, this spirit, there's no question about that. It's been taking the piss right from the beginning. Why do you think it filled up the Lavender Hill cop shop with millions of flies? Why do you think it killed my Maureen, and Dr Crowe? Okay – it knows *you* know about it, but it's been showing us that it knows exactly what we've been doing to try and track it down. It wouldn't surprise me if Vincent Narrow's been giving it a fair amount of inside information. He's always had dozens of contacts in the Met – officers who were happy to turn a blind eye to his housebreaking because he gave them a nice pair of Meissen vases that he'd lifted from some gaff in Chelsea.'

Jamila and Jerry took their coats down from the pegs on the back of the door.

'If anything else useful occurs to you, father, we'd appreciate it if you'd give us a call,' said Jamila. 'Even the smallest hint can be helpful when we're dealing with a case like this.'

Father Devine said nothing but stood up and followed them to the front door. They all stood in silence for a moment, as if they had been attending the funeral of a well-loved friend. Then Jamila and Jerry stepped out into the rain and walked over to their car.

'Well, what do we do now, guv?' asked Jerry, as he switched on the engine. 'It looks like we're up excrement creek without a paddle. We're going to go busting into a house that may not be the house we've busted into, looking for something that we don't know what it is.'

'We can set up surveillance outside the house for two or

three days,' said Jamila. 'We can watch to see who comes in and out, if anybody, and we can use a laser microphone to hear what's going on inside. Perhaps this evil spirit will chant some kind of incantation that will help us to identify it, or perhaps Vincent Narrow will call it by name. And we may be able to use cameras to give us an idea of what the house is going to look like inside, before we enter.'

'It depends, doesn't it? Maybe this spirit can change the whole house with a snap of its fingers. It probably doesn't have any fingers, but you know what I mean.'

They were about to drive off when the front door of the care home opened and Father Devine came hurrying out, one hand raised to keep the rain out of his face.

He knocked on Jamila's window, and she put it down. It was obvious that he was deeply distressed because he was having trouble speaking.

'What is it, father?'

'I'll come!' he gasped. 'When you break into the house again, I'll come!'

'Really? Are you sure?'

'I can't allow anyone else to die! And if I have to give my own life to defeat this spirit, then so be it! Jesus died in order to save mankind, and it is my duty as a priest to follow his sacred example!'

'Well, to be fair, it'll save us a hell of a lot of hassle,' said Jerry. 'I mean, if we're sure that we're entering the right house, and we know what we're up against once we're in there. So what *are* we up against?'

A raindrop dripped off the end of Father Devine's nose. 'I can't tell you. Not yet, anyway. If it's aware that I've told you its name, it could very well find a way to stop me from helping you.'

'What are you saying?' asked Jamila.

'Like Bishop Knight, and all those other clergy, it could kill me. Send some corpse to strangle me, or fling me into the air, or who knows what.'

'We can arrange for twenty-four-hour security for you, until we enter the house.'

'I don't think you understand yet how powerful this spirit actually is. No amount of security would be able to protect me. You could lock me inside a steel box and it would still be able to find me and kill me. No – I *will* tell you its name, but only when we have opened up the front door and are about to enter.'

'If it's as powerful as you say it is, do you think you'll be able to exorcise it?'

'We're not really talking about an exorcism here, Jamila. This spirit has not possessed anybody, as far as I can tell. We're talking about an *ultima exitium* – a final destruction – rather than an exorcism. It is likely that it has lived in one form or another for thousands of years, wreaking discontent and death whenever it can. But now is the time for it to be destroyed for good. If we can manage to wipe it off the face of the Earth for ever, believe me, the Earth will be a much safer and happier place.'

'What if we can't?' said Jerry. 'Come on, admit it, father. It's scaring the shit out of you, isn't it? What if we go into that house and find it, and you go through all your holy rigmarole, and it doesn't work? And it kills the lot of us?'

Father Devine crossed himself. 'We must try,' he said. 'Jesus gave His life, to save humanity, and we must be prepared to make the ultimate sacrifice too.'

Jerry looked at Jamila. 'That's all very well, but Jesus was only dead for the weekend. After that it was off back home to see Daddy.'

'In the post office in Lavender Hill I saw there was a vacancy for a Sunday school teacher,' said Jamila. 'You're not thinking of applying for it, are you?'

Jerry smiled as they drove off. He was pleased that Jamila was beginning to acquire his sarky sense of humour. In the investigations that they had been working on together, it was a good way of staying reasonably sane.

27

Later that afternoon, Jamila and Jerry held a meeting at the station with DCS Chance, DCI Butcher, DI Fairbrother, six detectives, nine uniformed officers and six specialist firearms officers from MO19.

Jamila stood up and said, 'The reason we've brought you all together is that we're now fairly certain we know where the instigator of all these fatal fly attacks is located. It's the same address that we searched before, Ekron, on Atherton Street, but much of what I'm going to tell you now you're going to find to be incredible, to say the least.'

'But that's why we called you in, isn't it, to work with DS Pardoe,' put in DCS Chance. 'You two can deal with the incredible, so that we don't have to.'

'That's quite right,' said Jamila. 'But in this case we're going to need you to back us up, without question, regardless of what we ask you to do, even if you do find it incredible. We're asking you to suspend your disbelief, no matter what you're confronted with, and respond as you normally would in dealing with any dangerous offender.'

'I'm not sure I understand,' said DI Fairbrother, from the back of the room. 'We've thoroughly searched that house, Ekron, but there was nobody there. Has the suspect returned there, and if they have, how do we know that?'

'We believe the suspect was always there and never left. The house we searched the first time looked real, but it wasn't real. I know – by all means raise your eyebrows. But we were all hallucinating. That's the only way I can describe it to you, because we don't know ourselves how it was done. The suspect was somehow making us believe that the house looked this particular way, but in actual fact it was deceiving us, and hiding behind it.'

'Are you serious?' asked DCI Butcher.

'Everything I'm going to explain to you now is serious. As I told you, you may find some of it hard to believe, but we've seen it with our own eyes. We're not speculating about it and we're not inventing anything.'

'You called the suspect "it". Does that mean you have some idea of what we're up against here?'

'Let me put it this way, sir. As far as we know, it's not a person in the usual sense of the word. On the other hand, it may share the same kind of feelings that a person might, such as hatred and revenge, and it certainly has intelligence. It has power, too. Extraordinary power. If it's responsible for raising dead bodies out of their graves and sending so many swarms of flies out to kill people and cause such havoc, then I think we have to treat it with a great deal of caution.'

Edge raised his hand. 'Think about it. It used flies to cover up CCTV cameras in the streets, one after the other, so that we wouldn't have any record of where these dead bodies were coming from, or where they were going. If that's not intelligent and powerful, then I don't know what is.'

Jamila proceeded to describe to the assembled officers their visit to Ekron this morning. She told them how the house had looked as they had first expected it to, like the home of Humphrey Bly. As she spoke, the officers listened in complete silence, except for some foot-shuffling, but Jerry could see the increasing incredulity on their faces, especially when it came to telling them about the appearance of Vincent Narrow, and how he had miraculously descended from the landing to the library.

'Must've been a trapdoor,' said DC Battersby. 'Same as those stage magicians.'

'You think so?' retorted DC Okeke. 'Come on, bro! If the suspect can change the entire house to look like another house, I don't think he's going to need any trapdoors. He can probably go through some other dimension.'

'So is Vincent Narrow the suspect?' DC Battersby asked Jamila.

'He's involved in this, for sure. But we believe he's only a pawn, so to speak.'

She then recounted everything that Father Devine had said to them about the malevolent spirit he felt was hiding inside Ekron – how he had been too terrified to enter the house with them, and how he was still withholding the spirit's name, in case it sent the flies out to kill him. But she also told them that he had volunteered to come with them when they went back into the house, regardless of the risk to his life.

When Jamila had finished, DCS Chance stood up. 'This has been the most entertaining briefing that I've attended in a long time, I must admit. I must also admit that you were right, Detective Inspector Patel, and that none of it was easy to believe. But this investigation has been hard to believe right from the very beginning, and it's obvious we have to take drastic and immediate action to prevent any more graverobbing and any more fatal attacks by swarms of flies. As it's been described several times on the news, it's like a biblical plague.'

He looked around the room like a general assessing his

army, and then he said, 'You've asked for our support, whether we believe what you've been telling us or not. Both you and Detective Sergeant Pardoe have established a remarkable record in closing offbeat investigations, which is why the two of you are affectionately nicknamed the Ghostbusters. For that reason, we'll give you all the backup you require. When do you plan to go back to this house?'

'Tomorrow morning,' said Jamila. 'An early start, six o'clock, while it's still dark. We'll have Father Devine with us, so hopefully the house will still look like Humphrey Bly's. We need to be armed, and we need to have at least two pest control technicians with us, with spray pesticides, just in case.'

She switched on a projector to show the assembled officers a floorplan of Ekron. It had been sent to her by the estate agent who had sold the house to Humphrey Bly.

'Here—' she said, pointing to the room that he had made into his library. 'I have a feeling that this is where this spirit is hiding itself, in whatever form, so we need to hit here first. At the same time, we go for the study – here – and occupy the rest of the house as quickly as possible, in case Vincent Narrow tries to escape from one floor to the other, or the spirit itself attempts to change the whole house back into another property altogether.'

Jerry stood up beside Jamila and said, 'Hands up all those who think this is all totally bonkers.'

There was a ripple of nervous laughter, but nobody raised their hand.

'Right then,' said Jerry. 'See you at the crack.'

They were back in Jerry's office when Jamila received an email from Dr Simon Dorset, the forensic pathologist who specialised in criminal causes of death. He was sending her the results of the autopsies on Maureen Glover and Dr John Crowe.

Both bodies had been covered all over in *Conicera tibialis*, or coffin flies, and the flies had also penetrated their nasal cavities, their oesophagi and their anuses. In Maureen's case, the flies had entered her vagina and had crawled up as far as her cervix. The flies, however, were not the primary cause of death. Both Maureen and Dr Crowe had been strangled.

After she had showed him the email, Jamila laid her hand on Jerry's shoulder.

'Do you want to go for a drink?' she asked him.

'No, I'll be all right, guv. Thanks anyway. We have to get up bright and early tomorrow, don't we, and I don't want a hangover. And what would you do? Sit there in the Fox and Hounds with a cup of lemon tea watching me get steadily gazeboed?'

Jamila kept her hand on his shoulder and gave him a regretful smile, and when she smiled he was just about to suggest that, yes, maybe they could go for a drink after all. But before he could say anything, his phone warbled.

It was DCI Butcher. 'Jerry? I've just had a call from Sergeant Bill Wilkins from the Marine Policing Unit at Wapping. They've lifted a body out of the river by China Wharf – an Asian male in his mid-twenties by the look of him.'

'Really? When?'

'Only about an hour-and-a-half ago. Bill was the cox in charge, and he and I go way back. He said the deceased had probably surfaced after a day or two underwater because of gasses forming in his lungs. Bill was able to give him a quick once-over before they took him off to St George's. He saw severe bruising around his neck and in his opinion there's no doubt at all that he was strangled. Not only that, there were dead flies caught in his sweater. He had credit cards in his wallet in the name of Zahir Asadullah, and he was also carrying ID from the coroner's office.'

'Oh, shit. Dr Crowe's assistant. Must be.'

'I'm afraid so.'

Jerry lowered his phone. Jamila took her hand off his shoulder and said, 'What?'

'That was Butcher. And guess what? Those bloody flies have done for another one.'

By a quarter to six the next morning, while it was still dark and drizzling, the armed unit had cordoned off Atherton Street at both ends and gathered outside the front of the house named Ekron, ready to make a forced entry. They included two pest control technicians, with large canisters of fly killer.

They had tried to keep as quiet as possible, but they knew their arrival had disturbed some of the residents because they had switched on their bedroom lights and drawn back their curtains, and Jamila and Jerry could see them peering out. They would not have seen much. All the officers were wearing black, with black helmets and black body armour.

Jamila and Jerry were standing by the garden gate, with Father Devine between them. All three of them were wearing protective vests, too, and both Jamila and Jerry were armed with Glock automatic pistols. In one hand, Father Devine was carrying his burgundy leather case of exorcism accessories. In the other he was carrying a crucifix, more than a metre and a half high, with a silver figure of Jesus on it.

DCI Butcher came over to them. 'Are we ready to roll?' he

asked them. 'Has the reverend gentleman here informed us what we could be up against?'

'Not yet, sir,' said Jamila. 'Just give us a minute.'

DCI Butcher stayed where he was, with his arms folded. Jamila turned to Father Devine and said, 'I know you're afraid, father, but you've had the courage to come this far.'

'It knows I'm here,' Father Devine told her, in a fearful, clogged-up whisper. 'I can feel it. It knows that I'm here, and it's baiting me.'

'It can bait you all it likes, father,' said DCI Butcher. 'We have half a dozen AFOs here with SIG Sauer carbines that can fire over nine hundred rounds a minute.'

'Oh, believe me, it has survived far worse tribulations than a few bullets, detective,' said Father Devine. 'It was first mentioned in the Book of Kings, in the Bible, which was written about 540 BC.'

DCI Butcher counted on his fingers. 'Oh... so it's a bit more than two and a half thousand years old. It's lasted pretty well, then, all things considered.'

'Don't take this lightly, I warn you,' Father Devine told him. 'It has survived for so long because of its extraordinary power. I can feel it now, almost as if it's standing here close behind me, breathing its animal breath down my neck.'

'Remember what I said, please,' Jamila told DCI Butcher. 'You have to suspend your disbelief, no matter how unbelievable this seems to be.'

DCI Butcher lifted both hands in surrender. 'Okay, I'm with you. Just for today, I'll believe that black is white and England won the World Cup.'

'That's stretching it a bit, guv,' said DC Noakes.

Father Devine glanced towards the front door of Ekron and took two or three deep, steadying breaths. 'This spirit has many different names, as so many spirits do. It is not only mentioned in Kings, in the Old Testament, but by Matthew in the New Testament too. It appears in various forms in the Testament of Solomon, in Canaanite and Ugaritic texts, and in countless historical descriptions of demonic possession and exorcisms, leading right up to the Salem witch trials in America in 1692.

'Cardinal Bellotto, who taught me the ritual of exorcism, told me that if I were to come across it, ever, I should stay well clear, and whatever I did, I should not attempt to confront it. He warned me that if I did, I would die an unimaginable death – those were his exact words. I always doubted that I ever would come across it, though, because it was last seen or heard of around 1917, and this is the first time that it has appeared since then.'

DCI Butcher said, 'It's raining, father. It's cold. It's coming up to six o'clock. Do you think you can cut the RE lesson and just tell us what its name is?'

The fluffy tuft on top of Father Devine's biretta was soaked, and so was his straggly white hair. He lifted the crucifix that he was carrying in his left hand, kissed it, and then said, 'It's commonly known in English as Beelzebub.'

'What?' said Jamila. 'Beelzebub, the demon they call the lord of the flies?'

'Now you know why. Some historians suggest his name was really Ba'al zevul, which means "lord of the heavenly dwelling", but the Israelites always called him Ba'al zebub, "lord of the flies", as a derogatory pun, to insult him.'

'Whatever his name is, I don't think there's any question that he's lord of a good many flies,' said Jamila. 'I wish you'd been able to tell us this earlier. There must be so much literature about Beelzebub, going right back to the Old Testament. And if he hasn't been seen since 1917, that's well over a hundred years ago. Did an exorcist like you find a way to lock him up, or put him into a coma, and if they did, how did they do it?'

'Are we going in, or do you want to postpone this whole operation while you do some more research?' asked DCI Butcher. He was growing increasingly impatient, and all the other officers in the unit were looking restless too, standing in the rain.

'We should go in now,' said Father Devine. 'If we delay, even for a day, Beelzebub will seize the opportunity to send out his flies to kill even more people, and the trouble is that we don't know who he might have in mind. It could be a rabbi or it could be a robber.'

'You're sure?' Jamila asked him.

Father Devine kissed his crucifix again. 'I'm sure. I know the Lord wants me to do this, as frightened as I am.'

DCI Butcher turned around and beckoned to the officer carrying a battering ram. They had decided on breaking their way in through the front door to give them an element of surprise, instead of fiddling around with a skeleton key. Father Devine may have said that Beelzebub was aware that they were there, but they had no way of knowing that for certain.

'All right, you lot!' shouted DCI Butcher. 'Go! Go! Go!'

Three officers kicked open the garden gate and ran up the steps into the porch. One was swinging the bosher and the other two had their carbines pointing at the front door. With three loud bangs and the sound of cracking door panels, they smashed their way into the hallway. To Jerry's relief, he could see that they had knocked over the coat stand, which had been in the same place as it was on their visit yesterday morning. That was a good sign that the house would look like Humphrey Bly's, and not some hallucination.

'Right, come on, father,' said Jerry, and he and Jamila helped Father Devine to climb the front steps. Father Devine was panting by the time they stepped over the front door, which was lying broken on the floor. DCI Butcher and the rest of the unit came crunching over the splinters close behind them.

Although the overhead lights had been switched on, the officers were shining a chaotic criss-cross of high-power torch beams all over the walls and the ceiling. Two officers had already opened the door to the library and were looking inside, where it was dark.

'Take care!' cried out Father Devine, and he quickened his pace along the hallway. 'Don't try to go inside yet! I must first petition the Lord to protect us!'

The two officers stepped back, but one of them shone his LED torch straight into the doorway. Even though the torch was so powerful, it completely failed to illuminate the interior of the library – not even the carpet by the open door. The darkness seemed to swallow up the beam of light like a shark swallowing a swimmer.

Father Devine approached the door, setting down his exorcism case on the floor but keeping his crucifix raised up high. Jamila and Jerry stayed close to him, on either side. They could smell that lemony tang of *za'atar*, but out of the library they began to smell something else – something putrid, like rotting meat. It filled their nostrils, and it seemed to grow stronger and more sickening with every breath they took.

One of the officers standing beside the doorway flapped his hand in front of his face and said, 'God almighty! Sorry, reverend, but you have to admit, whatever's in there, it doesn't half pen-and-ink!'

Father Devine peered into the library. 'He's here. He won't

allow us to shine a light on him because he was born and bred in darkness, and has always lived in darkness. He is not only the lord of the flies, he is the lord of the blind, and the hopelessly lost, and those who will never see another sunrise.'

He was trembling, and he had to use both hands to hold up his crucifix, or he might have dropped it. Jerry could tell that he was terrified.

Jamila narrowed her eyes and squinted into the darkness. 'I can just about make out a desk in the middle of the room. Black, and shiny. Is it a desk?'

'Yes, I can see that too,' said Jerry. 'Is it a desk, father, or is it something to do with Beelzebub?'

Father Devine didn't answer them, but began his petition. 'I lift the flag of praise high and declare Thou art my King. I walk boldly forward and trust in you as my fortress. I ride triumphantly upon Thy grace and thank Thee that the battle will be won. I worship Thee!'

He was still praying when there was a horrifying scream from inside the library, partly a screech of pain and partly a roar of rage. Even in the darkness, Jamila and Jerry could see a dark shape rising out of the shiny black furniture they had thought was a desk. It was the shape of a huge man, but its outline appeared to be blurred, so that they were unable to focus on it. It screamed, and screamed again, and Father Devine laid down his crucifix and sank to his knees to the floor, with his head bowed.

'It's not a desk,' he wept. 'It's the casket that he must have been held in. But now it's open.'

There was another ear-splitting scream. DCI Butcher looked into the library and said, 'Is that him? Is that your Beelzebub? Why don't our fucking flashlights work?'

'He kills light, as well as people,' sobbed Father Devine.

'So what do we do now? Taser him, shoot him – what?'

The dark shape appeared to have risen out of his casket, although he had not yet started to approach the doorway.

'We must get out of this house, as fast as we can,' said Father Devine. 'Please, help me up.'

'Are you kidding me?' protested DCI Butcher. 'We've set up this whole operation but now you're saying we have to pack it in, and scarper? I've already deployed officers in every other room, including upstairs.'

He turned to Jamila. 'You asked us to believe in anything we found in this house and deal with it like a normal shout. Well, you've got your wish, and I believe in that screaming thing in there, and whatever it is I don't see why we can't go in there and try to knock it out. Shoot it, if necessary.'

Father Devine was standing up again now. He pointed with his crucifix into the library and shouted, with spit flying from his lips, 'You don't understand! It's Beelzebub!'

The second he said the name, they heard a buzzing from the library. In seconds, the buzzing began to grow louder and louder, and Jamila and Jerry looked at each other with an expression that said, *oh no, please*. But out of the library door burst a whole glittering blizzard of flies, thousands of them, possibly millions of them – so many that they filled up the hallway from floor to ceiling, and Jamila and Jerry and Father Devine and DCI Butcher and all the other officers were instantly covered all over. Flies landed on their faces and started to crawl into their eyes and up their nostrils. Flies landed on their uniforms and started to crawl underneath their protective vests.

'*Pest control!*' bellowed DCI Butcher, spitting flies off his lips. '*Everybody else – get out now!*'

More and more flies came storming out of the library, with that relentless droning noise. They felt as hard as a shower of gravel, as if Beelzebub had somehow invested each one of them with some of his own angry power.

The two pest control technicians came scrambling up the steps and into the front doorway. They had to stand aside, though, as Jamila and Jerry and Father Devine and DCI Butcher pushed their way past them, followed by the rest of the officers. Once the police had all left the house and gathered in the street, still frantically brushing flies off their sleeves, the pest control technicians started to spray the hallway with DEET fly killer. Almost immediately, though, they had to stop. They, too, were being pelted by a mass of flies, which completely covered their PVC face masks.

They stopped spraying and staggered back down the steps. Not only had they been blinded by the flies, but their fly spray appeared to have had no effect at all, even though they had brought a formula nearly double the strength of the spray they had used at Lavender Hill police station.

Jamila and Jerry stood beside Father Devine, watching the flies whirling in the broken-open doorway of Ekron. Jamila was holding on to Father Devine's arm because he was shaking so much.

'It looks like we're going to need a plan B,' said Jerry. 'B for Beelzebub.'

DCI Butcher came up to them. He still had a fly crawling across his cap badge.

'So what do we do now?' he asked them. 'You've converted us. We all believe in this Beezle bloke now. But how the hell do we get the bugger out of there and stop him sending out all these fucking flies?'

At that moment, one of the upstairs lights in Ekron was

switched on. Jamila and Jerry looked up at it and saw Vincent Narrow standing at the bedroom window. Even though he was too far away for Jerry to be able to see his expression, he was sure that he must be smiling. He watched them for a while, and then he switched the light off and closed the curtain.

28

After they had propped up a plywood barrier to cover the broken door and left two constables to keep a watch on Atherton Street, they returned to the station. They all changed their clothing and showered and then went into the canteen for breakfast. Jerry had called an Uber for Father Devine so that he could return to Our Lady Help of Christians.

At ten thirty, they assembled in the operations room for a detailed debriefing. They were all unusually quiet, and there was none of the usual banter. Most of them were still trying to assimilate what they had seen and how they had been attacked by such a blizzard of flies.

They had several minutes of video and bodycam footage to watch, not only from the moment the flies had come exploding out of the library, but upstairs, too, where five officers had carried out a hurried but thorough search.

DC Woods said, 'That Vincent Narrow, he came to the window after we'd vacated the house. Perhaps he wanted to have a bit of a gloat. But we have absolutely no clue where he could have been hiding himself, because we went through every room upstairs, attic included.'

'We've identified our suspect now, if you can call him that,' said DCI Butcher. 'He's known as Beelzebub, and we're guessing that he was brought to the UK from Palestine by

Humphrey Bly, whose house this is – or *was*, before he got himself chopped into pieces and ended up in Battersea Park. The question now is not who Beelzebub is, but *what* he is, and until we know what he is, he isn't going to be easy to deal with.'

'I've been doing some quick background research on Beelzebub since we got back here,' said Jamila. 'He has many different names and a whole host of different identities. The name Beelzebub comes from Ekron, where he was worshipped by the Philistines. In Christian theology, he was one of the seven princes of hell. Some even identify him as Satan himself, while others believe his name was derived from the Canaanite god Baal. That makes sense, because in some accounts Baal was permanently covered in flies, and he could send them out to inflict sickness or death on any of his enemies.'

'But you're talking now about a god or a demon or a spirit,' protested PC Sadza. 'I'm not sure I can get my head round this. It's not a movie, you know. It's not like *Exorcist 8*. Surely there's some biological reason for all those flies.'

Jamila said, 'Just because we call something a god or a demon or a spirit doesn't make its existence any less scientifically feasible. For example, it was only in 1892 that the first virus was discovered. Before then, many diseases were thought to have been caused by witchcraft. In Ghana, a large percentage of the population still think that witches cause sickle cell anaemia and diabetes and HIV and many other illnesses. One day they'll come to understand what really infects people. In the same way, I believe that sometime in the future we will find out that many things that we presently consider to be supernatural are real, such as ghosts and poltergeists.'

'That still doesn't solve the immediate problem of this Beelzebub, does it?' said DCI Butcher. 'I'm beginning to think that we should put on protective clothing and go into that house with all guns blazing. We're ninety-nine per cent sure that Beelzebub was responsible for the killing of all those wedding guests at the Palette, aren't we, as well as those clergymen, and Ronnie Gibbs, and Jock Maclean, and who knows who else. If we snuff him out, I'm sure we'll be able to find enough evidence to justify it afterwards, if anyone makes a complaint.'

'Do you think Chance will give us the green light to do that?' asked DI Fairbrother.

'He'll be in after lunch. I'll give him a full rundown on this morning's fiasco and show him the video footage. I don't see how he'll be able to say no.'

They were still discussing their failed operation when Jamila's phone rang. It was Professor Yearling, calling her from his temporary laboratory on Falcon Road.

'How did it go this morning?' he asked her. 'I've been on tenterhooks.'

'Disastrous,' said Jamila. She stood up and went out into the corridor so that she could describe to him what had happened in detail.

'And the fly spray?' he asked her. 'Did that have no effect at all?'

'None. Perhaps it did later, but not at once, even though it was much stronger than the one that was used before, when all those flies invaded the station.'

'I believe I may have the answer to your prayers,' said Professor Yearling. 'I've been running a series of tests on the various living flies that you've given me as samples, using a variety of toxins, and I've found one that makes them drop dead at the drop of a hat, so to speak.'

'We're having a debriefing at the station now,' Jamila told

him. 'Do you think you could join us and tell all of us about it? I have to admit that after our raid this morning we're completely stumped about what we should do next. It's even been suggested that armed officers enter the house and shoot Beelzebub on sight, without any warning. But since he's a god, or a demon, or some kind of supernatural manifestation, I'm not at all sure that will have any more effect on him than our fly spray had on the flies.'

'Give me half an hour, and I'll be with you.'

When he arrived, Professor Yearling was carrying a large black ceramic jar with a label stuck on it. He was wearing a three-piece brown tweed suit and looked even more like Peter Cushing's twin than he had before. He greeted the assembled officers and placed the jar on the table at the side of the room. Jerry saw that the label had *Steatoda nobilis x 9* scrawled on it, in the kind of nearly illegible handwriting that would have done a doctor justice.

'There's no question that the flies that have been causing all this mayhem are far stronger than one would expect a normal fly to be,' he told them. 'That's why it takes only a few thousand of them to dig a dead body out of its grave and enable it to walk and to commit acts of murder. As we have seen, they are also capable of lifting people both living and dead high up into the air.'

'So how did they manage to get so strong?' asked DCI Butcher. 'When they were hitting us this morning, it was like being hit by airgun pellets, I can tell you.'

'I've analysed their structure,' said Professor Yearling. 'They are all coffin flies, *Conicera tibialis*, but I've been unable to detect any significant anatomical difference between them and any other coffin flies that I've studied in the past. Detective Inspector Patel has informed me about the supernatural element involved in this investigation, and the possibility that these flies are being created and controlled by the spirit Beelzebub. As far-fetched as this might seem to be, it would be at least one explanation for the unusual strength of these flies and the way in which they have been directed – almost like an army.'

'Could there be some other explanation that's *not* supernatural?' asked PC Sadza. 'You know, like the way that hundreds of starlings all fly together in those what-do-you-call-them, those murmurations. You couldn't call them an army, because they're up in the air, but they all fly together like an aerobatic display team, don't they? And what about shoals of fish? There's nothing supernatural about shoals of fish, yet they all swim together.'

'Maybe they do,' said Jerry, turning around to face him. 'But you've never seen a thousand sardines come jumping out of the water to strangle anybody, have you?'

Professor Yearling couldn't help giving the briefest of smiles. 'Whatever gives these flies so much strength, and whatever directs them, the number one priority has been for us to find a way to eliminate them, and I believe I have achieved that.'

He reached into his pocket and produced a pair of nitrile gloves. Then he took the lid off the black ceramic jar, reached inside it, and carefully drew out a wriggling spider. The spider had a bulbous body, black with yellow spots. Another two spiders were trying to climb out, so Professor Yearling gently flicked them back down and closed the lid.

'This is a noble false widow, *steatoda nobilis*. It's fairly common in the UK these days, and even more so in Ireland. It's the most poisonous of British spiders and it can bite you, especially if it gets tangled up in your bedding or your clothes. Its venom contains about forty-nine per cent latrodectus toxins, which can cause pain, muscle rigidity and vomiting, although its bites are very rarely fatal.'

He dropped the spider on to the table and it scuttled across and hid itself in the corner next to the wall.

'However, don't let's worry ourselves about the effect that its venom can have on humans. The reason I've come here today is to tell you that it kills coffin flies – instantly. I've extracted the venom from all these nine spiders and mixed it with a strong pyrethroid to make a spray. Even though the amount of noble false widow venom is almost infinitesimal, it's enough to make these flies drop dead on the spot.'

There were murmurs of approval all around the operations room, although two or three of the officers were looking anxiously over at the table where the spider had hidden itself, just to make sure that it was still there and had not started crawling around in search of someone to bite.

Jamila raised her hand and said, 'This is most encouraging, professor. With any luck, it means that we might be able to go back and enter the house without being overwhelmed with flies, like we were this morning. But there is still the problem of Beelzebub. Will *he* be susceptible to this spider toxin, do you think? What if it has no effect on him at all?'

'I admit that what I'm going to say now is purely guesswork,' Professor Yearling told her. 'On the other hand, from my experience as an entomologist, it's educated guesswork. From what you've told me about the huge swarms of flies that suddenly appear when this Beelzebub wants to attack someone, or when he obviously feels that he's being threatened, I can only deduce that they're already mature and that they're originating from him. Coffin fly eggs are often laid in large numbers, and they develop in only a few days into larvae, and then pupae, and then fully grown flies, but they don't all instantly hatch in their thousands just because someone has walked into the room.'

'When you say "they're originating from him", what do you mean by that, exactly?'

'You told me, didn't you, that the library in which you found him smells fetid?'

'That's right. It stinks like a mortuary, only worse.'

'It's highly likely that the smell is coming from him. He's in a constant state of decomposition. And all the flies that attacked you, they could have been crawling all over him already.'

'Oh, Jesus,' said Jerry. 'How are we supposed to deal with somebody who's rotten already?'

'We use *steatoda nobilis*,' said Professor Yearling. 'Noble false widows. In sufficient numbers, they could bite him to death, and of course his flies wouldn't be able to protect him, not from them.'

'But what would be "sufficient numbers"?' asked Jamila. 'We're talking about a being with the power to make dead bodies walk and people fly up in the air.'

Professor Yearling shook his head. 'I have no idea, to be honest with you. But I certainly know that if ten noble false widows were to bite a normal adult male, he would be at risk of paralysis, and death. So to be on the safe side with Beelzebub, why don't we say one hundred?'

'Are you having a laugh?' said Jerry. 'Where the hell are we going to find a hundred noble false widows?'

Professor Yearling seemed quite unconcerned. He leaned across the table, cupped his hand, and the spider ran into it. Then he took the lid off the black ceramic jar and dropped it back inside.

'We can find them in the same place that these nine beauties came from,' he said. 'There's a spider farm down in Sussex that has more spiders of more different species than you could ever imagine. You want a tarantula, or a black lace-weaver, or a cricket thief? They have them all.'

Jamila turned to DCI Butcher. 'Have you been taking this in, sir?'

'Yes, I have, and my head's still spinning. It's not spinning spider webs, by the way.'

'What do you think about Professor Yearling preparing some of his toxic fly spray for us, and seeing if we can get hold of these false widow spiders? Then we could go back to Atherton Street and have another crack at Beelzebub.'

'If you'd suggested this to me last week, Jamila, I would have said that you needed therapy.'

He looked around at all the other officers. DI Fairbrother shrugged, as if to say, *Why not, guv, this can't get any more insane than it is already.*

'There really is a spider farm?' asked DCI Butcher.

Professor Yearling nodded. 'The owner's a chap called Noel Billings. I'll give you his contact number and his address. I don't know how much you want to tell him about why you need a hundred noble false widows, but he's very obliging. He didn't ask me why I wanted nine of them, and I didn't tell him.'

It was already dark when Jamila and Jerry drove down to Crawley, a sprawling town of terraced houses built after the war to house people bombed out of the East End of London by the Blitz. The spider farm was located on an industrial estate, Manor Royal – a nondescript single-storey concrete building that looked more like a bank than a spider farm, except for the initials BSF on the roof and a spider web painted on its satellite dish.

Noel Billings was waiting to greet them in the reception area, wearing a white surgical coat with a face mask around his neck. He was bald, with wiry eyebrows, bulging eyes and a sharply curved nose. Jamila couldn't stop herself from thinking that he must have been breeding spiders for so long that he had started to look like one. She hardly dared to look down in case he had more than the usual number of legs.

'You won't mind if I ask you to wear masks, will you?' he said. 'The atmosphere inside is controlled. We don't want our spiders to catch anything – or vice versa, of course.'

He took them through one brightly lit laboratory after another. In the first, large long-legged spiders were contained in a whole wall of individual glass boxes. In the next, baby spiders were being grown in hundreds of circular plastic containers.

'We've been farming spiders for over six years now,' Noel Billings explained. 'They're probably the most unappreciated creatures on God's earth. These beauties are Australian Blue Mountains funnel-web spiders. We milk them for toxins, which we can mix with yeast to make pesticides. The good thing about spider pesticides is that they're highly effective and yet their toxic effect lasts only for a very short time after use, so you can return to your treated premises almost immediately.

'In *this* lab we're growing Madagascar silk spiders for their golden silk. Considering how fine it is, it's comparatively stronger than steel, and it can be woven into gorgeous fabrics. We feed them on crickets because I'm not too keen on having maggots in the farm.

'Here we have *theraphosidae*, or tarantulas, which we sell

online as pets. Of course they're big and hairy and they look scary, but they're quite harmless and they live longer than most spiders. We probably sell thirty or forty every week, at about thirty-five pounds each.'

He lifted a tarantula out of its plastic box and stuck it on to his cheek. 'See? Quite harmless. Unless you're an arachnophobe.'

In the last laboratory, which was gloomier, but warmer, he showed them all the noble false widows. Jamila and Jerry looked into their six glass terraria, where scores of them were crawling all over each other.

'We breed these for their toxins too,' Noel Billings told them. 'My assistant has already picked out a hundred for you and they're waiting for you in reception.'

'I'll let you know where to send the bill,' said Jamila.

'Really? I thought you *were* the Bill.'

Jamila and Jerry stared at Noel Billings as if he had taken the name of the Lord God in vain.

'Sorry,' he said. 'That was supposed to be a joke. It's not actually a laugh a minute, breeding spiders, as you can imagine.'

29

They returned to Atherton Street even earlier the next day, at 5 a.m. The rain had held off but it was foggy, so that the street lights looked like thistledown, and they felt more like a company of ghosts than a unit of armed police. This time they were all wearing riot gear, with helmets, which made them look even more sinister.

As before, Father Devine had come down from Ilford to join them, so they could be reasonably certain that Ekron would appear as it really was, the home of Humphrey Bly. He was the only one not wearing a protective vest and a helmet, because he was concerned that they would insulate him from the power of God. His shield would be his holy cassock.

Two pesticide technicians were backing up the police, but this time their spray cans were filled with the mixture of noble false widow toxins and pyrethroid that Professor Yearling had spent most of the small hours concocting in the Falcon Road laboratory.

The spiders themselves were contained in two large transparent polythene boxes, which were being carried by a pair of officers in protective Tyvek suits. DCI Butcher had asked for volunteers for this detail, not only because of the unknown risk of confronting Beelzebub face to face, but in case any officers had a morbid fear of spiders.

Standing outside the front gate of Ekron, Jamila lifted her Perspex face mask and said, 'Right. You've all been briefed on what we're attempting here this morning. We're praying that if those flies attack us again, our new pesticide is going to bring them all down. And we're also praying that our noble spiders are going to live up to their name and do for Beelzebub what generations of holy men and scientists could never do.'

Usually, one or two officers would make some jocular remark, even if the break-in was going to be dangerous. This morning, in the fog, nobody spoke.

Two officers climbed up the front steps and lifted away the temporary plywood barrier that had covered the doorway overnight. Once that had been removed, three more armed officers entered the hallway, followed by the pest control technicians. Behind them came Jamila and Jerry with Father Devine, and the two officers carrying the boxes of noble widow spiders.

The light in the hallway was still switched on from yesterday, and the door to the library was still open. On the wall, the picture still hung with the weeping woman holding up her dead dog. Inside the library it was pitch dark, as it had been before, except for the faintest glimmer of reflection from the black varnished casket.

The three armed officers stood back so that Jamila and Jerry could approach the library door and peer inside. Jerry sniffed and the stench of decomposing flesh was even stronger, almost completely overwhelming the lemony aroma from the kitchen.

'I think Professor Yearling might have been right about Beelzebub,' he whispered to Jamila. 'He smells like he's well past his sell-by date.'

Father Devine set down his burgundy leather exorcism case and raised up his crucifix. 'O Lord,' he said, but then he froze, with his mouth half open.

'Father?' said Jamila. 'Father – are you all right?'

Father Devine remained paralysed, still holding up his crucifix, but unable to speak.

Jerry turned to the armed officers. 'I think we need to get him out of here. He looks like he's had a stroke or something.'

'*Father?*' Jamila repeated, reaching out for his arm.

Before she could take hold of him, there was a scream so loud that all of them felt as if their eardrums had been torn out. It went on and on, and then a shrieking hurricane of freezing-cold air came blasting out of the library doorway. It flattened two of the armed officers back against the wall, and it forced Jamila to stumble into Jerry and almost knock him on to the floor.

Father Devine flung up both his arms. His crucifix was snatched out of his hand and sent spinning back along the hallway, hitting one of the pest control technicians on the shoulder before it spun away into the street. Father Devine remained standing, but his cassock was rippling and his white hair was flying and his face was grotesquely distorted. His eyelids were dragged back by the force of the wind so that he was staring up at the ceiling as if he were beseeching God to save him.

'*The spiders!*' Jerry shouted. Jamila was still clinging to him. '*Bring up the fucking spiders!*'

But the screaming went on and the hurricane grew stronger and stronger, so that none of them could move and it was so cold that they were all starting to feel numb. For only the second time in his career with the Met, Jerry believed that he could die – that all of them could die. It looked as if they had totally underestimated the raging power of Beelzebub, and his sheer malevolence.

Father Devine's cassock was slowly ripped open by the wind, bottom to top. Each one of its thirty-three buttons represented a year in the life of Christ, and it looked as if his belief was being deliberately picked apart, one year at a time.

Once the last button was opened up, his cassock was dragged right off him, and went flapping out of the front door like a wounded black raven. Next, his grey woollen vest was torn into shreds. Jerry could see that he was trying to cry for help. He kept opening and closing his mouth but no words came out, and even if he had been able to speak, the screaming and the wind would have drowned out what he was trying to say.

'Get him out of here!' Jamila shouted. 'He's going to be killed!'

Jerry and one of the armed officers managed to reach across and snatch Father Devine's upraised arms, but when they tried to pull him backwards, they were unable to move him. It felt as if his feet were nailed to the floor, like Christ's feet had been nailed to the cross.

They were still attempting to drag him away from the library doorway when there was a crackling noise and Father Devine's chest split open. His breastbone broke with a snap and his ribs all suddenly stuck upwards, like the frame of an old wooden ship. Inside his gaping torso his lungs and his heart were crushed into a bloody, shapeless pulp, and then his stomach split open too. His bowels began to unravel as if they had a life of their own. His small intestines wriggled furiously, and then the icy-cold wind lifted them out of his abdomen, right up to the ceiling like a rope trick, and wrapped them around the lampshades, around and around.

Father Devine was still alive to witness his slippery bowels pulled up out of him. Jerry could see the agony and the despair in his eyes. He had predicted that Beelzebub would try to inflict this grisly fate on him, and he had prayed that he would be spared, but it seemed as if his God had forsaken him.

'Spiders!' Jerry shouted again. 'For Christ's sake, can we get those spiders up here?'

The hurricane had been so strong that the two officers in their Tyvek suits had found it impossible to reach the library, and they had been shielding themselves in the living-room doorway. As abruptly as it had come blasting out, though, the hurricane died away, and the screaming gradually faded, as if the screamer were walking away down a tunnel. Father Devine pitched sideways on to the floor, dragging his intestines down with him. For a few seconds, the house was dead silent, and the officers could only look around at each other in shock. None of them had ever seen anyone killed like that before.

The silence didn't last long, though. Now they began to hear that familiar buzzing of flies. Jerry frantically beckoned the two officers to bring their boxes of spiders up to the library doorway, but he was too late. Thousands of flies came pouring out into the hallway, as they had before, and the air was so thick with them that Jerry could hardly see from one side of the hallway to the other. They rattled against the sides of his helmet and crawled all over his face mask.

'Pesticide!' shouted DCI Butcher, from where he was standing on the porch. 'Pesticide *now*!'

The two pest control technicians hurried into the hallway through the cloud of flies. They lifted up the nozzles of their fly sprays and started to release a fine mist of Professor Yearling's formula, filling the air in the hallway with it. It smelled strongly of petroleum and cloves.

Jamila stood back against the wall, praying that this mixture of pyrethroid and noble false widow toxin would work. She, too, was almost blinded by the flies covering her face mask and she was sure she could feel them trying to crawl down the back of her neck and into her gloves.

The pest control technicians sprayed again and again, up and down and from side to side. It seemed at first as if the flies were equally resistant to this formula as they had been to DEET. More and more of them kept storming out of the library, and their persistent droning even drowned out DCI Butcher shouting for paramedics.

Suddenly, though, some of the flies began to circle aimlessly around and drop to the floor. Only a few at first, but then more and more, spiralling down to the parquet and gradually creating a thick shimmering carpet of dead flies.

It took only three or four minutes, and then every fly in the hallway had fallen to the floor. The house was silent again. DCI Butcher came up to Father Devine's body. Two attenuated strings of his intestines were still hanging from the lights on the ceiling.

'Let's get this poor bugger moved out of here, shall we?' he said. 'I've called the paramedics. Then let's get in after this Beelzebub.'

The three armed officers entered the library first, carbines raised, ready to open fire on anything that looked remotely hostile. The officers carrying the two boxes of noble false widows came close behind them, followed by Jamila and Jerry and five more officers. They all carried flashlights or LED lights on their helmets, and they were all switched on, but the library remained in absolute darkness, except for the reflection from the casket and a faint gleam from the spines of some of the books.

The smell of rotting flesh was so strong in here that Jamila felt as if she would have to vomit. And as they approached the casket, they could hear breathing. Thick, laboured breathing, like some beast that was angry, or hungry, or both.

They stopped, and listened. Then Jerry took a step towards the casket and said quietly, '*Beelzebub.*'

For a moment, there was no response. Only the breathing. Then, without warning, all their torches and LED lamps lit up the library, so brightly that they were dazzled.

In front of them, on a long trestle, rested the black lacquered casket. It was at least twice as wide as a normal casket, and at least half as long again. Its lid lay at an angle on the floor beside it, covered with deep scratches, as if it had been forced open. A few flies were circling above it, but lazily, as if they were drugged.

Jerry approached the casket with an armed officer on either side of him, their carbines still raised. He had taken only two more steps when the library was filled with another ear-splitting scream. The casket rattled and shook, and the trestle creaked.

Out of the casket rose a creature that had the shape of a man but was nearly nine feet tall. He had long tangled hair and a brutish face that was pockmarked and pitted. He was naked, but his flesh was ragged and partly eaten away, and his skin was scarred and purple and wet in places as if it had once been severely burned, but had healed, only to be burned again. He was covered all over with a crawling mass of flies, which appeared to be voraciously feeding off him.

His eyes were tightly closed but his mouth was wide open, revealing broken and blackened teeth. He kept on screaming and screaming and never taking a breath, and as he screamed, Jamila and Jerry could feel a chilly wind beginning to rise again, although it was impossible to tell where it was coming from.

'Spiders!' shouted Jerry. 'Chuck 'em into his coffin!'

The two officers in Tyvek suits peeled the lids off their polythene boxes, bustled up to the casket and tipped all their spiders into it, fifty from each box. They had to knock their boxes once or twice to dislodge the last of the spiders, but at last they were all emptied out.

Beelzebub carried on screaming, but now he opened his eyes and looked down in horror at the scores of bulbous spiders that were crawling all over his feet and starting to climb up his legs. They were after the flies that were feeding on his decomposing flesh, but when he swung his arms and tried to beat them off, they started to bite him.

Neither Jamila nor Jerry nor any of the officers had heard a sound like the roar that came out of Beelzebub's throat. It sounded more like a landslide than a scream. The noble false widow spiders scurried up his legs and up his back and nestled in his groin, biting him over and over again. The flies that had been feeding on him began to fly away, and as they flew away, pieces of Beelzebub's flesh dropped off him.

What happened next was so unexpected that Jamila and Jerry took several steps back, and then both they and the officers retreated towards the library door.

Standing in his casket, covered all over in biting spiders, Beelzebub not only stretched his arms wide apart, but out of his back he opened up a pair of wings. The wings were grey and tattered, and they were deeply creased, as if they had been folded away for decades and never opened. But he flapped them, with a sound like opening up an umbrella, and then he flapped them again, and again.

'Jesus,' said Jerry. 'He's only trying to fly!'

Beelzebub flapped his wings harder and harder. By now, the last few flies that had been crawling all over him had flown away, and he was covered in noble widows, even in his tangled hair. Jamila could see their bulbous black-and-yellow bodies around his neck, as if he were wearing a necklace made of living spiders.

He gave a last desperate flap and tried to launch himself out of his casket. As he lifted himself up, though, he started to fall apart. One of his arms dropped out of its socket on to the floor, and then the other arm. His wings collapsed and then he gave a last piercing scream and imploded, with bones and lumps of rotten flesh scattering all over the carpet. His head ended up at one end of his casket, staring with bloodshot fury at his green and putrid liver, his hair still infested with spiders. The smell of death was unbearable.

Jamila said, 'Now I *am* going to be sick.'

'But we've done for him,' said Jerry. 'We've only bloody done for him. I reckon it was the flies that were holding him together. Maybe it was the same as those dead bodies that he covered in flies so that they could walk around and strangle people. No wonder they called him the lord of the flies.'

DCI Butcher was standing in the library doorway, shaking his head. 'Case closed,' he said. 'But I didn't see this – none of this. I didn't see a bloke with wings on try to fly out of a coffin and then fall to bits. It won't be in my report, you can bet your life on that. The suspect was an unregistered immigrant who took a fatal overdose before he could be taken into custody. Do you go along with that?'

Outside in the hallway, the remaining flies that had escaped from the noble false widows had been sprayed by the pest control technicians. Father Devine's body had been covered with a sheet and was being carried away by paramedics.

Jamila and Jerry took a last look at the pelvis and ribs and rotten chunks of flesh that were strewn around the floor of the library. They looked like the remains of someone who had fallen from the top of a thirty-storey skyscraper. It was extraordinary to think this had once been an ancient god. From the moment they had been called in to help with the investigation into the murder of the Reverend Wymarsh, this case had seemed to both of them to be one of the worst nightmares they could have imagined. Now, though, they felt that the nightmare was over, and that they had woken up.

As they left the library, DI Fairbrother and two uniformed officers came down the stairs into the hallway. They were escorting Vincent Narrow, who was handcuffed and looking aggrieved. He was not wearing his usual trilby hat and underneath his camel coat it looked as if he was barefoot, and wearing no trousers.

'Blimey,' said Jerry. 'Where did you find that piece of shit?'

'He was in his scratcher, fast asleep.'

'You're kidding me. So, no Houdini escape for him this time?'

'I don't know what the fuck you're talking about,' said Vincent Narrow. 'All right, I broke in, I admit it. Old habits die hard. I looked around to see if there was anything worth nicking, but that was all. I haven't taken nothing and I haven't done no damage.'

'He says he saw a box in the library and opened it up to see what was in it,' said DI Fairbrother. 'That's the last thing he remembers.'

'Not to worry,' put in Jamila. 'There are plenty of people who can bear witness to all the offences he has committed since he opened that box.'

'What offences?' Vincent Narrow protested. 'I opened the

box, then the next thing I knew you lot were shaking me awake.'

Jerry and Jamila left the house. The fog had cleared now, and it was a dull November morning, with a relentlessly grey sky.

'I think we should leave DCI Butcher to write this one up,' said Jamila.

'Fancy breakfast somewhere?' asked Jerry.

'No. No, thank you. It is going to be a while before my stomach forgets what we have seen today. One lesson I have learned, though.'

'What's that?'

'Beelzebub would have fallen to pieces a long time ago if it hadn't been for those flies. Sometimes it's your own worst enemies who keep you together.'

About the Author

GRAHAM MASTERTON is best known as a writer of horror and thrillers, but his career as an author spans many genres, including historical epics and sex advice books. His first horror novel, *The Manitou*, became a bestseller and was made into a film starring Tony Curtis. In 2019, Graham was given a Lifetime Achievement Award by the Horror Writers Association. He is also the author of the Katie Maguire series of crime thrillers, which have sold more than 1.5 million copies worldwide.

Visit www.grahammasterton.co.uk

Don't miss the other books in the spine-tingling Patel & Pardoe series.

From the master of horror and million-copy bestseller

GRAHAM MASTERTON

Available to enjoy in eBook, paperback and audio